CROSS COUNTRY

JAMES PATTERSON is one of the best-known and biggest-selling writers of all time. He is the author of some of the most popular series of the past decade: the Women's Murder Club, the Alex Cross novels and Maximum Ride, and he has written many other number one bestsellers including romance novels and stand-alone thrillers. He lives in Florida with his wife and son.

James is passionate about encouraging both adults and children alike to read. This has led to him forming a partnership with the National Literacy Trust, an independent, UK-based charity that changes lives through literacy.

James
Patterson
CROSS
COUNTRY

arrow books

Published in the United Kingdom by Arrow Books in 2009

3 5 7 9 10 8 6 4 2

First published in Great Britain in 2008 by
Century

Arrow Books
Random House, 20 Vauxhall Bridge Road,
London SW1V 2SA

www.rbooks.co.uk

Addresses for companies within The Random House Group Limited can be found at:
www.randomhouse.co.uk/offices.htm

The Random House Group Limited Reg. No. 954009

A CIP catalogue record for this book
is available from the British Library

ISBN 9780099514572
ISBN 9780099538936 (export edition)

The Random House Group Limited supports The Forest Stewardship
Council (FSC), the leading international forest certification organisation. All our
titles that are printed on Greenpeace approved FSC certified paper carry the FSC logo.
Our paper procurement policy can be found at:
www.rbooks.co.uk/environment

Printed and bound in Great Britain by
CPI Bookmarque Ltd, Croydon, CR0 4TD

For Jill and Avie Glazer

Prologue

HOME INVASION

One

The surname of the family was Cox, the father a very successful trial lawyer, but the target was the mother, Ellie Randall Cox. The timing was right now, tonight, just minutes away. The payday was excellent, couldn't be better.

The six-foot-six, two-hundred-fifty-pound killer known as "The Tiger" had given out guns to his team—also a gram of cocaine to share, and the only instruction they would need tonight: *The mother is mine. Kill the rest.*

His secondary mission was to scare the American meddlers. He knew how they felt about home invasions, and their precious families, and murders in cold blood. They had so many rules for how life ought to be conducted. The secret to beating them was to break all their silly, sacred rules.

He settled down to watch the house from the street. Wood blinds in the first-floor windows drew horizontal lines across the family members as they moved around inside, unaware of the murderous forces gathered outside.

The boys waited restlessly at the Tiger's side, and he waited for *instinct* to tell him it was time to move on the house.

"Now," he said, "we go!"

Then, with only the slightest bend and whack of the knees, he began to run, breaking out of the camouflaging shadow of an evergreen, his strides almost too fast to count.

A single, powerful leap and he was up on the stoop of the house. Next came three splintering blows to the front door. It seemed to explode open, and they were inside, the kill team, all five of them.

The boys, none older than seventeen, streamed in around him, firing Berettas into the living room ceiling, waving crude hunting knives, shouting orders that were hard to understand because their English was not at the level of the Tiger's.

The children of the house screamed like little piglets; their lawyer father leapt up and tried to shield them with his flabby, overfed body.

"You are pitiful!" the Tiger shouted at him. "You can't even protect your family in your own house."

Soon enough, three family members were corralled against the living-room mantel, which was covered with birthday cards addressed to "Momma" and "My Darling Ellie" and "Sweetness and Light."

The leader nudged the youngest of his boys forward, the one who had chosen the name Nike and who had a contagious sense of humor. "Just do it," the Tiger said.

The boy was eleven years old and fearless as a crocodile in

a muddy river. He raised a pistol much larger than his own hand and fired it into the shivering father's forehead.

The other boys howled their approval, shooting off rounds in all directions, overturning antique furniture, breaking mirrors and windows. The Cox children were weeping and holding one another.

One particularly scary, blank-faced boy in a Houston Rockets jersey emptied his magazine into the wide-screen television, then reloaded. "Rock da house!" he shouted.

Two

THE MOTHER, "DARLING Ellie," "Sweetness and Light," finally came running and screaming down the stairs for her *Akata* babies.

"Leave them out of this!" she yelled at the tall and very muscular leader. "I know who you are!"

"Of course you do, Mother," said the Tiger as he smiled at the tall, matronly woman. He had no desire to harm her really. This was just a job to him. A high-paying one, *important to somebody here in Washington*.

The two children scrambled to get to their mother, and it became an absurd game of cat and mouse. His boys shot holes in the sofa as the wheezing American young ones squeezed behind it.

When they emerged on the other side, the Tiger was there to pluck the squealing son off the floor with one hand. The young girl in the Rugrats pajamas was a little more clever and ran up the stairs, showing little pink heels at every step.

"Go, baby!" her mother yelled. "Get out a window! Run! Keep running!"

"Won't happen," said the Tiger. "No one gets away from here tonight, Mother."

"Don't do this!" she begged. "Let them go! They're just children!"

"You know who I am," he said to her. "So you know how this will end. You knew all along. Look at what you brought on yourself and on your family. You did this to them."

Part One

LATE TO THE PARTY

Chapter 1

THE HARDEST MYSTERIES to solve are the ones you come to near the end, because there isn't enough evidence, not enough to unravel, unless somehow you can go all the way back to the beginning—rewind and replay everything.

I was riding in the lap of comfort and civility, my Mercedes R350. I was thinking about how odd it was to be going to a murder scene now. And then I was there, leaving my vehicle, and feeling conflicted about going over to the dark side again.

Was I getting too soft for this? I wondered for an instant, then let it go. I wasn't soft. If anything, I was still too hard, too unyielding, too uncompromising.

Then I was thinking that there was something particularly terrifying about random, senseless murder, and that's what this appeared to be, that's what everyone thought anyway. It's what I was told when the call came to the house.

"It's rough in there, Dr. Cross. Five vics. It's an entire family."

"Yeah, I know it is. That's what they said."

One of the first responders, a young officer I know named Michael Fescoe, met me on the sidewalk at the murder scene in Georgetown, not far from the university where I'd gone as an undergrad and which I remembered fondly for all sorts of reasons, but mostly because Georgetown had taken a chance on me.

The patrolman was visibly shaken. No surprise there. Metro didn't call me in special at eleven o'clock on a Sunday night for run-of-the-mill homicides.

"What have we got so far?" I said to Fescoe and flashed my badge at a patrolman seemingly guarding an oak tree. Then I ducked under the bright yellow tape in front of the house. Beautiful house, a three-story Colonial on Cambridge Place, a well-heeled single block just south of Montrose Park.

Neighbors and looky-loos crowded the sidewalk—but they stayed at a safe distance in their pajamas and robes, keeping up their white-collar reserve.

"Family of five, all of them dead," Fescoe repeated himself. "The name's Cox. Father, Reeve. Mother, Eleanor. Son, James. All on the first floor. Daughters, Nicole and Clara, on the third. There's blood everywhere. Looks like they were shot first. Then cut up pretty bad and piled into groupings."

Piled. I sure didn't like the sound of that. Not inside this lovely home. Not anywhere.

"Senior officers on site? Who caught it?" I asked.

"Detective Stone is upstairs. She's the one asked me to page you. ME's still on the way. Probably a couple of them. Christ, what a night."

"You've got that right."

Bree Stone was a bright star with the Violent Crimes branch, and one of the few detectives I went out of my way to partner with, pun intended, since she and I were a couple and had been for more than a year now.

"Let Detective Stone know that I'm here," I said. "I'm going to start downstairs and work my way up to where she is."

"Will do, sir. I'm on it."

Fescoe stuck with me up the porch steps and past an ALS tech working on the demolished front door and threshold.

"Forced entry, of course," Fescoe went on. He blushed, probably because he'd stated the obvious. "Plus, there's a hatch open to the roof on the third floor. Looks like they might have left that way."

"They?"

"I'd say so — based on the amount of damage, whatever the hell happened in there. Never seen anything like it, sir. Listen, if there's anything else you need—"

"I'll let you know. Thank you. It's better if I do this alone. I concentrate better."

My reputation seems to attract hungry cops on big cases, which can have its advantages. Right now, though, I wanted to take in this scene for myself. Given the grim, steely-eyed look on the face of every tech I'd seen coming from the back of the house, I knew this was going to get harder in a hurry.

Turns out I didn't know the half of it. The murder of this family was much worse than I'd thought.

Much, much worse.

Chapter 2

THEY WANTED TO scare somebody, I was thinking as I entered a brightly lit, warmly decorated alcove. *But who? Not these dead people. Not this poor family that had been slaughtered for God only knew what reason.*

The first floor told a grim and foreboding story that delineated the murder. Nearly every piece of furniture in the living and dining rooms had been either turned over or destroyed—or both. There were gaping holes punched in the walls, along with dozens of smaller ones. An antique glass chandelier lay scattered in splinters and shards all over a brightly colored Oriental rug.

The crime scene made no sense and, worse, had no direct precedent in my experience as a homicide detective.

A bullet-riddled Chesterfield couch and settee had been pushed up against the wall to make room in front of the fireplace. This was where the first three bodies were *piled.*

While it's safe to say that I've seen some horrendous shit in the line of duty, this scene, the monstrosity of it, stopped me instantly.

As promised, the stacked victims were the father, mother, and son on top, all lying faceup. There were blood streaks and stains on the nearby walls, furniture, and ceiling, and a pool had formed around the bodies. These poor people had been attacked with sharp cutting instruments of some sort, and there had been amputations.

"Jesus, Jesus," I muttered under my breath. It was a prayer, or a curse on the killers, or more likely both.

One of the printing techs answered under his breath, "Amen."

Neither of us was looking at the other, though. This was the kind of homicide scene you just gutted your way through, trying to get out of the house with a minute piece of your sanity intact.

The blood patterns around the room suggested the family members had been attacked separately, then dragged together in the middle.

Something had fueled whatever savage rage brought these killers to this and I agreed with Fescoe that there had been several killers. But what exactly had happened? What was the cause of the massacre? Drugs? Ritual? Psychosis?

Group psychosis?

I stashed the random thoughts to consider at another time. *Methods first, motive later.*

I slowly circled the bodies and parts, picking my way around the pools of blood, stepping on dry parquet where I could. There didn't seem to be any cohesion to the cutting, or the killing for that matter.

The son's throat was slit; the father had a bullet wound to the forehead; and the mother's head was turned away at an unnatural angle, as if her neck had been broken.

I went full circle to see the mother's face. The angle was such that she seemed to be looking right up at me, almost hopeful, as if I could still save her.

I leaned in for a closer look at her and all of a sudden felt dizzy. My legs went weak. I couldn't believe what I was seeing.

Oh no! Oh my God, no!

I stepped back blindly, my foot hit a slick spot, and I fell. As I went down, I reached to break my fall. My gloved hand smeared deep red across the floor.

Ellie Randall's blood. Not Cox — Randall!

I knew her — at least I once had.

Long, long ago, Ellie had been my girlfriend when we'd been students at Georgetown. She had probably been my first love.

And now Ellie had been murdered, along with her family.

Chapter 3

ONE OF THE printing techs moved to help me, but I got myself up quickly. I wondered if maybe I was in shock about Ellie. "No harm. I'm fine. What's the name here again?" I asked the tech.

"Cox, sir. Reeve, Eleanor, and James are the victims in the living room."

Eleanor *Cox*. That was right; I remembered now. I stared down at Ellie, my heart racing out of control, tears starting at the corners of my eyes. She had been Ellie *Randall* when I met her, a smart, attractive history major looking for anti-apartheid signatures from Georgetown University students. Definitely not someone whose story would end like this.

"Need anything?" Fescoe was back and he was hovering.

"Just...get me a garbage bag or something," I told him. "Please. Thank you."

I peeled off my Windbreaker and tried to wipe myself

with it, then stuck the coat in the bag Fescoe brought me. I needed to keep moving and to get out of this room, at least for now.

I headed toward the stairs and found Bree just coming down.

"Alex? Jesus, what happened to you?" she asked.

I knew if I started to explain, I wouldn't be able to finish. "We'll talk about it later, okay?" I said. "What's going on upstairs?"

She looked at me strangely but didn't push it. "More of the same. Bad stuff. Third floor, Alex. Two more kids. I think they were trying to hide from the killers, but it didn't work."

A photo flash ghosted the stairwell as we climbed. Everything seemed hallucinogenic and unreal to me. I was outside the scene, watching myself stumble through it. *Ellie had been murdered.* I tried again but couldn't process the thought.

"No blood on the stairs, or in the hall," I noticed, trying to focus on evidence, trying to do the job. It was freezing cold, with a hatch door open overhead. November third, and the forecast was for single-digit temperatures overnight. Even the weather had gone a little crazy.

"Alex?"

Bree was waiting up ahead, standing at the doorway to a room on the third floor. She didn't move as I approached. "You sure you're okay to be here?" she asked, speaking low so the others wouldn't hear.

I nodded and peered into the room.

Behind Bree, the two little girls' bodies were crisscrossed on an oval rag rug. A white canopy bed was broken into pieces, collapsed in on itself as if someone had jumped too hard on it.

"I'll be fine," I said. "I need to see what happened here. I need to begin to understand what it all means. *Like who the hell was jumping on that bed?*"

Chapter 4

BUT I DIDN'T even *begin* to understand the horrible murders of five family members. Not that night, anyway. I was as baffled as everybody else about the possible motivation of the killers.

What made the mystery even deeper was something that happened about an hour after I got to the crime scene. Two officers from the CIA showed up. They looked around, then left. *What was the CIA doing there?*

It was a little after three thirty in the morning when Bree and I finally got back home to Fifth Street. In the stillness of my house, I could hear Ali's little-boy snores wafting down from upstairs. Reassuring and comforting sounds, to be sure.

Nana Mama had left the hood light on over the stove, and she'd Saran Wrapped a plate of the last four hermit cookies from dessert. We took them upstairs, along with glasses and a half-full bottle of wine.

Two hours later I was still awake and still messed up in the head. Bree finally sat up and turned on the light. She found me sitting on the edge of the bed. I could feel the warmth of her body against my back, her breath on my neck.

"You sleep at all?" she asked.

That wasn't really what she wanted to know.

"I knew the mother, Bree. We went to Georgetown together. This couldn't have happened to her. Shouldn't have, anyway."

She breathed in sharply at my revelation. "I'm so sorry, Alex. Why didn't you say so?"

I shrugged, then sighed. "I'm not even sure if I can talk about it now," I said.

She hugged me. "It's okay. No need to talk. Unless you want to, Alex. I'm here."

"We were best friends, Bree. We were a couple for a year. I know it was a long time ago, but..." I trailed off. But *what*? But—it hadn't just been kid stuff, either. "I loved her for a while, Bree. I'm blown away right now."

"You want to get off the case?"

"No." I'd already asked myself the same question, and the answer had come just as quickly.

"I can get Sampson or somebody else from Violent Crimes to cover. We'll keep you up to the second—"

"Bree, I can't let go of this one."

"This one?" She ran a hand softly up and down my arm. "As compared to...what, Alex?"

I took a deep breath. I knew where Bree was going with this. "It's not about Maria, if that's what you mean." My wife, Maria, had been gunned down when our kids were small.

I'd managed to close the case only recently. There had been years of torture and guilt before that. But Maria had been my wife, the love of my life at the time. Ellie was something else. I wasn't confusing the two. I didn't think so anyway.

"Okay," she said, stroking my back, soothing me. "Tell me what I can do."

I folded us both under the covers. "Just lie here with me," I said. "That's all I need for now."

"You got it."

And soon, wrapped in Bree's arms, I went off to sleep — for a whole two hours.

Chapter 5

"I SPY, WITH my little eye, a *pink* newspaper," said Bree.

"Over there!" Ali was quick to spot it. "I see it! It *is* pink. What kind of crazy newspaper is that?"

To my family's surprise and delight, I hadn't left for work at some obscene hour the morning after I found Ellie and her family dead in their home. Today, I wanted to walk the kids to school. Actually, I wanted to do it most every day, but sometimes I couldn't, and sometimes I didn't. But today I needed lots of fresh air in my life. And smiles. And Ali's giggles.

Jannie was in her last year at Sojourner Truth, all ready for high school, while Ali was just starting out in the school world. It seemed very circle-of-life to me that morning, with Ellie's family gone in a blink, and my own kids coming up strong.

I put on my best cheerful dad face and tried to set aside the gruesome images of last night. "Who's next?"

"I've got one," Jannie said. She turned a canary-eating grin on Bree and me. "I spy, with my little eye, a POSSLQ."

"What's a *possel-cue*?" Ali wanted to know. He was already looking around, moving his head like a bobblehead doll's, trying to spot it, whatever *it* was.

Jannie practically sang out the answer. "P, O, S, S, L, Q. Person of the opposite sex, sharing living quarters." She whispered the word *sex* in our direction, presumably to safeguard her little brother's innocence. No matter, I could feel myself blushing slightly.

Bree tagged Jannie's shoulder. "Where exactly did you pick that one up?"

"Cherise J. She says her mom says you two are, you know, living in sin."

I exchanged a look with Bree over the top of Jannie's head. I guessed this was bound to come up in some way or another sooner or later. Bree and I had been together for more than a year now, and she spent a good amount of time at the house on Fifth Street. Part of the reason was that the kids loved having her around. Part was that I did.

"I think maybe you and Cherise J. need to find something else to talk about," I told her. "You think?"

"Oh, it's okay, Daddy. I told Cherise her mom needs to get over herself. I mean, even Nana Mama's down with it, and her picture's in the dictionary under 'old-fashioned,' right?"

"You wouldn't have any idea what's in a dictionary," I said.

But Bree and I had stopped trying to be politically correct with Jannie, and we just let ourselves laugh. Jannie had that "crossroads" thing going on these days; she was right at the intersection of girl and woman.

"What's so funny?" Ali asked. "Somebody tell me. What is it?"

I scooped him up off the sidewalk and onto my shoulders for the last half block of our walk to school. "I'll tell you in about five years."

"I know anyway," he said. "You and Bree love each other. Everybody knows. No big deal. It's a good thing."

"Yes it is," I said and kissed his cheek.

We dropped him at the school's east entrance, where the rest of his class of minicuties were lining up outside. Jannie called to him through the fence. "See you later, alligator! Love you."

"In a while, crocodile! Love you back."

With their older brother, Damon, off at prep school in Massachusetts, these two had grown closer than ever lately. On weekend nights, Ali often slept on an air mattress at the foot of his sister's bed, in what he called his "nest."

We left Jannie at the opposite side of the school building, where all the older kids were streaming in. She gave us both hugs good-bye, and I held on a little longer than usual. "I love you, sweetie. There's nothing more special to me than you and your brothers."

Jannie couldn't help but look around to make sure no one had heard. "Me too, Daddy," she said. Then, almost in the same breath, "Cherise! Wait up!"

As soon as Jannie was gone, Bree took my arm in hers. "So what was that?" she said. "'Everybody knows you and Bree love each other'?"

I shrugged and smiled. "What do I know? That's the big rumor going around, anyway."

I gave her a kiss.

And because that worked out so well, I gave her another.

Chapter 6

BY NINE A.M. I was all kissed out and getting ready to enter a most unpleasant multiple-homicide briefing at the Daly Building. It was being held in the large conference room right across from my office. Handy, anyway. Every available D-1 and D-2, and a contingent from Second District, which covered most of Georgetown, would be there.

I still couldn't get it in my head that Ellie was the victim. *One of the victims.*

The ME's Office had sent over a representative in the person of Dr. Paula Cook, a bright investigator who had the personality of tapioca pudding. The corners of Dr. Cook's mouth actually twitched when we shook hands. I think it was an attempted smile, so I smiled back. "Thanks for coming, Paula. We need you on this one."

"Worst I've seen," she said, "in fourteen years. All those kids, the parents. Turns my stomach. Senseless."

We had picked up a stack of crime scene photos on the way in, and now Paula and I pinned some of them up in the situation room. I made sure they were all 11 × 14s. I wanted everyone to feel some of what had happened last night in Georgetown, the way I still did.

"This might be an isolated incident," I stood in front and told the assembled group a few minutes later. "But I'm not going to assume it is. The more we understand, the more prepared we'll be if this happens again. It might not be an isolated incident." I figured some of the more jaded homicide detectives wouldn't agree; they'd be thinking I'd worked one too many serial cases. I didn't much care what they thought at that point.

For the first fifteen minutes or so, I ran through the primary facts of the case for those who hadn't been there the night before. Then I turned it over to Paula. She bounced up and talked us through the photos on the wall.

"The cutting styles indicate a variety of weapons, strength, and ability," she said, using a red laser pointer to highlight the slashes, punctures, and severing that had been done to the Cox family.

"At least one blade had a serrated edge. One was unusually large—possibly a machete. The amputations, wherever they occurred, were never done cleanly. Rather, they were the result of repetitive trauma."

A detective named Monk Jeffries asked a pretty good question from the front row. "You think they were practicing? Had never done this before?"

"I couldn't say," Paula told him. "Wouldn't surprise me."

"Yeah," I put in. "It's like they were practicing, Monk." I had my own opinion about the murders. "There's something very *young* about this crime scene."

"As in inexperienced?" Jeffries asked.

"No. Just *young*. I'm talking about the cutting, the broken bed, the vandalism in general. Also the fact that this was probably done by a group of five or more. That's a big group of intruders. When I intersect all those factors, I get a few possibilities: gang, cult, OC. In that order."

"Gang?" another D-1 asked from the back. "You ever see gang violence like this massacre?"

"I've never seen violence like this, period," I said.

"I've got twenty bucks on OC. Any takers?" It was Lou Copeland, a competent but thoroughly obnoxious D-1 with Major Case Squad. A few of his cronies laughed.

Not me. I threw my clipboard across the room. It struck the wall and fell onto the tile. That wasn't like me, so it made an impression.

The room was quiet. I walked over to pick up my notes. I saw Bree and Sampson exchange a look I didn't like. They weren't sure that I could handle this.

Bree took it from there, and she started handing out assignments. We needed people recanvassing the Cambridge Place neighborhood, riding the lab for fast turnaround, and calling in any chits we had on the street for information about last night.

"We need your best work on this one," Bree told the group. "And we want some answers by the end of the day."

"What about —?"

"*Dismissed!*"

Everyone looked around. It was Sampson who'd spoken.

"You all have any more questions, you can reach Stone or Cross on their cells. Meanwhile, we've got a buttload of fieldwork to do. This is a major case. So get started! Let's hit it, and hit it hard."

Chapter 7

THE TIGER WAS the tallest and strongest of ten well-muscled black men racing up and down a weathered asphalt basketball court at Carter Park in Petway. He understood that he wasn't a skillful shooter or dribbler, but he rebounded like a pro and defended the basket fiercely, and he hated to lose more than anything. In his world, *you lose, you die.*

The player he guarded called himself "Buckwheat" and the Tiger had heard that the nickname had something to do with an old TV series in America that sometimes made fun of black kids.

Buckwheat either didn't mind the name, or he'd gotten used to it. He was fast on the basketball court and a steady shooter. He was also a trash-talker, as were most of the young players in DC. The Tiger had picked up the game in London instantly while he was at university, but there wasn't much trash-talking in England.

"You talk a good game, but you're going to lose," the Tiger finally said as he and his opponent ran up the court, shoulder to shoulder. Buckwheat turned off a screen and took a bounce pass in the left corner. He proceeded to bury a long, perfectly arced jump shot even though the Tiger bumped him hard after the release.

"Fuckin' ape," the other man yelled as the two of them ran back the other way.

"You think so?"

"Oh hell, I know so. 'Nother minute, you be the big monkey watchin' on the sideline!"

The Tiger laughed but said nothing more. He scored on a rebound, and then Buckwheat's team raced the ball up the court on a fast break.

Buckwheat caught a pass in full stride and brought it hard to the hoop. He had a step on the Tiger and called out, "Game!" even before he went up for the winning dunk.

He was airborne, graceful and athletic, when the Tiger hit him with all his force and weight. He took the six-foot-three man down, drove him into the metal pole supporting the basket. The man lay sprawled on the asphalt with blood streaming from his face.

"*Game!*" shouted the Tiger and raised both arms high over his head. He loved to play basketball—what great fun it was to beat these loudmouthed *African Americans* who didn't know anything about the real world.

On the sidelines, his boys cheered as if he were Michael Jordan and Kobe Bryant rolled into one. He wasn't any of that, he knew. He didn't want to be like Mike or Kobe. He was much better.

He decided life and death on a daily basis.

He walked off the court, and a man came up to him. This particular man couldn't have been more out of place, since he wore a gray suit and he was white.

"Ghedi Ahmed," said the white devil. "You know who he is?"

The Tiger nodded. "I know who he *used* to be."

"Make an example of him."

"And his family."

"Of course," said the white devil. "His family too."

Chapter 8

I PUT IN a call for help to my friend Avie Glazer, who headed up the Gang Intervention Project in the Third District. I told Avie why it was important to me.

"'Course I'll help. You know me, Alex. I'm more tapped into *La Mara R, Vatos Locos,* Northwest gangs. But you can come over here and ask around Seventeenth and R if you want. See if anybody's tuned in."

"Any way you could meet us?" I asked him. "I'll owe you one. Buy you a beer."

"Which makes it how many total? Favors *and* beers?"

That was his way of saying yes, though. Bree and I met Avie at a shitty little pool hall called Forty-Four. The owner told us that was how old he was when he opened the place. Avie already knew the story but listened politely anyway.

"Seemed like as good a name as any," the owner said. His *what-ev* attitude struck me as that of a long-term stoner. For sure, he wasn't making his nut on billiards and sodas. His name was Jaime Ramirez, and Avie Glazer had advised me to give him room and a little respect.

"You know anything about the murders in Georgetown last night?" I asked Ramirez after we'd chit-chatted some. "Multiple perps?"

"That was some awful shit," he said, leaning on the bottom half of a Dutch door, a brown cigarette held between stubby fingers and tilted at the same angle as his body.

He chinned up at the television in the corner. "Channel Four's all I get in here, Detective."

"How about any new games opening up?" Bree asked. "Players we might not have heard about? Somebody who would wipe a family out?"

"Hard to keep up," Ramirez said and shrugged. That's when Glazer gave him a look. "But yeah, matter of fact, there has been some talk."

His dark eyes flicked almost involuntarily past me and Bree. "Africans," he said to Avie.

"African American?" I asked. "Or—"

"African African." He turned back to Avie. "Yo, Toto, I'm gonna get something for this? Or this a freebie?"

Avie Glazer looked at me first and then at Ramirez. "Let's say I owe you one."

"What kind of African?" I asked.

He shrugged and blew out air. "How'm I supposed to know that? Black-guys-from-Africa kind of African."

"English speaking?"

"Yeah," he said, nodding. "But I never spoke to them. Sounds like they're into a little bit of everything. You know, four-H club? Hits, ho's, heroin, and heists. This ain't your graffiti-and-skip-party kind of gang."

He opened a glass-fronted cooler and took out a can of Coke. "Anyone thirsty? Two dollars."

"I'll take one," Glazer said. He cupped a couple of bills into Ramirez's hand, and they didn't look like singles.

Then Glazer turned to me. "And I *will* collect from you too. Count on it."

"Africans," Ramirez repeated as we headed toward the door, "*from Africa.*"

Chapter 9

THIS WAS THE last place I wanted to be in DC, or probably anyplace else.

So unbelievably sad, and eerie, and tragic. So many memories rising to the surface for me.

Ellie's office was up on the second floor of the house in Georgetown. It was as tidy and meticulously organized as I remembered her being back when we thought we might love each other.

A copy of Sidney Poitier's *The Measure of a Man* was open on the arm of an easy chair. I'd liked the autobiography and remembered that Ellie and I had similar tastes in books, music, and politics.

The shades were all drawn to exactly the same height. The desk held an iMac, a phone, an appointment book, and a few family photos in silver frames. The room felt strange compared with the downstairs of the house, which had been ransacked by the killers last night.

I started with Ellie's appointment book and then went on to the desk drawers. I wasn't sure yet what I was looking for, only that I'd had to come back here with a clearer head than I'd had last night.

I booted up Ellie's computer and went into her e-mail— checking the inbox, sent items, and deleted folders, working backward in time. I was trying to get as close as possible to the moment of the murders. Had Ellie known the killers?

The first thing to catch my attention was a note from an editor at Georgetown University Press. It concerned her completion schedule for "the new book."

Ellie had a new book coming out? I knew she was on the history faculty at Georgetown, but I didn't know much more than that. We had seen each other at a few charity events during the past fifteen years or so, but that was about it. She was married, I wasn't for much of that time, and that fact can sometimes cut down contact and communication.

I ran her name through Amazon and Barnes & Noble and found three book titles. Each had something to do with African sociopolitics. The most recent one, *Critical Juncture*, had been published four years ago.

So where was the new book? Was there a partial manuscript I could read?

I swiveled around to look over the floor-to-ceiling bookcases that took up two entire walls of the office. Ellie had hundreds of volumes here, mixed in with a collection of awards and citations.

Kids' artwork and framed photos covered the rest of the space.

Then all of a sudden *I was looking at a picture of myself.*

Chapter 10

IT WAS AN old snapshot from our college days. I remembered the time as soon as I saw it. Ellie and I were sitting on a blanket on the National Mall. We had just finished finals. I had a summer internship lined up at Sibley Memorial, and I was falling in love for the first time. Ellie told me that she was too. In the photograph, we were smiling and hugging one another, and it looked as if we could be that way forever.

Now here I was in her house, responsible for Ellie in a way I never could have imagined.

I let myself stare nostalgically at the picture for a few more seconds, then forced myself to move on, to come back to the present mess.

It didn't take long to find three hundred typed pages of a manuscript titled *Deathtrip*. The subtitle on the title page read *Crime as a Way of Life, of Doing Business, in Central Africa*.

A copy of a plane ticket had been inserted in the manuscript. The ticket was round-trip from Washington to Lagos, Nigeria. Ellie had returned from there two weeks ago.

I looked through the index at the back of the manuscript and found a listing for "Violence, African Style," and a subhead, "Family Massacre."

I turned to the relevant manuscript page and read: "There are gang leaders for hire all through Nigeria and especially in Sudan. These brutal men and their groups—*often made up of boys as young as ten*—have an unlimited appetite for violence and sadism. A favorite target is entire families, since that spreads both news and fear the farthest. Families are massacred in their huts and shacks, and even boiled in oil, a trademark of a few of the worst gang leaders."

I decided to take the partial manuscript with me to get it copied. I wanted to read everything that Ellie had written.

Was this what had gotten her killed—her book?

Next, I stared for a long time at a striking, poignant picture of Ellie, her husband, and their three beautiful children.

All dead now.

Murdered right here in their home. At least they hadn't been boiled in oil.

I took one more look at the photo of the two of us on the National Mall. Young and in love, or whatever it was that we were feeling.

"Ellie, I'll do what I can for you and your family. I promise you that."

I left the house, thinking, *What did you find in Africa? Did somebody follow you back?*

Chapter 11

EVERYBODY THERE KNEW there was trouble, but no one knew what kind or how bad it was.

A dark green panel van had screeched to a stop in front of a low-level mosque in Washington called Masjid Al-Shura. More than one hundred fifty peaceful congregants were crowding the sidewalk in front.

Even so, the very moment Ghedi Ahmed saw the gunmen scrambling out of the van, saw their gray hoodies, their black face masks and jaunty sunglasses, he knew they had come for him. *They were just boys—the Tiger's boys.*

The first gunshots were aimed into the sky. Just warnings. Men and women screamed, and some scurried back into the mosque.

Others flattened themselves on the sidewalk, shielding their children's bodies as best they could.

His hands held high, Ghedi Ahmed made his decision and

moved away from his family. *Better to die alone than to take them with me,* he was thinking, shaking like a leaf now.

He hadn't gotten far when he heard his wife, Aziza, scream, and he realized what a terrible mistake he'd made. "Ghedi! Ghedi!" He turned as the wild boys carried, then threw, Aziza into the waiting van. And then—his children! They were taking the children, too! All four of them were hustled into the van.

Ghedi reversed direction quickly, and now he was screaming more loudly than anyone in the crowd, even more than Aziza.

A courageous man from the congregation took a swing at one of the kidnappers. The boy yelled, "Dog!" and shot the man in the face. Then he fired again, where the man lay spread-eagled and already dying on the sidewalk.

Another bullet took down an elderly woman just as Ghedi pushed past her.

The next shot found his leg, and running became falling. Then two of the boys snatched him up off the ground and threw him into the van with his family.

"The children! Not our children!" sobbed Aziza.

"Where are you taking us?" Ghedi screamed at the kidnappers. "Where?"

"To Allah," came the answer from the driver, the Tiger himself.

Chapter 12

THE MYSTERY WAS deepening and getting worse each day, but much of Washington didn't seem to care, probably because this one happened in Southeast, and only black people were killed.

Lorton Landfill is the final destination for much of Washington's garbage. It is two hundred and fifty acres of foul and disgusting refuse, so we were fortunate the bodies had been found at all. I drove the R350 in through valleys of trash that rose thirty feet high on either side. I continued on to where the response team was parked around an orange-and-white DC sanitation truck. The gauze masks they'd provided Bree and me at the gate didn't do much against the nauseating smell.

"A drive in the country, Alex. This is so romantic," Bree said as we plunged forward through the muck. She was good at keeping things upbeat, no matter what the circumstances.

"I'm always thinking of new things for us to do."

"You've outdone yourself this time. Trust me on that."

I finally spotted Sampson talking to the truck's driver as we got out of the car. Behind the two of them and a ribbon of crime scene tape, I could see yellow sheets covering the six bodies where they had been found.

Two parents and four more kids here. That made four adults and seven children in just the past few days.

Sampson walked over to brief us. "Garbage truck started on the empty streets this morning and made stops all over midtown. Forty-one Dumpsters at eighteen locations, some of them as close as a few blocks from the mosque. That's a shitload of follow-up work for us."

"Any other good news?" I asked him.

"So far, only the bodies have been found. *No word on the heads.*" We hadn't released *that* so far to the press: All six of the victims had been decapitated.

"I love my job, I love my job," Bree said quietly. "I can't wait to get to work in the morning."

I asked Sampson where the father's body was, and we started there. When I pulled back the sheet, the sight was horrific, but I didn't need an ME to tell me that the cutting was much cleaner this time. There were no extraneous wounds: no bullet holes, no slashes, no punctures. Plus, the lower body had been burned badly.

Senseless murders, but probably not random, I was thinking.

But what did the Ahmed killings have to do with Ellie and her family?

"We've got some similarities and some real differences

here," Sampson told us. "Two families taken out suddenly. Multiple perps. But one behind closed doors, the other outside a mosque. Heavy cutting in both cases."

"But different cutting," Bree said. "And if the heads don't turn up—"

"Something tells me they won't," I said.

"Then, maybe we're talking about trophies, keepsakes."

"Or proof of purchase," I said.

They both looked at me. "Maybe this one was business, and the other was personal. Also, CNBC just broke a story that Ghedi Ahmed was the brother of Erasto Ahmed, who's Al-Qaeda, operating out of Somalia."

"Al-Qaeda?" Bree whispered and looked momentarily stumped. "Al-Qaeda, Alex?"

We stood there, silent for a moment, trying to comprehend something as horrible as these murders. I thought of Ellie again. I couldn't stop thinking of her the past few days. *Did her trip to Africa have something to do with her murder?*

"So, what are we looking at?" Sampson finally spoke again. "Two sides of a war?"

"Could be," I said. "Or maybe two teams."

Or maybe one very smart killer, trying to keep us guessing.

Chapter 13

THERE WAS NO question there was federal interest in these cases. They were inflammatory and international in scope, and the CIA probably knew something. Two of their people had shown up at Ellie's house the night of the murders. The question was, How much could I get them to tell me, if anything at all?

I pulled in a few favors from my days with the bureau and got a meeting set up at Langley. The fact that they not only agreed to meet but also waived the first in what was normally a two-meeting protocol told me this was no back-burner issue for them. Usually, the CIA started you with somebody who couldn't do anything for you before you even got close to anybody who could.

I was given a whole team: Eric Dana from the National Clandestine Service; two spit-shined analysts in their mid twenties who never spoke a word the whole time I was there;

and one familiar face, Al Tunney, from the Office of Transnational Issues.

Tunney and I had worked together on a Russian mafia case a few years back. I hoped he would advocate for me here, but this was clearly Eric Dana's meeting, his case. We sat at a gleaming wood table with a view of nothing but green forests and lawns as far as I could see. Peaceful, serene, *very misleading.*

"Detective Cross, why don't you tell us what you know so far?" Dana asked. "That would be helpful to get things going."

I didn't hold back, saw no reason to. I walked them through all three crime scenes—the Cox house, the street outside Masjid Al-Shura, and, finally, the landfill out in Lorton.

I also passed around a set of photos, keeping them chronological.

Then I covered everything I'd learned or heard about gang leaders in Africa, including what I'd read in Ellie's book. Only then did I mention the CIA officers who had shown up at the first murder scene.

"We won't comment on that," said Dana. "Not at this point."

"I'm not looking for you to open your files to me," I said to Dana. "But I'd like to know if you're tracking a killer stateside. And if you are, do you have any idea where he is?"

Dana listened to what I had to say, then shoved a stack of papers back into a file and stood up.

"Okay. Thank you, Detective Cross. This has been most helpful. We'll get back to you. Let us do our thing here for a few days."

It wasn't the response I wanted. "Hold on, what are you talking about? Get back to me *now*."

It was a bad moment. Dana stared at his analysts with a look that said, *Didn't anyone brief this guy?*

Then he looked back at me, not impolitely. "I think I understand your urgency, Detec —"

"I don't think you do," I cut in. I looked over at Al Tunney, who was shifting uncomfortably in his seat. "Al, is this a joint decision?"

Tunney's eyes played tennis between me and Dana. "No one's decided anything, Alex. We just can't turn over information that quickly," he finally said. "That's not how we work. You knew that when you came here."

"You can't or you won't?" I asked, looking at Tunney first, then at Dana.

"We won't," Dana said. "And it's my decision, no one else's. You have no idea what kind of damage this man and his team are responsible for."

I leaned across the table. "All the more reason to drop any turf wars, don't you think? We're here for the same reason," I said.

Dana stood at the table. "We'll get back to you." Then he left the room. *How very CIA of him.*

Chapter 14

BUT I COULDN'T let it go like that, and I didn't.

In the wide, mostly empty corridor outside the conference room, I called to Al Tunney before he could get away. "Hey, Al! I meant to ask you how Trish and the kids are doing." I held up a hand to my building escort. "I'll just be a second."

Al was giving me a disgusted look as I walked over to him. I knew he had a wife, but unless I was psychic, her name probably wasn't Trish.

I started right in with him. "You know something, or you wouldn't be at that meeting. Neither would Dana. Your guys were at the murder scene. Help me out here. Anything, *something*, Al."

"Alex, I can't. This case is even hotter than you think it is. You heard my boss in there. It goes right to the top of our group. Steven Millard is involved. Trust me, there *is* an investigation going on. We're taking it very seriously."

"Eric Dana doesn't know me, and neither does Steven Millard, but you do. You know what I can get done. I don't have to prove that to you, do I?" A large department seal loomed over us in the hall. I took a step to the side so Tunney wouldn't be looking up at it.

"Very funny," he said.

"Come on, Al. Two families have died already. Doesn't that mean anything?"

Then Tunney said a really odd thing. "Not as much as you might think. There are other monsters."

My escort called over from the intersection in the corridor. "Detective Cross? This way?"

"One second." I turned back to Tunney again. "Ellie Cox was a dear friend. Nicole Cox was thirteen. Clara was six. James ten. The four Ahmed kids? All younger than twelve. They didn't just die, Al. *Their heads were cut off.* Whoever did it is on a par with Hannibal Lecter. Only this is *real*."

"I know the case by heart," he said. "I've got it."

"You have kids, right? I've got three. Damon, Jannie, and Ali. What about you?"

"Jesus." Tunney shook his head at me. "You got mean somewhere along the way."

"Not mean, Al. I'm trying to solve some horrific murders. Something tells me the trail might go to Africa. Is that true?"

I could tell he was close to giving me something. I put a hand on his shoulder and ratcheted down my tone a little. "I'm not asking for any deep agency secrets. I'm talking about existing police business. In my own jurisdiction. At least for now."

Tunney looked down at the floor tile for a few seconds,

then over at my escort, then back at the floor. Without looking up, he said, "There's been some talk about a deal going down. We got this from the FBI. Service Plaza in Virginia. Chantilly, Virginia. Might be your guy. You'd be within your rights to intercept."

"What kind of deal?"

Tunney didn't answer. He put out his hand, with a smile broad enough for the escort to see. His voice rose just a notch. "It was good seeing you again, Alex. And say hello to Bree for me. Like I said, I know this case by heart. It *is* horrific. Boy shot your friend. And please remember this, we're still the good guys, Alex. No matter what you might read or see in the movies."

Chapter 15

BY EIGHT O'CLOCK that night, I had gathered together a half dozen handpicked officers from Major Case Squad, plus Bree, Sampson, and myself. We wore Kevlar vests under plain clothes and were heavily armed and wired, waiting at the service plaza in Chantilly, Virginia, where something might be going down involving my killer.

We were scheduled for a twelve-hour shift, eight to eight if we needed it. The team was already spread out over five sectors: front car park, restaurant, gas station, and both sides of the big truck lot in back. Sampson had a hip problem, so he was on the roof observing for us. Bree and I traded off roaming and covering the communications van parked near the entrance, with another good view of the service plaza.

There was no sign of the CIA. *Had they not shown up yet?*

For the first five hours, there was nothing but radio silence and lots of bad coffee.

Then just after one in the morning, the silence broke.

"Twenty-two-oh-one. Over."

"Go ahead, twenty-two-oh-one."

I looked over from the communications van toward the far corner of the truck lot, where a detective named Jamal McDonald was stationed.

"I got two Land Cruisers. Just pulled up to a tanker in the back. Northeast corner."

"How long has the tanker been there?" I asked McDonald.

"Hard to say, Alex. At least half an hour. Most of these tankers been pulling in and out."

We hadn't known what to expect tonight, but stolen gas or crude would make sense, especially if Nigerians were involved. I was already out of the van and walking quickly in Jamal's direction. Two dozen or more semis, lined up in rows, were temporarily blocking my view of the corner.

"Nicolo, Redman, pull in tighter. Bree, where are you right now?"

"I'm behind the buildings. Headed east."

"Good. Everyone else hold position. What about you, John? See anything yet?"

"Nothing from here," Sampson radioed back. "Nobody's moving around over there. Just you guys."

"Jamal, how close are you?"

"Hang on. Just coming around a semi." I caught sight of him briefly up near the last row of trucks as I crossed the parking lot. Bree fell in silently beside me.

I had my Glock out, low at my side. So did she. *Was the killer here with his team? Were they the same ones who had killed the Coxes and the Ahmeds?*

"Somebody's getting out of the cab," Jamal McDonald whispered. "No, two people. There's four others I can see approaching from the Land Cruisers. Looks like a satchel of some kind. This must be it. Hang on." There was a brief silence and then, "Shit! I think they see me. Looks like little kids—teenagers!"

Bree and I were running now. "Jamal, what's going on? We're on our way, *almost there!*"

The next thing we heard were gunshots, lots of them.

Chapter 16

BREE AND I began to sprint at full speed in the direction of the first volley of shots. I could still hear Jamal McDonald—but he was making a wet, gasping sound, as though he might have been hit in the throat and was possibly suffocating.

The other officers were shouting "twenties" over the wireless and also converging on the tanker. Sampson stayed put on the roof and radioed Fairfax County for more help.

We were only halfway there when three or four fast-moving shadows ran across our path. Maybe fifty feet ahead. *They looked like kids to me,* just like Jamal had said.

One of them fired from the hip as he went, not even trying to keep covered. Then they all opened up on us. It was like some kind of Old West shoot-out; they appeared to have no fear at all, no concept of dying.

Bree and I dropped down and fired back from ground

level. Bullets sparked off the asphalt and trucks in the dark, but we couldn't see who we were shooting at now or where they were headed.

"Kids," Bree said.

"Killers," I corrected her.

A second heavy exchange of fire came from the next row over of trucks. One of the team members, Art Sheiner, shouted out that he'd been hit too.

Then everything was quiet again.

"Sheiner?" I radioed.

He didn't respond.

"McDonald?"

No response either.

"Sampson, we need medical with that backup."

"On its way. I'm coming down now."

"Stay up there, John. We need a spotter, more than ever. Stay where you are!"

"Sir, it's Connors." He was the rookie of the group and his voice was tight. "I found Jamal. He's down. There's a lot of blood."

"Stay with him! But watch yourself."

"Twenty-two-oh-four." It was Frank Nicolo. "Sheiner's here. He's down. No pulse. I think he's gone."

Then, suddenly, there were more shots!

Chapter 17

WE WERE UP and running again. Two officers had been shot, and an unknown number of assailants were at the service plaza. A second ambush opened up on us. A bullet streaked by my face.

Someone had fired from the roof of a tractor trailer — as he ran down the length of it. I shot back and couldn't tell if I'd hit the sniper or not. Everything was happening like fireworks — there and gone — then quiet again.

"What the fuck?" somebody shouted on radio. He didn't explain. *Couldn't?*

"Alex! Bree!" It was Sampson again. "By the pumps! To your left!"

I ran out to where I could see the main buildings. Three of the gunmen had a good fifty yards on us and were running toward the gas canopy, firing as they went. They had black balaclavas pulled over their heads.

Two were short—*boys*, if the height was any indication. A larger person—huge—was in the first position. Was that the gang leader? Ellie's killer. It had to be him, didn't it? I wanted to get the bastard, no matter what else happened tonight.

Innocent people ran screaming away from their cars and semis. There was too much confusion for us to fire.

A woman in a red parka and baseball cap went down, clutching her stomach. The large man shot her a second time! *Was he crazy?*

Then he plucked the gas nozzle out of her SUV. He definitely *was* mad. He locked it in the on position, then left the gas running on the ground.

Then he stepped over to the next car in line and did the same thing.

His team of boys was getting clear of the area, running and shouting as if this were some kind of out-of-control sports match. His pistol was pointed at the pooling gas, and that was all the warning I needed.

"Hold fire! Hold fire!" I yelled, then pulled up short of the pumps. "Bree, take Brighton. Go around the other side. Nicolo, get somebody to shut those things off."

The large man held a third nozzle in his hand now, just letting the gasoline flow onto the pavement. I could smell the vapors, even at this distance.

What the hell was he thinking?

"Just put it down. Walk away!" I shouted. "We won't fire on you."

He didn't move, just stared back at me. No fear in him. A second later, someone shouted behind him. Then came three short blasts of a car horn.

Finally he did what I'd asked. He kept his gun pointed my way, but set the gas nozzle down. He backed away slowly, moving out of the light of the canopy.

We were clear—*he was leaving!*

Then several shots were fired out of the darkness. It was him—the bastard!

A wall of flame burst from the concrete. It almost seemed like a magic trick. In seconds, the forecourt was burning, flames licking under and around the empty cars.

A white Corolla went up first. It exploded right where the large male had been standing a few seconds ago. Then a black pickup on the other side of the pumps caught fire.

"Clear! Clear! Clear! Clear!" I was shouting and waving both arms over my head, trying to get everybody, civilians and police, away from there.

That's when the first pump head blew.

And then—*Armageddon in Virginia.*

Chapter 18

THE PLAZA WITH its lines of gas pumps exploded from underneath, the pavement rising like a carpet being rolled. Flames shot at least eighty feet into the air, a ball of bright yellow and orange, followed by a heavy black coat of smoke. Burning vehicles rolled around like toy cars; truckers and families fled screaming from the restaurant, where the fire had already spread and with it *the panic*.

I was running as close to the blast site as I could. Heat singed my face, my eyes, and my hearing felt like it was half gone.

Up ahead I could see two SUVs speeding out toward Route 50. They were getting away!

I spotted Bree coming around from the far side of the building and breathed a sigh of relief. She was all right. She ran toward my car and so did I.

I got in the R350 and punched it up to ninety in a hurry.

For a few uneasy seconds, there was nothing ahead of us, nothing I could see.

"*There!*" Bree pointed at the two SUVs. They must have spotted us because just then they peeled off from each other.

The first Land Cruiser went left. The second SUV turned right. I followed the lead vehicle, hoping I had made the right choice.

Chapter 19

I BARRELED DOWN a dark two-lane road, gaining ground quickly on the Land Cruiser. A deep drainage culvert curled along our left side. I came up on the Cruiser's taillights, and the driver appeared to panic. Suddenly it flared to the right, then cut back nearly ninety degrees without slowing. Then the Land Cruiser flew straight toward the ditch.

For a second I thought he'd make it across. The Land Cruiser had air under it, but the front end came down too fast. It crashed hard and loud, the undercarriage fracturing.

The front wheels were lodged into the far bank. The rear tires continued to spin fiercely.

Bree and I were already out of our car and crouched behind the open doors.

"Out of the vehicle! Now!" I yelled across the ditch.

Finally, I could see bodies moving inside the Land Cruiser.

The adult was in the driver's seat. Next to him was someone barely tall enough to be seen.

The smaller figure reached through the passenger-side window. He put one palm on the roof, then the other. He started lifting himself up and out.

"Down on the ground! Now!" Bree shouted at him. "Get down, I said!"

But he didn't! He torpedoed himself up onto the roof, skinny and cat-quick. His gun was out now, pointing our way. He slid across the roof, firing three quick shots at us.

We fired back. A round caught him and he dropped to the ground. But not before he'd given the adult enough cover to get outside. The driver's door was open. I couldn't see the large man, but I knew he was getting away.

Bree stopped beside the kid; I kept going. Down into the ditch, then up the other side.

I'd thought there were woods beyond the gulley, but now I saw there was just cedar screening and tall weeds.

Suddenly I heard the rattle of a chain-link fence. The large male was climbing it. By the time I pushed through the trees, he was over the top and running across the rear yard of some kind of storage facility.

I leveled my Glock against the chain link, then emptied the magazine. He was too far away. I didn't think I'd hit him and then he turned. He waved contemptuously, then disappeared like a cat into the darkness.

I called in the location and then ran back to see about Bree. She was still crouched near the ground, right where I had left her. She'd put her jacket over the dead boy's face. It was an odd thing for a cop in a shoot-out to do, but Bree liked to go her own way.

"You okay?" I asked.

She didn't look up. "He was maybe twelve, Alex. Maybe that old. He ran suicide for the prick adult."

"Was he alive when you got to him?" I asked her. Bree nodded.

"He say anything?"

"Yeah." She finally looked up at me. "He told me to fuck myself. His last words on this earth."

Chapter 20

I DIDN'T SLEEP more than a couple of hours that night. An officer and two civilians were dead—not to mention one of the boy killers, the *"world's youngest terrorist,"* according to a *Washington Post* headline the next morning. On top of everything else, I had an eight o'clock psych client to see at St. Anthony's.

Ever since the Tyler Bell case the year before, when I was literally stalked in my own office, I'd had to seriously re-evaluate my life. The upshot: I'd decided my criminal cases were too high-profile too often for me to keep the private in private practice anymore. Now, I saw only two or three patients a week, usually pro bono, and I was satisfied with that. Most days, anyway.

But I didn't want to see this particular patient—not today.

It was ironic that I had a session with Bronson "Pop-Pop"

James that morning. He was eleven years old and probably the most advanced sociopath at that age I'd ever seen. Four months before, he'd made headlines when he and a seventeen-year-old beat two homeless men half to death. They had used a cinder block. It was Pop-Pop's idea. The district attorney hadn't figured out how to try the case yet, and Bronson was being held in juvenile custody. The one thing he had going for him was a very good social worker from Corrections, who made sure he got to his appointments with me.

At first I thought it best to keep the events of the last night out of my head. Once the session got going, though, I changed my mind.

"Bronson, you hear about what happened at the service plaza in Virginia last night?"

He sat across from me on a cheap vinyl couch, fidgeting the whole time, hands and feet always in motion. "Yeah, right, I heard. They was talking 'bout that shit on the radio. What of it?"

"The boy who died . . . he was twelve."

Bronson grinned and put two fingers to his head. "Heard he got X-Boxed."

His confidence was prodigious; it gave him a strange adult quality — while his feet dangled about six inches off the floor in my office.

"You ever think something like that might happen to you?" I asked him.

He snorted. "Every day. It's no thing."

"That's okay with you, though? Makes sense? That's how the world should be?"

"That's how the world be. *Bam*."

"So then"—I looked around the room and back at him—"why bother to sit here and talk to me about it? That doesn't make much sense to me."

"'Cause that bitch Lorraine fuckin' make me come."

I nodded. "Just because you come here doesn't mean you have to say anything. But you do. You talk to me. Why do you think that is?"

He made a thing of getting all impatient. "You the witch doctor, you tell me."

"You envy kids like the one who died? Working for a living? Running around with guns?"

He squinted at me, pulled the Lebron James Cleveland Cavaliers sweatband around his head a little lower. "Whaddya mean?"

"You know, are you jealous of them?"

He smiled again, but only to himself. Then he slouched down on the couch and reached out with a toe to casually tip over the orange juice I'd given him. It spilled across the table between us. "Yo, they got any Skittles in the machine downstairs? Go get me some Skittles!"

I did no such thing. After the session, I escorted Pop-Pop out to his social worker and told the boy I'd see him on Friday. Then I went home and picked up Nana.

We went to the Cox family funeral together. We held each other and cried with everybody else.

I didn't care if people saw me cry anymore. I just didn't care. If they were friends, they would understand. If they weren't, what did it matter what they thought of me?

That philosophy, to give credit where credit is due, was a Nana-ism.

Chapter 21

"THIS IS DETECTIVE Alex Cross. I'm with the Metro police here in Washington. I need to speak with Ambassador Njoku or his representative. It's important, *very important*."

Late that night, I was in the car with Bree, speeding to the Bubble Lounge in the heart of Georgetown. Four people were dead at the club. Two were Nigerian citizens, and one was the son of the ambassador. Advance reports had twenty-one-year-old Daniel Njoku as the gunman's primary target. That meant one thing to me: The Njoku family didn't need just notification; they might also need protection—if it wasn't already too late. So far, all of the gang's murders had involved families.

A night deputy from the Nigerian embassy was on the line with me. I kept one ear covered, trying to hear what she was saying above the wail of Bree's siren.

"Sir, I am very sorry, but I will need more information than simply—"

"This is an emergency call. Their son Daniel was just murdered at a nightclub. We have reason to believe the ambassador and his wife may be in danger too. We're sending police cruisers right now."

"But, sir . . . the Njokus are not in the country. They are at a symposium, in Abuja."

"Find them, then. Tell them to get somewhere secure. Please, do whatever you can do. Then call me back at this number. I'm Detective Cross."

"I'll do what I can, sir. I will call you back, Detective Cross."

I hung up, feeling a little helpless. How was I supposed to stop a murder that could happen six thousand miles away?

Chapter 22

"I WANT TO talk to the witnesses first. As many of them as I can. No one goes home."

The Bubble Lounge had been a lively place, but by the time I got there it was a wrecking yard. There were overturned tables, smashed and scattered chairs, broken shards of glass everywhere. Body teams were working both floors; we had six GSW, one broken neck, and one suffocation. EMTs were still busily triaging the wounded. Young people were moaning and crying, and everyone I passed looked dazed, even the police officers.

Members of Daniel Njoku's party were being held in the coat-check area. I found them sitting close together on sofas, huddled. One girl, wearing a tiny black dress with a man's blazer over her shoulders, had blood smeared all over her neck and cheek.

I knelt down next to her. "I'm Detective Cross. I'm here to help. What's your name?"

"Karavi," she said. She had beautiful long hair and scared

dark eyes, and I thought she might be East Indian. She looked to be early twenties at most.

"Karavi, did you get a look at the people who did this?"

"Just one man," she whimpered to me. "He was huge."

"Excuse me, sir," one of the others interrupted, "but we need to speak with our lawyers before we say anything to police." The speaker had an air of privilege about him; these twenty-somethings spent their Saturday nights in private boxes at a private club.

"You can talk to me," I said to the girl.

"Nonetheless, sir—"

"Or," I interrupted, "we can do this later tonight and tomorrow. After I'm done here with all of the others."

"It's all right, Freddy," Karavi said, waving off the boy. "I want to help if I possibly can. Daniel is dead."

We sat off to the side for a little privacy, and Karavi told me she was a grad student in cell biology at Georgetown. Both her parents were in the diplomatic corps, which was how she knew Daniel Njoku. They had been best friends but were never a couple. Daniel's girlfriend, Bari Nederman, had been shot tonight too, but she was alive.

Karavi described the gunman as a lone black man, maybe six six, at least that tall, wearing dark street clothes. "And he just looked...strong," she said. "He had huge, muscular arms. Everything about him was powerful."

"How about his voice? Did he speak to anyone? Before he started to shoot?"

Karavi nodded. "I heard him say something like 'I have an invitation' just before he..." She trailed off, not able to finish the thought.

"What kind of accent?" I asked. "American? Something else?" I was pushing because I knew I'd never get a better, truer account than right now.

"He wasn't from here," she said. "Not American, I'm certain of that."

"Nigerian? Did he sound like Daniel?"

"Maybe." Her jaw clenched as she fought back the tears. "It's hard to think straight. I'm sorry."

"Anyone else here Nigerian?" I turned back toward the others. "I need someone with a Nigerian accent."

One of the boys spoke up. "I'm sorry, Officer, but there's no such thing." He had a Jimi Hendrix 'fro and an open tuxedo shirt showing off his skinny chest and jewelry. "I speak Yoruban, for instance. There is also Igbo, and Hausa. And dozens of other languages. I'm not sure it's appropriate for you to suggest—"

"That's it!" Karavi put a shaking hand on my arm. I noticed a few of the others in the party were nodding too. "That's how the killer sounded. *Just like him.*"

Chapter 23

I WAS STILL at the nightclub murder scene around two in the morning, conducting interviews that had begun to blend one into another, when the cell in my trousers pocket rang. I figured it might be the Nigerian embassy and answered it right away.

"Alex Cross, Metro," I said.

"Dad?"

Damon's voice on my cell shocked me a little. *At two in the morning, why wouldn't it?* What was up now?

"Day, what's going on?" I asked my fourteen-year-old, who was away at school in Massachusetts.

"Uh...nothing really," Damon said. I think my tone had taken him off guard. "I mean—I've been trying to call you all day. I've got some good news."

I was relieved, but my pulse was still racing. "Okay, I need some good news. But what are you doing up so late?"

"I had to stay up. To catch *you*. I called home, talked to Nana. I didn't want to call you on your cell."

I took in a slow breath and walked over to the hall by the bathrooms, away from the crime scene techs. No matter the time, it was always good to hear Damon's voice. I missed our talks, the boxing lessons I gave him, watching his basketball games. "What's your news? Let me hear it."

"Nana already knows, but I wanted to tell you myself. I made the varsity. As a freshman. That's pretty good, right? Oh, and I got As on my midterms."

"Listen to you — 'Oh, and I got As.' Nice one-two, Damon. I guess you're doing pretty good up there," I said, and suddenly I found myself smiling.

It was weird to be having this conversation under neon lights in a hallway that smelled of liquor and death, but it was still great news. Cushing Academy's sports *and* academic program had been a real draw for Damon. I knew how hard he'd been working to do well at both.

"Sir?" A uniform leaned her head into the hallway. "Nine-one-one dispatch for you?"

"Listen, Damon, can I call you later? Like in daylight, maybe?"

He laughed. "Sure, Dad. This is a big one, isn't it? Your case at that club. I saw you online."

"It is a big one," I admitted. "But it's still great to hear your voice. *Any time.* Get some sleep."

"Yeah, I will. You get some sleep too."

I hung up, feeling guilty. If this is what work meant — two a.m. conversations with my son — then I better make the work count. Dispatch relayed the call over to me, and I got the same woman from the Nigerian embassy as before. This time, though, her voice was thick with emotion.

"Detective, I'm sorry to tell you, but Ambassador and Mrs. Njoku were killed tonight. We're quite in shock."

I didn't feel shocked, I felt sick. "When did it happen?" I asked her.

"We're not entirely sure. Within the past few hours, I believe."

And within minutes of their son's murder? Had that been the plan all along? And whose plan? To what end? What was going on here?

I slid down against the wall until I rested on my haunches. Another family dead. And this time, the murder had crossed two continents — two completely different worlds. At least I thought so at the time.

Chapter 24

THE BIG HEAT was on all of us now. It took me all of the next day to locate the CIA's Eric Dana again, and then I found him only because he showed up at the Daly Building.

I caught Dana coming out of Chief Davies's office, and I saw the boss sitting inside before the door closed again. He wasn't smiling, and he didn't look up at me, though I was pretty sure he knew I was there.

I walked up to Dana. "Where have you been all day? I called at least half a dozen times. I need your help on this case. What's the problem?"

The CIA man didn't even break stride. "Talk to your CO. Metro is out of this. Chantilly was a disaster from our point of view. Our division head, Steven Millard, is involved at this point."

Millard. I'd heard that name from my buddy Al Tunney.

I caught up with Dana at the elevator and elbowed my

way through the closing door. "Where is the killer?" I asked him. "What do you know about him?"

"We believe he's left the country. We'll let you know if he heads this way again," the CIA man said, and he actually looked at me for the first time. "Stick to your own crime scenes, Cross. Do your job. I'll do mine."

"Is that advice or a threat?" I asked Dana.

"As long as you're working in DC, it's advice. I have no control or influence over you here."

His superior attitude was no surprise, and it didn't steam so much as focus me. I reached over and flipped the red toggle in the elevator. We jerked to a stop, and a warning bell went off.

"*Where* did he go, Dana?" I shouted. "Tell me where the hell he is!"

"What's the matter with you? This isn't how the game is played."

When Dana reached for the switch, I grabbed his arm and held it.

"Where did he go?" I asked again. "This isn't a game to me."

Dana looked at me with hard eyes. He said, very evenly, "Let go of my arm, Cross. Get your hand the hell off me. He went back to Nigeria. The killer is out of your jurisdiction."

I knew I'd taken this too far, and it made me realize how emotional I was about this case, maybe even more than I knew. I let go, and he flipped the elevator back on without a word. We rode to the lobby in silence and I watched the CIA prick leave the building.

The only question now was whether or not I could get

around him. Maybe if I hurried. I dialed my cell phone from right there in the lobby of the Daly Building.

"Al Tunney," I heard a voice on the other end answer.

"It's Alex Cross. I need a favor," I said.

Tunney said, "No," and groaned.

Then he asked, "What is it?"

I told him, and he groaned again, and I really couldn't blame him.

Chapter 25

"ALEX, YOU'RE TAKING this too far," Bree said.

"I know that. It's what I do. It's what I've always done."

Late that night, Bree and I were taking a ride around town. I like to drive late at night when the traffic thins out, and sixty, even seventy, isn't a dangerous speed on most of these avenues. Once we got back to Fifth Street I was feeling better, but Bree was still wound up. She couldn't stop pacing up in the bedroom. I had never seen her like this, agitated and unsure of herself.

"See, the thing is, I've always been the one on the *other side* of this particular argument, the one trying to do the convincing. I've never been the person sitting there not buying it. You're going over the top here, Alex. This latest plan of yours. Chase the killer back in Africa? Even under the circumstances, it's — I don't even know what to call it."

I started to speak, but she went on.

"And you know *why* I don't buy your arguments now, Alex? Because sometimes in your position, I'd lie. I don't know how many times I've told my family there was nothing to worry about, or how safe I was going to be, when really I had no idea. *You* have no idea what you'll find in Africa."

"You're right," I said, and not just to get her to stop pacing. "I won't try to sell you some bill of goods here, Bree. But I will tell you that I'm not going to do anything stupid over there."

It was about eight hours after my confrontation with Eric Dana and my subsequent conversation with Tunney. Tunney had gone as far as setting me up with a CIA officer stationed in Nigeria — just before he told me never to call him again.

I had the frequent flier miles, so that wasn't a problem. I had vacation time banked with the MPD. Now I just had to convince two of the strongest women I'd ever known that it made sense for me to do this — *Bree tonight, Nana Mama tomorrow.*

The air, the tension, between Bree and me was as thick as I'd ever felt it.

"What exactly are you hoping to accomplish over there?" she finally asked me.

"Ultimately? Use Tunney's guy to set up some local co-operation. Then steer the killer into custody if I can. I can get this guy, Bree. He's arrogant, thinks he can't be caught. That's his weakness."

"Kyle Craig was a lifer, several times over. It's no guarantee, Alex. That's *if* you catch him."

I allowed myself a sheepish grin. "And yet we keep doing our jobs anyway, don't we? We keep trying to catch these killers."

I finally reached out and took her hand. Then I pulled her over to sit next to me on the bed.

"I have to go, Bree. He's already killed more people in Washington than anyone I've seen. Eventually he'll come back and start up again."

"And he killed your friend."

"Yes, he killed my friend. He killed Ellie Cox *and her entire family.*"

Finally Bree shrugged. "So, go. Go to Africa, Alex." And we hugged each other for a long time, and I was reminded again of why I loved her. And maybe why I was running away from her now.

Chapter 26

HE MET UP with the white devil in a wood-paneled cigar bar just off Pennsylvania Avenue, half a dozen blocks from the White House. They ordered drinks and appetizers, and the white man selected a Partagás cigar.

"Cigars aren't a vice of yours?" the white man asked.

"I have no vices," said the Tiger. "I am pure of heart."

The white man laughed at that.

"The money has been transferred, three hundred and fifty thousand. You're going back now?"

"Yes, later tonight, in fact. I'm looking forward to being home in Nigeria."

The man nodded. "Even in such troubled times?"

"Especially now. There's lots of work for me. I like being lazy. Oil rich. Getting there anyway. By my standards."

The white man clipped his expensive cigar and the Tiger sipped his cognac. He wasn't certain, but he thought he knew who his employer was. It wouldn't be the first time. This group's contractors in Africa weren't always reliable—*but he was. Always.*

"There's something else."

"There always is," said the Tiger, "with you people."

"You're being followed by an American policeman."

"He won't go to Africa after me."

"Yes, actually he will. You might have to kill him, but we would prefer you didn't. His name is Alex Cross."

"I see. Alex Cross. Not smart to travel all the way to Africa just to die."

"No," said the white man. "Try to remember that yourself."

Part Two

SIGN OF THE CROSS

Chapter 27

THE TIGER WAS an enigma in every way, a mystery no one had ever solved. Actually, there were no tigers in Africa, which was how he got his nickname. He was like no other, one of a kind, superior to all the other animals, especially humans.

Before he went to school in England, the Tiger had lived in France for a couple of years, and he had learned French and English. He discovered he had a gift for languages, and he could remember almost everything he learned or read. His first summer in France, he'd sold mechanical birds to children in the parking areas outside the palace at Versailles. He'd learned a valuable lesson there: to hate the white man, and especially white families.

This day he had a mission in a city he didn't much like because the foreigner had left too much of a mark here. The city was Port Harcourt in the Delta region of Nigeria, where most of the oil wells were located.

The game was on. He had another bounty to collect.

A black Mercedes was speeding up a steep hill toward the wealthy foreigners' part of the city—and straight toward the Tiger as well.

As always, he waited patiently for his prey.

Then he wandered out into the street like some poor drunkard on a binge. The Mercedes would either have to stop very quickly or strike him head-on.

Probably because he was so large and might dent the car, at the last possible moment, the chauffeur applied the brakes.

The Tiger could see the liveried black scum cursing him from behind the spotlessly clean windshield. So he raised his pistol fast and shot the driver and a bodyguard through the glass.

His boys, wild, were already at both rear doors of the limousine, breaking the side windows with crowbars.

Then they threw open the doors and pulled out the screaming white schoolchildren, a boy and a girl in their early teens.

"Don't harm them, I have other plans!" he yelled.

An hour later, he had the boy and girl inside a shack on a deserted farm outside the city. They were dead now, unrecognizable even if they were found eventually. He had boiled them in a pot of oil. His employer had ordered this manner of death, which happened to be common in Sudan. The Tiger had no problem with it.

Finally, he pulled out his cell phone and called a number in town. When the phone was picked up on the other end, he didn't allow the American parents to speak.

Nor would he ever talk to the local police, or to the private contractor who worked for the oil company and was supposed to protect them from harm.

"You want to see young Adam and Chloe again, you do exactly as I say. First of all, I don't want to hear a word from you. *Not a word.*"

One of the cops spoke, of course, and he hung up on him. He would call back later, and have his money by the end of the day. It was easy work, and Adam and Chloe reminded him of the obnoxious and greedy white children who used to buy his mechanical birds at Versailles.

He felt no regret for them, nothing at all. It was just business to him.

Just another large bounty to collect.

And just the start of things to come.

Chapter 28

I WAS DETERMINED to follow the psycho killer and his gang wherever it took me, but I could see this wasn't going to be easy. Quite the opposite.

"You *took* my passport? Did I get that right?" I asked Nana. "You actually stole my passport?"

She ignored the questions and set a plate of scrambled eggs in front of me. Overdone and no toast, I noticed. *So this was war.*

"That's right," she said. "You behave like an obstinate child, that's how I treat you. Purloined," she added. "I prefer *purloined* to stole."

I pushed the plate away. "Ellie Cox died because of this man, Nana. So did her family. And another family here in DC. Don't pretend this has nothing to do with us."

"You mean *you*. And your job, Alex. That's what this has

to do with." She poured a half cup of coffee and then headed for her room.

I called after her. "You know stealing someone's passport is against the law?"

"So arrest me," she said, and slammed shut her door. Six in the morning and round one of the new day was already over.

We'd been building up to this ever since I first mentioned the possibility of my going to Africa. At first she'd been coy, with news articles cropping up around the house. I found a *Time* cover story, "The Deadly Delta," snipped out and left with my laundry one night; a BBC news piece with the headline "Many Factions, No Peace for Nigeria" in an envelope next to my keys the next morning.

When I ignored them, she moved on to lecturing—with a list of what-ifs and potential risks, as if I hadn't considered nearly every one of them myself. Muslims killing Christians in the north of Nigeria; Christians retaliating in Eastern Nigeria; students lynching a Christian teacher; mass graves found in Okija; police corruption and brutality; daily kidnappings in Port Harcourt.

It's not that she was all wrong. These murder cases were already dangerous, and I hadn't even given up the home-court advantage yet. The truth was, I didn't know what to expect in Africa. All I knew was that if I had a chance to shut this butcher down, I was going to take it. The CIA contact there had signaled the murder suspect was in Lagos right now, or at least he had been a few days ago.

I'd pulled some strings to expedite my visa application.

Then I had cashed in seventy-five thousand miles for a last-minute ticket to Lagos.

Now the only obstacle was my eighty-eight-year-old grandmother. Big obstacle. She stayed in her room until I left for work that morning, refusing to even talk about the *purloined* passport.

Obviously, I couldn't get far without it.

Chapter 29

THAT NIGHT, I gave Nana Mama a little taste of her own medicine. I waited until late, after the kids had gone to bed. Then I found her in her favorite reading chair, huddled over a copy of *Eats, Shoots & Leaves*.

"What's this?" She squinted at the manila folder in my hand as if it might bite her.

"More news articles. I want you to take a look at them. They tell a horrible story, Nana. Murder, fraud, rape, *genocide*."

The article I'd given Nana included coverage of the gang's DC murders. There were two long and well-written stories from the *Post*, one on each family, including pictures from happier times — like when they'd had their heads.

"Alex, I already told you. I know what's going on there. I don't want to discuss this anymore."

"Neither do I."

"You don't have to solve every single case. Let it go for once in your life."

"I wish I could."

I put the folder flat on her lap, kissed the warm top of her head, and went up to bed. "Stubborn," I muttered.

"Yes, you are. *Very.*"

Chapter 30

IN THE MORNING, I went downstairs around five-thirty. I was surprised to see that Jannie and Ali were already up. Nana stood fiddling around at the stove with her back to me. She was cooking something cinnamony and irresistible.

I sensed a *trap*.

Jannie ferried glasses of orange juice from the counter to the table, where there were already silverware and cloth napkins for five.

Ali was already sitting at his place, working on a big bowl of cereal and milk. He saluted me with a drippy spoon. "He's here!"

Et tu, Ali.

"Well, this is a pleasant surprise," I said, loud enough for the whole room.

Nana didn't respond, but she had heard me, for sure.

Only then did I notice a yellow-bordered National Geographic map of Africa Scotch taped to the refrigerator door.

And also, set down with the napkins and silverware on the table, *my passport*.

"So," said Nana. "It was nice knowing you."

Chapter 31

A CIA OPERATIVE named Ian Flaherty was "babysitting" a hysterical family down in Port Harcourt, Nigeria. The parents' teenaged son and daughter had been kidnapped. They were gathered together in the living room, waiting to learn the ransom demands, and the atmosphere couldn't have been more desperate.

Oh no, Flaherty had thought.

His cell rang, and everyone crowded into the room looked at him with anxious faces and deep concern.

"I'm sorry, I have to take this. It's another case," he said, then walked out into the lush gardens just off the living room.

America was calling—another kind of emergency.

Flaherty recognized the voice on the other end as that of Eric Dana, his superior, at least in rank.

"We have quite a situation on our hands. A homicide

detective named Alex Cross is on his way there. He'll arrive on Lufthansa flight 564 at four thirty p.m. The Tiger is in Lagos?" Dana asked.

"He's here," said Flaherty.

"You've seen him yourself?"

"I have, actually. Do you want me to meet the detective's plane?"

"I'll leave that up to you."

"Probably be best if I meet him. Alex Cross, you say. Let me think about it."

"All right, but you have to watch over him. Don't let anything happen to him...when it can be helped. He's well liked here and connected. We don't want a mess over there."

"Too late for that," Flaherty said and snickered a nasty, cynical laugh.

He went back to comfort the family whose children were probably already dead.

But they would pay anyway.

Chapter 32

WELL, THE INVESTIGATION had definitely taken a turn now. But was it for better or for worse?

The plane from Washington to Frankfurt, Germany, was nearly full, and it was incredibly noisy for the first hour anyway. I spent some idle time guessing who might be continuing on to Africa, but it wasn't too long before I fell back into my own dark reveries.

Everything that had led to this trip ran through my head like extended case notes, going all the way back to my Georgetown days with Ellie, and then up to Nana's grudging consent that morning.

Nana's going-away gift, such as it was, sat open on my lap. It was a copy of Wole Soyinka's memoir, *You Must Set Forth at Dawn.*

She'd bookmarked it with a family photo—Jannie, Damon, and Ali, cheesing with Donald Duck at Disneyland a year or so back—and she had underlined a quotation on the page.

T'agba ba nde, a a ye ogun ja.

As one approaches an elder's status, one ceases to indulge in battles.

It was her version of getting the last word, I suppose. Except that it had the opposite effect on me. I was more determined than ever to make this trip count for something.

Whatever the odds against me, I was going to find the killers of Ellie's family. I had to; I was the Dragon Slayer.

Chapter 33

"AH, SOYINKA. AN illuminating writer. Have you read him before?"

I didn't realize that someone had stopped in the aisle alongside my seat. I looked up, though just barely, at the shortest priest I'd ever seen. Not the shortest man, but definitely the shortest priest. His white collar came just to my eye level.

"No, this is my first," I said. "It was a going-away gift from my grandmother."

His smile got even brighter, his eyes wider. "Is she a Nigerian?"

"Just a well-read American."

"Ah, well, nobody's perfect," he said and then laughed before there could be any suggestion of an insult. "*T'agba ba nde, a a ye ogun ja.* It's a Yoruban proverb, you know."

"Are you Yoruban?" I asked. His accent sounded Nigerian

to me, but I didn't have the ear to tell Yoruban from Igbo from Hausa, or any of the other tongues.

"Yoruban Christian," he said and then, with a wink added, "*Christian* Yoruban, if you ask the bishop. But don't tell on me. Do I have your word on it?"

"I won't tell anyone. Your secret is safe."

He extended a hand as if to shake, and then sandwiched mine between both of his when I reached out toward him. The priest's hands were tiny, yet they communicated friendship, and maybe something else.

"Have you accepted Jesus Christ as your savior, Detective Cross?"

I pulled my hand back. "How do you know my name?"

"Because if not, considering the trip you're about to take, now might be a good time to do so. Accept Jesus Christ, that is."

The priest made the sign of the cross over me. "I am Father Bombata. May God be with you, Detective Cross. You will need His help in Africa, I promise you. This is a very bad time for us. Maybe even a time of civil war."

He invited me to come sit in the empty seat next to him, and we didn't stop talking for hours, but *he never did tell me how he knew my name.*

Chapter 34

EIGHTEEN HOURS—*WHICH seemed more like a couple of days*—after I left Washington, the flight from Frankfurt finally landed at Murtala Muhammed Airport in Lagos, Nigeria.

I had watched the unbelievable, and somewhat hypnotic, sweep of the Sahara from the plane; the savannas that buffered it from the coast; and the equally vast Gulf of Guinea just beyond the city.

Then, as I deplaned onto the tarmac, I suddenly felt like I was in Anytown, USA. It might have been Fort Lauderdale, for all I could tell.

"I'm sorry I can't help you here, brother." Father Bombata came up and shook my hand again before we separated. He had told me he had an escort meeting him to speed up his arrival. "Put two hundred naira in an empty pocket, my friend," he told me.

"What for?" I asked.

"Sometimes God is the answer. Other times it's cash."

Smiling as ever, the diminutive priest gave me his card, then turned and walked away with a final, friendly wave.

I found out what he meant around three hours later, which was the amount of time I had spent sweating on the immigration line. There were just two slow-moving officers at the counter for something like four hundred people.

Some passengers sailed through, while others were detained at the head of the line for as long as thirty minutes. Twice I saw someone taken away by an armed guard through a side door rather than being allowed to go out to the main terminal.

When it was finally my turn, I handed my landing card and passport to the officer.

"Yes, and your passport?" he asked.

I was momentarily confused, but then I remembered what Father Bombata had said and understood. I held a scowl in check. *The official wanted his bribe.*

I slid two hundred naira across the counter. He took it, stamped me through, and called out for the next person without ever looking at me again.

Chapter 35

THE LOW HUBBUB and frustration of clearing immigration was nothing compared with the instantaneous onslaught of noise and hurrying people that met me when I passed through the hand- and fingerprint-smudged glass doors and into the main terminal at Murtala Muhammed.

There's where I got my first real indication that I was in a metropolitan area of thirteen million people. I think at least half of them were there at the airport that day.

So this is Africa, I thought. *And somewhere out there is my killer, or rather killers.*

No fewer than five Nigerian "officials" stopped me on my way to the luggage carousels. Each of them asked for verification of my identity. They all basically said the same thing. "Visa, American Express, any card will do." Each of them clearly knew I was American. They all required a small bribe, or maybe they thought of it as a gratuity.

By the time I reached the baggage carousel, got my duffel, and pushed back out through the twenty-deep wall of people pressing in, I was tempted to fork over a few more naira to a raggedy-looking kid in an old skycap hat who asked where I wanted my bags taken.

I thought better of it, however, and pushed on, hauling my own luggage, keeping everything close to the chest. *Stranger in a strange land,* I thought, though I was also strangely pleased to be here. This promised to be quite an adventure, didn't it? It was completely new territory for me. I didn't know any of the rules.

Chapter 36

THERE WAS NO relief outside, where the air smelled of diesel, and no wonder: There was a raft of old cars, trucks, and bright yellow buses everywhere that I looked. Locals of all ages walked alongside the traffic, selling everything from newspapers to fruit to children's clothing and used shoes.

"Alexander Cross?"

I turned around, expecting to see and meet Ian Flaherty, my CIA contact here in Nigeria. The CIA was good at sneaking up on you, right?

Instead, I came face-to-face with two armed officers. These were regular police, I noticed, not immigration. They had all-black uniforms, including berets, with insignia chevrons on the epaulets of their shirts. Both of them carried semiautomatics.

"I'm Alex Cross, yes," I told them.

What happened next defied all logic. My duffel bag was

ripped from my arm. Then my small suitcase. One of the officers spun me around and I felt cuffs on my wrists. Then a hard pinch as they snapped down too tightly.

"What's going on?" I struggled to turn to look at the policemen. "What is this? Tell me what's happening."

The officer with my luggage raised a hand in the air as if he were hailing a cab. A white four-door Toyota truck immediately pulled up to the curb.

The cops yanked open a rear door, ducked my head, and pushed me in, throwing my travel bag after me. One officer stayed on the sidewalk while the other jumped in next to the driver, and we took off.

I suddenly realized—*I was being kidnapped!*

Chapter 37

THIS WAS SURREAL. It was insane.

"Where are you taking me? What is this about? I'm an American police officer," I protested from the back of the truck. No one seemed to be listening to a word I said.

I leaned forward in my seat and got a baton hard in the chest, then twice across the face.

I felt, and *heard,* my nose break!

Blood immediately gushed down my face onto my shirt. I couldn't believe this was happening—not any of it.

The cop in the front passenger seat looked back at me, wild-eyed and ready to swing the baton again. "You like to keep quiet, white man. Fucking American, fucking terrorist, fucking policeman."

I had heard that some people here didn't like American blacks referring to themselves as African American. Now I was feeling it firsthand. I breathed hard through my mouth, coughing up blood and trying to focus though my head was spinning. Humidity and diesel fumes washed over me as the truck weaved through airport traffic, the driver repeatedly sitting on the horn.

I saw a blur of cars, white, red, and green, and several more bright yellow buses. Women were walking on the side of the road with swaddled babies held low on their backs, some of them with baskets balanced on top of their *geles*. There were a great number of huts in view, but also modern buildings, plus more cars, buses, trucks, and animal-driven carts.

All around me, business as usual.

And business as usual inside this truck, I feared.

Suddenly the cop was on me again. He stretched over the seat and pushed me onto my side. I braced for another strike of his billy club. Instead, I felt his hands patting me down.

Then my wallet was sliding out of my pocket.

"Hey!" I yelled.

He pulled out the wad of cash I had—three hundred American, and another five hundred in naira—then threw the empty wallet back in my face. It sent a shudder of pain deep into my skull.

I coughed out another spray of blood, which hit the seat and earned me another baton strike across the shoulder.

The dark blue nylon sheet covering the backseat suddenly made sense to me. It was there for bloodstains, wasn't it?

I had no bearings, no idea why this was happening, no idea what to do about it either.

In spite of my own better judgment, I asked again, "Where

are you taking me? I'm an American policeman! I'm here on a murder case."

The officer barked out something in dialect to the driver. We swerved, and I fell against the car door as we came to a fast stop on the shoulder of the road.

They both got out! One of them tore open the door on my side and I dropped to the ground, cuffed and unable to break my fall.

A world of dust and heat and pain swam around me. I started to cough up dirt.

Powerful hands were under my arms now, lifting. The cop, or whoever he was, brought me up to my knees. I saw a little boy staring from the back of a packed Audi station wagon as it passed.

"You are a brave man. Just as brave as you are stupid, fucking white man."

It was the driver talking now, stepping in for his turn. He slapped me hard, once across the left side of my face and then back across the right. I struggled to stay upright.

"You two are doing an excellent job—" I was definitely punchy. Already I didn't care what came next.

It was a hard overhand fist to my temple. I heard a strange crunching sound inside my head, then another.

I don't know how many closed-fist blows came after that.

I think I passed out at four.

Chapter 38

UNREAL. UNPRECEDENTED. UNBELIEVABLE.

It was dark when I woke up, and I hurt all over, but especially around my nose. At first my mind was blank. I had no idea where I was; not Africa, not anywhere. I just thought *How the hell did I get here?*

And then, *Where is here? Where have I been taken?*

My hand went up to my temple. I felt a sharp sting where I touched an open wound, and then I remembered the handcuffs. *But they weren't on my wrists anymore.*

I was on my back, on a hard floor, stone or cement maybe.

Someone was looking down at me. I couldn't make out his expression in the nearly lightless room. I could only tell that he was a dark-skinned man.

Not one man, I realized. Many. A dozen or more men were

standing around me. Then I got it! They were *prisoners*—like me.

"White man is awake," someone said.

My clothes gave me away, I supposed. They had made me for an American. "White man," was meant to be an insult, one that I had heard already on the trip.

"Where am I?" It came out as a croak. "Water?" I asked.

The one who'd already spoken said, "Not until morning, my friend." He knelt down and helped me sit up, though. My rib cage felt like it was ready to explode, and I had a monster headache that wasn't going away by itself.

I saw that I was in a bleak, filthy holding cell of some kind. Even with my nose broken, the smell was unbelievably strong and foul, probably coming from a latrine in some unseen corner. I took shallow breaths through my mouth.

What little light there was came through a grated door on the far wall. The place looked big enough for maybe a dozen of us, but there were at least three times that number, all males.

Many of the prisoners were lying shoulder-to-shoulder on the floor. A relatively lucky few were snoring away on wall-mounted bunks.

"What time is it?" I asked.

"Midnight, maybe. Who knows? What's the difference to us? We're all dead men anyway."

Chapter 39

AS MY HEAD cleared some, I realized that my wallet was gone. And my belt.

And, I realized as I felt around some more, the earring from my left ear. The lobe was scabbed over where a small silver hoop had been, a birthday present from Jannie.

Where had they taken me? How far was I from the airport? Was I still in Nigeria?

Why hadn't anyone tried to stop them from kidnapping me? Did it happen all the time?

I had no idea about any of these questions, or their answers.

"Are we in Lagos?" I finally asked.

"Yes. In Kirikiri. We are political prisoners. So we have been told. I am a journalist. And you are?"

A metal scrape came from the direction of the door as it was unlocked, then opened wide.

I saw two blue-uniformed guards pause in the light of a

cement corridor before they stepped in and became shadows themselves. Seconds later, one of them played a flashlight over us.

It caught me in the eyes and hung there for several seconds.

I felt sure they were here for me, but they grabbed the man two down from me instead. The one who had said he was a journalist.

They pulled him roughly to his feet. Then one of the guards unholstered a pistol and pressed it to his temple.

"No one talks to the American. *No one,*" the guard told the room. "You hear me?"

Then, as I watched in disbelief, the man was pistol-whipped until he was unconscious. Then he was dragged out of the holding cell.

The reaction of the other prisoners around me was mostly silent acceptance, but a couple of men moaned into their hands. No one moved; I could still hear snoring from a few of them.

I stayed where I was, holding it all in until the vicious guards were gone. Then I did the only thing I could, which was ease back down to the floor, where every shallow, rapid breath produced another slice of pain through my chest.

What kind of hell had I gotten myself into?

Chapter 40

I WISH I could say that my first night in the prison cell in Kirikiri was a blur and that I barely remember it.

It's just the opposite, though. I will never forget any of it, not one second.

The thirst was the worst, on that first night anyway. My throat felt like it was closing up. Dehydration ate at me from the inside. Meanwhile, oversize mosquitoes and rats tried to do the same from the outside.

My head and torso throbbed like a metronome all night, and a sense of hopelessness threatened to overwhelm me the minute I let my guard down, or, God forbid, slept for half an hour.

I'd read enough from Human Rights Watch to know something about the conditions in this kind of prison—but the gap between knowing it and living it was enormous. It was possibly the worst night of my life, and I'd had some bad ones before this. I had spent time with Kyle Craig, Gary Soneji, and Casanova.

As dawn finally came, I watched the single barred window like a television set. Seeing its slow change, from black, to gray, to blue, was as close as I could get to optimism.

Just when the prisoners around me began to stir, the cell door opened again.

A wiry guard stood at the threshold. He reminded me of a very tall grasshopper. "Cross! Alexander!" he yelled at the top of his voice. "Cross! Over here! Now!"

It was a struggle to look halfway able-bodied as I slowly rose to my feet. I focused on the pain of my chest hairs being pulled out where they had fused with the dried blood in my shirt. It was just instinct, but it got me up on rubbery legs and across the floor.

Then I followed the guard into the corridor. He turned right, and when I saw the dead end ahead of us, I let go of any thoughts I'd had about getting out of the prison.

Maybe ever.

"I am an American policeman," I said, starting up my story again. "I'm here investigating a murder."

And then it struck me — *was that why I was in this prison?*

Chapter 41

THIS DEFINITELY WAS hell. We passed several foreboding, metal doors like the one to my cell. I wondered how many prisoners were kept here, and how many of them were Americans. Most of the guards spoke some English, which made me suspect that I wasn't the only American here.

The last door on the ward was the only one without a lock. An old office chair sat in front of it, its seat nearly rusted through.

"Inside," barked the guard. "Quickly now, go ahead, *Detective.*"

When I went to move the chair out of the way, he shoved it into my hands. Just as well. It was something to sit on besides the floor, and I didn't feel much like standing right now.

Once I was in, he closed the door and, from the sound of it, walked away.

This room was similar to the holding cell—except that

it was maybe half the size and empty. The cement floor and stone walls were streaked dark, which was probably where the putrefying smell came from.

There was no latrine here. Possibly because the whole area had been a latrine at one time.

I looked back at the gray metal door again. Given that there was no lock, was it more foolish to try to get out of here than to just sit and wait for whatever might come next?

Probably not, but I couldn't be sure about it, could I?

I was halfway to my feet when I heard footsteps again. I sat back down. The door opened and two police officers came in—wearing black uniforms instead of prison-guard blue. My stomach told me it was a bad trade-off.

So did the hard, pissed-off look on the guards' faces.

"Cross? Alexander?" one barked.

"Could I have some water?" I asked. There was nothing on earth that I wanted more. I could barely speak now.

One officer, in mirror shades, glanced over at the other, who shook his head no.

"What am I charged with?" I asked.

"Stupid question," said Mirror Shades.

To demonstrate, the second cop walked up and drove his fist into my stomach. My wind was gone, even before I hit the floor like a dry sack.

"Get him up!"

Mirror Shades hoisted me easily, then put his powerful arms around my shoulders from behind. When the next punch came, he kept me from falling over, and also made sure my body absorbed the full impact. I vomited immediately, a little surprised there was anything to bring up.

"I have money," I said, trying what had worked before in this country, back at Immigration.

The lead cop was huge—as tall as Sampson, with a flopping Idi Amin belly. He looked down the slope of his body right into my eyes. "Let's see what you have."

"Not here," I said. Flaherty, my CIA contact, had supposedly set up a money fund for me in a Lagos bank, which at this point was the equivalent of a million miles away. "But I can get it—"

The lead cop crushed his elbow into my jaw. Then came another wrecking ball of a punch to my chest. Suddenly I couldn't breathe.

He stepped back and waved Mirror Shades out of the way. With an agility I wouldn't have guessed at, the large, fat man kicked high with one boot and caught me square in the chest again. All the air remaining went out of me. I felt as if I'd just been crushed.

I *heard*, rather than *saw*, the two guards leave the room. That was it. They left me lying on the floor; no interrogation, no demands, no explanations.

No hope?

Chapter 42

BACK IN THE holding cell, I was given a bowl of cassava and a cup of water, only a few ounces, though. I bolted the water but found I couldn't eat the cassava, which is an important vegetable throughout Africa. My throat closed when I tried to swallow solid food.

A young prisoner hovered nearby and was staring at me. With my back to the wall, I whispered barely loud enough for him to hear, "You want it?" I held out the bowl.

"We hail the cassava, the great cassava," he wheezed as he took the bowl. "It's from a famous poem we learn in school."

He scrabbled over and sat next to me, both of us watching the door for guards.

"What's your name?" I asked.

"Sunday, sir."

He couldn't have been more than twenty, if that. His

clothes were dirty but seemed middle class to me, and he had a three-stripe tribal scar on each cheek.

"Here, Sunday. You'd better not be seen talking to me, though."

"Oh, fuck them," he said. "What can they do—throw me in a prison cell?"

He ate the cassava quickly, looking around like he expected someone to take it away from him. Or to rush in and beat him.

"How long have you been here?" I asked when he had finished eating.

"I come here ten days ago. Maybe it's eleven now. Everyone here is new prisoner, waiting for processing."

This was news.

"Processing? To where?"

"To the maximum-security unit. Somewhere in the country. Or maybe it will be worse. We don't know. Maybe we all goin' to a big ditch."

"How long does it take? The processing. Whatever happens here?"

He looked at the floor and shrugged. "Maybe ten days. Unless you have *egunje*."

"Egunje?"

"Dash. Money for the guards. Or maybe someone knows you're here?" I shook my head no on both counts. "Then you have big *wahala*, sir. Same as me. You don't exist. Shhhh. Guard is coming."

Chapter 43

WHEN THE GUARDS woke me on the third morning, they had to drag me to my feet. I wasn't going with them willingly. Not to my own execution. My chest still ached from the beating the day before. And my nose felt seriously infected.

This time, it was a *left* turn out of the cell. I didn't know if that meant good news or that the bad news had just gotten a lot worse.

I followed the human grasshopper down a steep, stone staircase, through another corridor, and around several more turns that had me thinking I never would have gotten out of this place on my own.

We finally came outside into an enclosed quad. It was just a wide expanse of sunbleached earth with a few tufts of weeds and a ten-foot-high fence topped with ribbons of barbed wire. If this was the exercise yard, it was a sad excuse for one.

Anyway, I could barely see anything in the bright light. And it was hot, at least a hundred degrees, give or take ten or twenty.

The guard didn't stop until he got to the high razor-wire-topped gate on the far side.

A locked door was opened to a passage through a building, through another door, then a gate, and to what looked like a parking area in the distance.

I asked Grasshopper Man what was going on. He didn't answer. He just opened the door and let me through.

He closed it behind me, locking me into yet another passageway.

"It's been taken care of," he said.

"What has?"

"You have."

He was already walking back the way we'd come, leaving me there. My heart sped up and my body tensed hard. This sure felt like an ending, one way or the other.

Suddenly a door opened on my right. Another guard stuck his head out. He gestured at me impatiently.

"Get in, get in!"

When I hesitated, he reached out and pulled me by the arm. "Are you deaf? Or are you stupid? Get inside."

The room I entered was air-conditioned. It was like a shock to my skin, and I realized that all he'd wanted was to get the door closed again.

I was standing in a plain office that seemed quite ordinary. In it were two wooden desks and several filing cabinets. A second guard, bent over some paperwork, ignored me. Also present was the first white man I'd seen since arriving at the airport.

He was a civilian dressed in light trousers, a loose button-down shirt, and sunglasses. My guess was CIA.

"Flaherty?" I asked, since he didn't bother to volunteer any information.

He tossed me my empty wallet. Then finally he spoke. "Jesus, you look like hell. Ready to get out of here?"

Chapter 44

I WAS WAY beyond ready to get out of this nightmarish prison, but I was also stupefied by everything that had happened to me since I had arrived in Lagos.

"What—? How did you find me?" I asked Flaherty before we were even out of the air-conditioned office. "What's going on? What just happened back there?"

"Not now." He walked over and opened a door and gestured for me to go out first. The two guards didn't even look up. One of them was scribbling in a file and the other was jabbering on the phone when we left. Business as usual here in the bowels of hell.

As soon as the door closed behind us, Flaherty took my arm. "You need some help?"

"Jesus, Flaherty. Thank you."

"They break your nose?"

"Feels that way."

"Looks it too. I know a guy. Here." He handed me a small bottle of water and I started to empty it down my throat. "Go slow, fella."

He steered me over to an old off-white Peugeot 405 parked under a shade tree nearby. My duffel was already in the backseat. "Thank you," I said again.

Once we were moving, I asked him, "How did you do this?"

"When you didn't show up on Thursday, I figured there were only a few possibilities. A hundred got me your name. Another five hundred got you out."

He took a business card from his breast pocket and handed it to me. It was from Citibank, with an address in Lagos. On the back in blue ballpoint was written ACROSS9786EY4.

"You're going to want to change that pass code. And probably wire in another grand or so if you can."

"What about my family?" They came rushing into my mind all at once. "Have you spoken with them? Do they know what's happening?"

"Listen, don't take this the wrong way, but I'm not your social worker. I know you probably feel like you've been through the eighteenth circle of hell or whatever, but you can't count on me for this kind of shit. Okay? I don't mean to be harsh. But that's the way it is here these days. There's a lot going on right now."

He tipped a Camel Light out of a pack, lit it, and blew twin streams of smoke through his nostrils. "You can call them from the hotel. Your family."

"I'm moved by your compassion."

He grinned straight ahead. I guess we understood each

other. Mine was obviously not the saddest or worst story Ian Flaherty had heard in Lagos. Probably not by a long shot.

"You have any food in this car?" I asked him.

He reached over and popped the glove compartment. There was a chocolate protein drink in a can. It was warm and a little gritty, and nothing had ever tasted better to me.

I threw my head back, closed my eyes, and tried for the first time in three days to relax and, maybe, think in straight lines about the murder investigation and what had just happened to me.

Chapter 45

A HEAVY THUD woke me from a hot, sweaty, and unpleasant sleep.

Maybe only a few minutes had passed. My eyes jerked open just in time to see an old Adidas sneaker bounce off the roof and onto the hood of the Peugeot.

"What the fuck?" Flaherty craned his head around.

We were caught in a bad traffic jam, with cars as far as I could see in front or behind us. "Area Boys. I should have guessed." He frowned and pointed.

I saw them in the side mirror first. There were at least half a dozen of them. Teenagers, it looked like. They were going from car to car, passing some and stopping at others, robbing drivers and passengers.

"Area Boys?" I asked.

"Like gangbangers, without the bling. Just cockroach thugs. Don't worry about them."

Two cars back, a flat-faced boy in an old Chicago Bulls jersey reached into someone's driver's-side window and threw a punch. Then his hand came out holding a briefcase.

"We should do something, shouldn't we?" I reached for the door handle, but Flaherty pulled me back.

"Do what? Arrest all of them? Put 'em in the trunk? Just let me handle this."

Another kid, shirtless with a shaved head and an angry spray of zits across his face, ambled up alongside our car. He leaned halfway into Flaherty's window and raised his fist.

"Give me ya fuckin' wallet, *oyinbo* man," he yelled at the top of his voice. "Give it now!"

Flaherty's hand was already reaching down under the seat. He pulled out a Glock and pointed it at the kid from his lap.

"How about you give me *your* fuckin' wallet, sucko?" he snapped. The kid stepped back, both hands up, with a sneer on his face. "Or maybe I should say *boy,* boy. That's right, keep moving before I change my mind."

"Not this one, bros," the kid called out to his friends and made a thumb and forefinger gun for them.

One of them drummed on the trunk anyway as they passed, but they kept going. Nobody else bothered us.

Flaherty saw that I was staring at him.

"What? Listen, when I come to DC, you can tell me what's what. Okay? Meanwhile, just try to remember where you are."

I turned and looked through the windshield and saw another driver getting robbed while we just sat there.

"Hard to forget," I said.

Chapter 46

I REALIZED WITH a jolt that my investigation could actually continue now, and that it was going to be something like a criminal investigation on Mars. That's how different life was here in Nigeria at this point in time.

The Superior Hotel, where Flaherty dropped me, was sprawling. There wasn't too much else to recommend it. It had probably been quite something in the fifties, or whenever. Now it had chipped stucco walls and a steady crew of locals in the parking lot hawking T-shirts, electronics, and phone cards.

It was also right near the airport. Three days in Nigeria, and I'd managed one small circle.

"Why'd you bring me here?" I asked as I changed my shirt in the backseat.

"I thought you might want to catch a plane in the morning. One can always hope."

"A plane to where?"

"To home, duh. You should leave now, Detective Cross. Before they get serious about hurting you. You're not going to get to the Tiger, but he could get to you."

I stopped talking and stared at Flaherty. *The Tiger?*

Chapter 47

"THAT'S HIS NAME, Detective Cross. Didn't you know? Actually, several of these gang bosses are called Tiger. But your guy was the first."

"So, do you know where he is?"

"If I did, I'd take you there right now and get this over and done with."

I tossed my bloodied shirt into a trash can and picked up my duffel. "What time can I meet you tomorrow?"

Flaherty grinned just a little. I think it was partial approval. "I'll call you."

"What time?"

"As early as I can. Get some rest. If you're not here in the morning, I'll know you're actually sane."

Before he took off, I borrowed some cash so I could pay for the first night at the Superior and also buy a phone card.

Forty-five minutes later, I was showered and fed, and waiting for my overseas call to go through.

The room was definitely nothing special. It was maybe 10 × 15, with chipped stucco walls, and the occasional water bug for company.

The bellhop hadn't been surprised to find the bathroom sink fixtures gone. He promised new ones soon. I didn't really care. After jail, the room felt like the presidential suite to me.

When Jannie answered the phone and I heard her voice for the first time, a lump rose in my throat. I forgot about the fact that my nose was throbbing and sporadically leaking blood.

"Well, look who's not in school today," I said, trying to keep it light and bright.

"It's Saturday, Daddy. Are you losing track of time over there? You sound like you have a cold, too."

I touched my sore and broken nose. "Yeah, I guess I'm a little stuffed up. I'll live. I'm actually staying at one of the best hotels in town."

"Alex, is that you?" Nana was on the extension now, and more than a little peeved, I could tell. "Where have you been for three days? That's unacceptable behavior to me."

"I'm sorry, Nana. It's been a lot harder getting a line out than I thought," I said and then started asking a lot of questions to avoid any more of my not quite lies.

Jannie told me about the fruit flies in her science experiment and about some new neighbors on Fifth Street. Nana was worried that the boiler noise in the basement was the same one that had cost nine hundred dollars the last time.

Then Ali got on to tell me that he could find Nigeria on the map and that the capital was Lagos, and he knew what the population was—more than one hundred thirty five million.

Then Nana said she was going to put Bree on.

"She's there?" I was a little surprised. Bree had planned on moving back to her apartment while I was away.

"Someone's got to watch over us around here," Nana said pointedly. "Besides, she's one of us now. Bree is family."

Chapter 48

I LIKED WHAT Nana had just said and also the sound of Bree's voice when she got on the line. I heard a door close and knew we were being given some privacy.

"Finally," I said.

"I know. Nana's tough, isn't she? But she can be sweet too."

I laughed. "She's pulling punches because you're there. She's manipulating you already."

"Speaking of which, don't bullshit me now, Alex. Where have you been for the past three days?"

"*Detective* Stone, is that you?" I said. "I guess you missed me?"

"Of course I did. But I asked a serious question. I've been worried sick for three days. We all have, *especially* Nana."

"Okay, here's what happened, and it's part of the case. It has to be. I was arrested at the airport."

"Arrested?" Bree said it in a whisper that registered new concern. "By who? At the airport? On what possible grounds?"

"On the grounds that due process is a relative concept around the world, I guess. I was in a holding cell for two and a half days. They never charged me with anything."

Her voice slipped a little—more Bree and less Detective Stone. "How bad was it?"

"Scale of ten, I'd give it a fifteen, but I'm mostly okay now. I'm at the Superior Hotel. Of course, that's just a name. There's nothing superior about this joint."

I looked out the window, where dark thunderheads were rolling in over the gulf. The pool area, ten stories down, was starting to clear out. It was hard to believe I'd woken up in Kirikiri just that morning.

"Listen, Alex, I don't know if you want to hear this right now, but we had another multiple last night. Another family was slaughtered over in Petway. This time, the parents were Sudanese nationals."

I sat down on the bed. "Same MO as the first two?" I asked.

"Yeah. Large knives, possibly machetes, extreme malice. Just ugly for the sake of ugly, cruel for the sake of cruel. Whether or not your boy and his gang were here, I'll bet his people were involved."

"Apparently the murderer is called the Tiger. So I'm playing Catch a Tiger. He could have ordered a hit from anywhere."

"That's right. Or he could be back in Washington, Alex. You could be over there, while he's *here*."

Before I could respond, there was a sudden flash from outside and a huge smack of thunder overhead. The lights in the room flickered, then went out, taking the phone with them.

"Bree?" I said. "Bree, are you there?"

But the line was dead. *Shit*. I hadn't even told Bree how much I missed her.

I'd seen candles and at least one propane generator in the lobby, so I guess they were used to this kind of thing at the Superior. I lay back on my bed and closed my eyes, figuring I'd go down and check things out if the power didn't come back on soon.

Meanwhile, what was the upshot of the new murders in DC? And what did they mean for me?

Was the killer I was chasing—the Tiger—still here in Nigeria?

Or had I come all this way...just to get my nose broken?

Chapter 49

MY PHONE WAS ringing.

And ringing.

I finally blinked awake, starting to come out of a deep comalike sleep. The clock flashed *12:00, 12:00, 12:00* on the bedside table next to my face.

It was morning, and the power at the hotel was obviously back on.

When I rolled over to answer the phone, my whole body resisted with an aching stiffness and the pain of severe bruising. It brought everything back into focus. Jail, the beatings, the murder of Ellie and her family, the investigation.

"Alex Cross," I said.

"Don't do that."

"Who is this?"

"It's Flaherty. Don't answer the phone with your name. You never know who—"

"What time is it?" I asked Flaherty. Too early for a lecture anyway.

I stared up at the ceiling, then down the length of my body. I was still in my clothes, and my mouth felt like paste. My busted nose was throbbing again too. There were bloodstains all over the pillow, both dark and bright red.

"Eleven o'clock. I've been calling all morning. Listen. I can give you a couple of hours if you make it soon, and then I'm out on assignment till next Monday."

"What have you got? Anything at all?"

"Besides the eczema on my ass? I've got the closest thing to a cooperative contact you're going to find in Lagos. You been to the bank yet?"

"I haven't been to the john yet."

"Yeah, well, sleep when you're dead, right? Get yourself a driver. The front desk'll set it up, but tell them you want it for the day, not by the hour. You're welcome for the travel tip.

"Go to the Citibank on Broad Street. And tell the guy to take the causeway so it'll sound like you know what the hell you're talking about. If you get going, you can make it by one. I'll meet you there. And don't be late. *Citibank on Broad*."

"Yeah, I got it the first time."

"I could tell you were a quick study. Get going!"

Chapter 50

BY THE TIME I pulled away from the Superior with a steaming and delicious cup of dark Nigerian coffee in one hand, I felt like someone had hit my "reset" button.

Not counting the way my face looked or half my muscles felt, it was as though I were getting a first day in Africa all over again. I thought about Ellie's being here just a few weeks ago and wondered what had happened to her. Had she come into contact with the Tiger? If so, how?

There was no case file or intelligence to go over — my clothes and passport and empty wallet had been the only things returned to me — so I spent the slow crawl over to Lagos Island just taking in the sights.

"You know they call Lagos the 'go-slow city,'" my driver told me with a friendly smile. All the many abandoned cars on the side of the road, he said, came from people running out of gas in perpetual jams, or "go-slows," as they called them.

Our pace picked up somewhat on the mainland bridge, where I saw downtown Lagos for the first time. From a distance, its cityscape was typical of large cities, all concrete, glass, and steel.

As we got closer, though, it started to look more like something out of an Escher painting, with one impossible cluster of buildings tucked in and around the next, and the next, and the next. The density here—the crowds, the traffic, the infrastructure—was startling to me, and I had been to New York many times and even to Mexico City.

When we finally got to the Citibank on Broad Street, Flaherty was standing out front, smoking. The first thing he said to me was, "Jack Nicholson in *Chinatown*." He grinned at his little joke, then said, "You squeamish?"

"Not so much. Why?"

He pointed at my nose. "We can make a quick stop after this. Fix you right up."

Meanwhile, he said, I should go in and get my replacement cards and also the cash I owed him. Plus whatever I needed for myself and at least two hundred American, in small bills if I could get them.

"What for?" I asked.

"Grease."

I took him at his word and did what he said.

From there, my driver took us across Five Cowrie Creek to the more upscale of the city's major islands—Victoria—and to a private medical practice on the fifth floor of an office building. *Very* private.

The doctor saw me right away. He examined my face and then gave me one quick, and excruciating, adjustment. It was the strangest doctor visit I've ever had, hands down. There were no questions about my injury and no request for payment. I was in and out in less than ten minutes.

Back in the car, I asked Flaherty how long he'd been based in Lagos. He had obvious juice here, and plenty of it. He also knew enough not to answer my questions.

"Oshodi Market," he said to the driver, then sat back again and lit another cigarette.

"You might as well chill," he said to me. "This is gonna be a while, trust me. You know what they call Lagos?"

"The go-slow city."

He turned down the corners of his mouth and exhaled a cloud of white smoke.

"You learn fast. Some things, anyway."

Chapter 51

VISUALLY OSHODI MARKET was a lot like the rest of Lagos—crammed end to end with busy, hurrying people, either buying something or selling something, and possibly doing both.

Flaherty curled his way through the crowds and the stalls like a skinny white rat in its favorite maze.

I had to keep my eyes on him to stay with him, but the exotic food smells and the sounds of the market still came through loud and strong. I took it all in—and liked it very much.

There were grilled meats and peanutty things and sweet-spicy stews over open fires, all of it reminding me of how hungry I was. Accents and languages came and went like radio stations, or maybe jazz. Yoruban was the most common; I was starting to pick that one out from among the many others.

I also heard livestock braying from the back of trucks, babies crying in a line for vaccinations, and people continually haggling about prices pretty much everywhere we went in the market.

My pulse ran high the whole time, but in a good way. Faced with squalor or not, I was finally pumped to be here.

Africa! Unbelievable.

I didn't think of it as my home, but the attraction was powerful anyway. Exotic and sensual and *new*. Once again I found myself thinking about poor Ellie. I couldn't get her out of my mind. What had happened to her here? What had she found out?

Flaherty finally slowed at a rug stall. The young seller, negotiating with a man in traditional oatmeal-colored robes, barely glanced over as we walked through the shoulder-high stacks to the back of the stall.

Less than a minute later, he appeared like an apparition at our side.

"Mr. Flaherty," he said and then nodded at me politely. "I have beer and mineral water in the cooler, if you like." It felt as though he were welcoming us into his home rather than selling Intel in the marketplace.

Flaherty held up a hand. "Just current events, Tokunbo. Today we're interested in the one called the Tiger. The massive one." I noticed that the name needed no more explanation than that.

"Anything in the last twenty-four hours gets you twenty American. Forty-eight gets you ten. Anything older than that gets you whatever you'd make selling rugs today."

Tokunbo nodded serenely. He was like Flaherty's polar

opposite. "They say he's gone to Sierra Leone. Last night, in fact. You just missed him—lucky for you."

"Ground or air?"

"By ground."

"Okay." Flaherty turned to me. "We're good here. Pay the man."

Chapter 52

I HAD PLENTY of other tough questions to ask Tokunbo about the Tiger and his gang of savage boys, but he was Flaherty's informant, and I followed his protocol. I owed it to him to keep my mouth shut until we were out of earshot anyway.

"What's with the quick in-and-out?" I said once we had left the rug seller's stall.

"He's in Sierra Leone. Dead end, no good. You don't want to go there."

"What are you talking about? How do you even know the information's good?"

"Let's just say I've never wanted my money back. Meanwhile, you're better off cooling your heels here for a few days, a week, whatever it takes. See the sights. Stay away from the prostitutes, especially the pretty ones."

I grabbed Flaherty's arm. "I didn't come all this way to cool my heels by the hotel pool. I've got one target here."

"*You* are a target here, my man. You ever hear the saying 'You've got to stay alive to stay in the game?' This is a very dangerous city right now."

"Don't be an ass, Flaherty. I'm a DC cop, remember. I've done this kind of thing a lot. I'm still standing."

"Just...take my advice, Detective Cross. He'll be back. Let him come. You can die then."

"What's your advice if I still want to go to Sierra Leone?"

He took a breath, feeling resigned, I think. "He'll probably go to Koidu. It's near the eastern border. Kailahun's a little too hot right now, even for him. If he went over ground, that means he's trading—which means oil, or maybe gas."

"Why Koidu?"

"Diamond mines. There's an unofficial oil-for-diamonds trading corridor between here and there. He's heavily into it, from what I hear."

"Okay. Anything else I should know?"

He started walking again. "Yeah. You got a best buddy back home? Call him. Tell him where you keep your porn, or whatever else you don't want your family to find when you're dead. But hey, have a good trip, and nice knowing you."

"Flaherty!" I called, but he refused to look back, and when I got outside the market, I found that he'd stranded me there.

So I wandered back inside and bought some fresh fruit—mangoes, guavas, and papayas. Delicious! Might as well live it up while I could.

Tomorrow I would be in Sierra Leone.

Chapter 53

ON A SUN-BEATEN dirt road that twisted through what used to be a forest outside Koidu, a fifteen-year-old boy was slowly choking to death.

Slowly, because that's exactly how the Tiger wanted it to happen.

Very slowly, in fact.

This was an important death for his boys to watch and learn from.

He closed his grip even tighter on the young soldier's esophagus.

"You were my number one. I trusted you. I gave you everything, including your oxygen. Do you understand? Do you?"

Of course the boy understood. He'd palmed a stone, a diamond. It was found under his tongue. He was probably going to die for it now.

But not at the Tiger's hand.

"You." He pointed to the youngest of the other boy soldiers. "Cut your brother!"

The lad of no more than ten stepped forward and unsheathed a clip-pointed Ka-bar, a gift for him from the Tiger's trip to America. With no hesitation at all, he shoved the blade into his brother's thigh, then jumped back to avoid the spurting blood.

The Tiger kept his own hand where it was on the thief's throat; unable to even scream, the boy just gagged.

"Now you," he said to the next youngest wild boy. "Take your time. No hurry."

Each of them took a turn, one at a time, any strike they chose, any kind of blow, except one that would kill the diamond thief. That right belonged to the oldest—or at least the one who would now be the oldest. "Rocket," they called him—on account of the bright red Houston Rockets basketball jersey he always wore, rain or shine.

The Tiger stepped back to let Rocket finish the murder. There was no need to hold the thief down anymore; his body was limp and broken, blood pooling in the dust around his shattered face. Black flies and puffy gnats were already settling on the wounds.

Rocket walked around until he was standing over the thieving boy's head. He was casually rubbing at the fuzz of beard he hadn't yet begun to shave.

"You shame us all," he said. "Mostly, you shame yourself. You were number one. Now you are nothing!" Then he fired once from the hip, gangsta-style, like in the American videos he'd watched all his life. "No more trouble with this dumb bastard," he said.

"Bury him!" the Tiger yelled at the boys.

All that mattered was that the carcass stay out of sight until they were gone. This dead boy was no one to anyone, and Sierra Leone was a country of pigs and savages anyway. Unclaimed bodies were as common as dirt weeds here.

He put the pilfered diamond back in its black leather canister with the others. This was the package a tanker of Bonny Crude had bought him—and it was a good trade. Certificates of origin could be easily purchased or faked. The stones would move with no trouble in London or New York or Tokyo.

He called Rocket over from the digging of the grave. "Pull his wireless—before you put him in the ground. Keep it with you at all times, even when you sleep."

Rocket saluted and went back to supervising the others, a bigger swagger in his walk than before. He understood what had just been said. *Pull his wireless. Wear it yourself.*

He was the Tiger's new number-one boy.

Chapter 54

MAYBE I ALREADY knew more than I wanted to about the small, sad country called Sierra Leone. The rebels there had murdered more than 300,000 people in recent years, sometimes lopping off their hands and feet first, or setting fire to homes where families slept, or tearing fetuses from the wombs of mothers. They created 'billboards of terror,' messages carved into the bodies of victims they chose to spare and then used as walking advertisements.

I took something called Bellview Air overnight to Freetown, and then a death-defying prop plane all the way to the eastern border of Sierra Leone, where we landed bumpty-bump on a grassy airstrip serving Koidu. From there, I took one of the two cabs available in the region.

Thirty-six hours after Ian Flaherty warned me not to go,

I was standing on the perimeter of Running Recovery, one of several working diamond mines in Koidu.

Whether or not the Tiger had done business with anyone from this particular mine, I didn't yet know, but Running Recovery had a rotten reputation according to Flaherty.

At home in DC, I'd start by canvassing. So that's what I decided to do here, one mine at a time if necessary.

I was a detective again.

I already knew that.

Running Recovery was an alluvial diamond field, not really a mine at all. It looked like a miniature canyon to me — two football fields' worth of pitted and trenched yellow earth, maybe thirty feet at the deepest.

The workers were bent over in the extreme heat, laboring with pickaxes and sieves. Most of them were up to their waists in muddy brown water.

Some looked to be about the size of grammar school kids, and as far as I could tell, that's what they were. I kept thinking about the Kanye West song "Diamonds from Sierra Leone," hearing the rap lyrics in my head. Damon used to listen to the tune a lot, and I wondered now if he or his friends ever considered the true meaning of the words.

Security up top was surprisingly light at the mine. Dozens of stragglers hung around the perimeter, working deals or just watching, like me.

"You a journalist?" someone asked from behind. "What you doin' here?"

I turned around to find three older men staring hard at me. All three were "war" amputees. They were probably not soldiers, but some of the thousands of civilians who had suffered a kind of trademark brutality during Sierra Leone's ten-year conflict, largely over control of the diamond industry.

Diamonds had already done to this country the kind of thing that oil was poised to do to Nigeria. There was no harsher reminder of that fact than the men standing in front of me right now.

"Journalist?" I said. "No, but I would like to speak with someone down there in the field, one of the workers. Do any of you know who's in charge?"

One of them pointed with the rounded stub of an elbow. "Tehjan."

"He won't talk to journalist," said one of the others. Both of that man's shirtsleeves hung empty at his sides.

"I'm not a journalist," I repeated.

"It don't matter nutting to Tehjan. You American, you journalist."

Given the kind of press coverage I'd seen about these mines, the sensitivity was almost understandable.

"Is there anyone down there who will speak to me?" I asked. "One of the workers? You know any of these men? You have friends down there?"

"Maybe tonight at the hall in town," said the first man who'd spoken to me. "After the keg comes 'round, tongues loosen up."

"The town hall? Where would that be?"

"I can show you," said the most talkative of the amputees. I looked at him and as he held my stare, I wondered how it was that paranoia hadn't eaten this part of Africa alive. And then I decided to trust him.

"I'm Alex. What's your name?"

We shook left hands. "I am Moses," he said.

I had to smile at that and thought of Nana. She would have smiled too and patted him on the back.

Show me the way, Moses.

Chapter 55

I WAS ON the job now, definitely working the case I had come here to solve.

The walk into town took about an hour. Moses told me a lot on the way, though he said he'd never heard of the Tiger. Could I believe him about that? I couldn't be sure.

Diamond trading for oil, gas, weapons, drugs, and any number of illicit goods was no secret around here. Moses knew that it went on the same way everyone knew that it went on. He'd been a diamond miner himself as a teenager and in his twenties. Until the civil war.

"Now, they call us 'san-san boys,'" he said. I assumed he meant those who could no longer do the work, like him.

At first I was surprised at the man's apparent openness. Some of his stories seemed too personal to share with a stranger, especially one who might be an American journalist, or maybe even CIA. But the more he spoke, the more I realized that talking about what had happened to him might be all he had left.

"We lived over that way." He pointed abstractly in a direction without looking.

"My wife sold palm oil at market. I had two fine sons. When the RUF soldiers came to Kono, they came for us like the others. It was at night, in the rain, so there were no torches. They say to me, if I watch them kill my boys, then they will spare my wife. And when I did as they told, they killed her anyway."

The RUF was the revolutionary force responsible for the death of thousands. He was devastatingly matter-of-fact about it—a terrible family massacre, not unlike the ones in Washington, I thought.

"And you lived," I said.

"Yes. They put me on a table and held me down. They asked if I want short or long sleeves for after the war. Then they cut my arm, here." He pointed, though of course it was obvious what had happened.

"They were to cut the other arm, but then an explosion came from the next house. I don't know what happened after that. I fell unconscious, and when I woke up, RUF soldiers were gone. And my wife too. They left my murdered sons. I wanted to die, but I did not. It was not yet my time."

"Moses, why do you stay here now? Isn't there anywhere else for you to go?"

"There is nowhere else for me. Here at least sometimes there is work. I have my friends, other san-san boys." He smiled at that revelation for some reason. "This is my home."

We had walked all the way into town by now. Koidu was a

sprawling village of dirt roads and low buildings, still recovering from "the war" six years ago.

I saw a half-finished hospital as we walked, and a mosque in decent shape, but other than that, I found mostly abandoned buildings, burned-out husks of small homes, everywhere I looked.

When I offered Moses money for his trouble, he said he didn't want it, and I knew not to force it on him.

"You tell the story I've told you," he said. "Tell it to America. Still, there are rebels who would like to kill all of us from the war. They want to make it so no one can see what they did." He held up what was left of his arm. "So maybe you tell people in America. And they tell people. And people will know."

"I will, Moses," I promised. "I'll tell people in America and see what happens."

Chapter 56

THE HALL IN town was named, incongruously, Modern Serenity. The name was scrawled in blue on an old wooden sign out front, and it made me think of an Alexander McCall Smith novel, *The No. 1 Ladies' Detective Agency*.

Maybe the building had been a church once. Now it was an all-purpose sort of place—one large, dingy room with tables and chairs that started to fill up as the sun went down.

Someone turned on a boom box, and the guy who showed up with a keg of Star Beer dispensed it into previously used plastic cups and took money.

Moses and his friends wouldn't come inside and let me buy them a drink. They said they'd be kicked out if they couldn't pay for their own beer. Instead, Moses told me, he'd hang out with some other men around an open fire, singing and talking, not far from the hall, and he pointed in the direction where he'd be.

I spent the next few hours casually asking around and mostly getting nowhere. Even the few people who would talk to me about mining shut up as soon as I moved my questions anywhere else . . . such as to the subject of the illegal diamond trade.

Twice I noticed men in camos and flip-flops licking their palms. *Diamonds for sale,* they were saying. *You need only swallow them to get them out of the country.* Both of them stopped and spoke with me, but just long enough to figure out I wasn't selling or buying.

I was starting to think this night might be a washout, when a teenage kid came over and stood next to me against the wall.

"I hear you lookin' for someone," he said, loud enough just for me. Busta Rhymes was doing his thing on the boom box at high volume.

"Who do you hear I'm looking for?"

"He's already gone, mister. Left the country, but I can't tell you where he is. The Tiger."

I looked down at the kid. He was maybe five foot nine, muscled, and cocky-looking. Younger than I'd first thought too — sixteen or seventeen maybe. Barely older than Damon. Like a lot of teenagers I'd seen on the continent, he wore an NBA jersey. His was a Houston Rockets jersey, an American basketball team that had once featured an excellent player from Nigeria named Hakeem Olajuwon.

"And who are you?" I asked the boy.

"You wanna know more 'bout anything, it's a hundred dollars American. I'll be outside. It's dangerous to talk in here.

Too many eyes and ears. Outside, mister. We talk out there. One hundred dollars."

He pushed off from the wall and pimp-strutted toward the front door, which was wide open to the street. I watched him drain his cup of beer, drop it on a table, and leave the hall.

I had no intention of letting him get away, but I wasn't going to walk outside the way he wanted me to either. It was his accent that told me what I needed to know. Not Sierra Leonean. *Yoruban*. The boy was from Nigeria.

I counted thirty, then slipped out the back of Modern Serenity.

Chapter 57

SURVEILLANCE. I WAS decent at it, always had been good at keeping a step ahead of an opponent. Even, hopefully, some as tricky and dangerous as the Tiger and his gang.

I worked a wide perimeter around to the front. When I got to the corner of the neighboring building, I had a pretty clear view of the town hall entrance.

The kid in the red Houston Rockets jersey was standing off to the side with another, younger boy. They were facing different directions, surveying the street while they talked.

An ambush? I had to wonder.

After a few minutes, the older one went back inside, presumably to look for me. I didn't wait to make my next move. If he had half a brain, he'd go exactly the way I'd just come.

I skirted the dirt intersection and changed position, moving to a burnt-out doorway on the opposite corner of the street. It was attached to the black concrete skeleton of whatever the building had once been, possibly a general store.

I pressed back into the empty door frame and hung there out of sight, watching, doing the surveillance as best I could.

Considering that I was working on Mars.

Sure enough, Houston Rockets came out a minute later, then paused right where I had been standing before.

His partner ran over and they conferred, nervously looking around for me.

I decided that as soon as they made a move, I'd follow them. If they split up, I'd stick with the older one, *Rockets*.

That's when a voice came from directly behind me.

"Hey, mister, *mister*. Want to buy a stone? . . . . Want to get your skull crushed in?"

I turned, and before I saw anyone in the dark, something hard and heavy clocked me in the head; a rock or a brick, maybe.

It stunned me and I fell to one knee. My vision whited out, then went black before it started to come back.

Someone grabbed my arm and yanked me away from the street—into a building. Then more rough hands—I didn't know how many—forced me to the ground and flat on my back.

My awareness swam in fast circles. I was working hard to get my bearings. I could feel several people gripping my arms and legs, holding me to the floor with their strong, lithe bodies.

As my vision got a little sharper, it was still hard to make any of them out in the dark. All I saw were vague, small shadows, but lots of them.

All the size of boys.

Chapter 58

"YO!" ONE OF the threatening shadows called out with a voice too cocky and young to be anything but a street punk's. "*Over here!* We got di bastard good now."

I was flying blind, almost literally, but I refused to go down for the count so easily. I figured that if I did, I was probably dead.

I shook off whoever was on my right arm and swung at whoever had my left. None of them was stronger than me, but collectively they were like fly paper covering every inch of my body. I fought even harder, fighting for my life, I knew.

I finally struggled to get halfway to my feet, each leg carrying an extra hundred pounds, when the other two bangers from the street came running in.

One of them shined a flashlight on me; the other smashed the butt of a pistol into my face.

I felt my nose snap. *Again!*

"Sonofabitch!" I yelled.

The blinding pain ran up into my brain and seemed to spread through my whole body. It was worse than the first time, if that was possible. My first thought was, *You've got to be fucking kidding me.*

The killer boys swarmed all over me, half as many this time, and brought me down. A sneakered foot came to rest on my forehead.

Then I felt the cold metal of a gun barrel pressed hard into my cheek.

"He da' one?" someone asked.

A flashlight's bright light sent another spike of pain through my eyes.

"He da' one, Azi." I recognized the voice from the town hall.

The speaker crouched down next to my head. "Listen, we gonna send you out of here with a message. No one fuck with us, you understand?"

I tried to raise my head and he fired a shot into the ground right next to my temple. "You understand?"

I stopped straining and lay back. I couldn't hear in one ear. *Was I deaf in an ear now too?* It was the pistol that kept me where I was. More than anything, I was seething mad.

"Go ahead," the lead punk said. I saw the silhouette of a long blade in somebody's hand. *A machete,* I thought.

Jesus, no!

Houston Rockets leaned in close again, rubbing his pistol up and down my temple. "You move, you die, Captain America. You stay still, *most* of you goin' home."

Chapter 59

"THIS GONNA HURT real *bad*. You gonna scream like baby girl. Starting now!"

They pulled my arm out straighter and held it tight so I couldn't move. Either they were getting stronger, or I was starting to lose it. I had never been closer to panic in my life.

"At the joint, Azi. Less bone," said Rocketman in the coolest, calmest tone.

The blade touched the crook of my arm softly once. Then the machete was raised high. The boy called Azi grinned down at me, enjoying this like the psychopath that he was.

No way. No way. Not going to happen, I told myself.

I wrenched my arm free and rolled hard to one side. The machete whiffed and the pistol fired, ringing sharply.

But at least I wasn't hit. Not yet, anyway.

I wasn't done. Or even started. I entwined my arm with

the shooter's and snapped his wrist. I heard it break, and the gun fell from his hand.

The first one to get to it was me!

Everything was shadows and noisy chaos after that. The punks were all over me again, which was lucky in a way. I think it kept the machete blade away long enough for me to get off a warning shot.

Then I scrambled up, my back to the door. *"Get over there!"* I shouted, motioning with the gun. I had them covered, but it was dark, and the layout of the building was a complete mystery to me. They would figure that out soon.

Sure enough, Rockets barked an order.

"Go! *Outside!*"

Two of the gang whipped away in opposite directions. One of them vaulted out an empty window frame. I didn't see where the other one went.

"What you gonna do, man?" Rockets said with a shrug. "Can't kill us all."

"I can kill you," I told him.

The others were doubling around behind me, I knew. I was either going to have to start shooting these boys—or run like hell.

I ran!

Chapter 60

I HAD ENOUGH of a head start and enough cover from the darkness to get out of sight fast. Suddenly I could smell a combination of things—*burning, rotting,* and *growing*—all at the same time. I flew down a couple of dirt streets and around a corner and eventually saw the light of a fire in a vacant lot.

Moses? I was in the vicinity of where he'd said he'd be.

I threw myself down in a stand of high weeds and waited for the thugs to run past. They shouted as they went, one small group to another, splitting up and looking for their prey—me. It was difficult to accept that boys this young could be hardened killers, but they were.

I'd seen it in their eyes, especially Rockets's. That boy had definitely killed before.

I waited several minutes. Then, keeping low, I cut around behind the fire until I was close enough to call out quietly.

Thank God Moses was there! He and his friends were eating crumbly rice and homemade peanut butter. He was tentative at first, until he saw who it was skulking in the tall brush.

"Come with me, sah," he told me in hushed tones. "It's not safe for you to be here now. Boys lookin' for you. Bad boys everywhere."

"Tell me about it." I wiped a stream of blood from my face with the back of my arm, forgetting how much it was going to hurt it. *"Shit!"*

"It's not much, ya'll be okay," said Moses.

"Easy for you to say." I forced a grin.

I followed him through the back of the lot and up the next road to a narrow side street. We were in a shabby tenement neighborhood, one long row of mud-brick hovels. Several huts had people in front, cooking and tending fires, socializing at this late hour.

"In here, sah. This way, please. Hurry."

I kept my head down and followed Moses through an open doorway into one of the huts. He lit a kerosene lamp and asked me to sit down.

"My home," he said.

The place was just one room with a single window cut into the back wall. There was a thin mattress on the floor, and a jumble of cookware, some clothing, and caved-in cardboard boxes stacked in the corners.

Moses deftly tossed a dirty cloth onto two hooks over the open doorway and said he'd be right back. Then he was gone again. I had no idea where he'd gone—or even if I could trust him.

But what choice did I have right now? I was hiding out for my life.

Chapter 61

IT TOOK A minute for me to catch my breath, and to check out the handgun I'd grabbed from the gang of boys. It was a subcompact Beretta, not a cheap piece. The magazine had the capacity for only seven rounds, and five were gone. With luck, I wouldn't need the other two to get through tonight. *Make that — with a lot of luck.*

I was sweating profusely and I was scared. No way around it. I'd almost lost an arm back there. Things could easily have gone the other way. Talk about close calls.

I heard a noise outside and raised the Beretta. Who was there? Now what was happening?

"Don' shoot me, sah." It was Moses, and he had a small pot of water. He gave me a rag to clean my face.

"What do you do now?" he asked me.

It was a good question. My instincts told me Houston Rockets hadn't lied; the Tiger was already gone. Most likely he was on his way to Nigeria with his diamonds. I'd missed him again. The killer and gang leader was no fool.

"I guess I need to see about a flight out of here in the morning," I said to Moses.

"The airport is small, sah. They can easily find you there. The boys, or maybe police."

He was right about that. It wasn't even an airport; it was just an airstrip with no cover anywhere that I could remember.

For that matter, I still didn't know who had arranged my little "Welcome to Lagos" party the first time around. If the Tiger knew where I was—and I had to assume he did now—I could be setting myself up for another round of the same hospitality, maybe with a worse ending.

Suddenly shouting rose up outside. Young men's voices. It was hard to tell how many—at least half a dozen, I was sure.

Moses ducked his head out the open doorway, then came back in and blew out the lantern.

"They are here," he said. "You should go. You *must* go, sah."

I had to agree, if for no other reason than to keep Moses out of this terrible mess.

"Tell me when it's clear."

He hung in the door sideways, watching. I stood opposite, ready to bolt at his signal.

"Now!" He motioned me out to the left. "Go now! Go quickly."

I darted across a narrow road and straight up another dirt alley. The next street I came to was wider, but completely deserted. I turned left and kept going that way.

It wasn't until then that I realized Moses was still with me.

"This way." He pointed straight into the dark. "I know where you can buy a truck."

Chapter 62

I FOLLOWED THE brittle-looking, one-armed man to an old stone house on the outskirts of the village, back toward Running Recovery. It was at least eleven o'clock by now, but the house lights were still on. I wondered if Moses was an anomaly, or if many people around here would help a stranger, even an American. From what I'd heard, most of the people in Sierra Leone and Nigeria were good, just victims of circumstances and greed.

A salt-and-pepper-haired man answered the door. "What do you want?" he asked.

A brood of kids was clustered behind him, trying to see who had come to the house in the middle of the night.

"The American wants to buy a vehicle," Moses said simply. "He has cash for it."

I hung back at first, at Moses' advice. Before I offered any money, we needed to see exactly what our options were.

"You're lucky," the man at the door said and smiled thinly. "We stay open late."

The best of the old wrecks he had out back was an ancient Mazda Drifter, with a tattered canopy over the bed and an empty space in the dash where the odometer used to be.

But the engine turned over, gingerly, on the first try. And the price was right—five hundred in leones.

Plus, he didn't mind our spending the night right there in the truck.

I told Moses he had done more than enough and that he should go home, but he wouldn't hear of it. He stayed with me until morning and then went out to secure the few things he said I'd need for my safe journey, including a police clearance sheet to leave the country.

While I waited, the gravity of this trip back started to sink in. I had to cover more than a thousand miles of unfamiliar countryside to Lagos, over multiple borders, with no more guidance than the maps that Moses only hoped he'd be able to find for me.

So when he came back, I had a proposition for him.

"Make this trip with me and you can keep the truck," I said. "As a fair trade for your services."

I expected a conversation, or at least a pause, but there was none.

He hoisted a goatskin bag of provisions from his shoulder into the truck, then handed me back the money he hadn't spent.

"Yes," he said simply. "I will do it."

Chapter 63

"SAMPSON?"

"Yeah?"

"This sucks big time, you know that? I hate you."

"Should have called tails, Bree."

The house on Eighteenth Street was quiet now, not the nasty hive of activity it had been on the night of the murders. Today, this morning, Bree and Sampson had it to themselves. Not that either one of them wanted to be here at the crime scene.

That was why they'd tossed a coin on the front stoop.

Sampson got *the master suite.*

Bree got *the children's bedroom.*

She blew into a latex glove, put it on, and unlocked the door, letting it swing to a stop before she stepped inside. Then she put her head down and hurried upstairs.

"I *hate* you, John," she called out.

The kids' bodies were gone, of course, but there was

the residue of printing powder everywhere. Otherwise, the murder scene looked the same: matching yellow comforters soaked through with blood; wide spatter pattern on the bunk bed, rug, walls, and ceiling; two small desks on the opposite wall, undisturbed, as if nothing unspeakable had happened here.

Ayana Abboud had been ten. Her brother, Peter, seven.

The hit on their father, Basel Abboud, was a hell of a lot easier for Bree to comprehend. His columns in the *Washington Times* had been an early and insistent voice for US military intervention in Darfur, with or without UN Security Council buy-in. He wrote of widespread bribes and corruption both in Africa and Washington. By definition, the man had enemies on at least two continents.

The kind of enemies who go after your wife and kids while they're at it? It sure looked that way. All four of them had been slaughtered in their house.

Bree turned a slow three-sixty, trying to see it all for the first time again. What jumped out at her now? What had they missed before? What would Alex see if he were here instead of in Africa?

Africa! For the first time, it made some sense to her for him to be there. This kind of violence—Africa was where it came from. This warning could only be fully understood in the context of Lagos, Sierra Leone, Darfur.

Certainly, the killers made no pretense of covering their tracks or hiding anything. Patent prints were visible everywhere that there was blood. Hundreds of latents had turned up as well, all over the house—the walls, the beds, the bodies of the dead.

Food had been hastily consumed in the kitchen: the remains of a pork chop dinner, Neapolitan ice cream scooped from a tub, soda pop, and liquor.

Imagine the level of stupidity, or the indifference to being caught, tried, and sentenced to a lifetime in prison for these unspeakable murders.

Bree didn't need results to know that none of these prints would flag in the FBI's fingerprint ID system. Her best guess was that the killers were young African nationals with no priors in the US and, most likely, no record of having entered the country either. Some of them would probably match prints taken at Eleanor Cox's home, some would not. They were savage ghosts whom someone older could use to do his dirty work, she thought. Very efficient. And very much fucked up in their heads. God, she hated him—whoever was behind this!

She came full circle and was staring at the children's beds again when a soft *tap-tap* sounded at the dormer window behind her.

Bree wheeled around and nearly cried out in surprise. She had always had a fear of getting shot in the back.

A young boy, small and wide-eyed, hung on to the fixed burglar bars outside, and he was looking in at her. When their eyes met he let go of the bars with one arm and beckoned her over.

"I saw the bad murders. I saw everyting," he said in a quiet voice meant only for her. "I know who the killers are."

Chapter 64

"PLEASE? I CAN tell you what happened in the house. Every-ting." The boy's small voice came muted through the glass. Bree was thinking that he couldn't be more than eleven or twelve.

He was either scared or a good little actor—or maybe he was both.

Sampson was in the bedroom behind her now. Neither of them drew a weapon; not that they trusted the boy for a second.

Bree had a hand on her piece.

"Tell me what you know about this," she said.

She and Sampson approached the window from opposite angles. Bree moved in first. She had to duck her head to get inside the dormer alcove.

From here, she could see that the boy had his feet on a lip of decorative brickwork outside.

Beneath that was the roof of the back porch, and a small, November-dead garden maybe ten feet below.

"No further," the boy warned, "or I run away. I can run very fast. You never catch me."

"Okay. Let me get this out of the way, though."

The old rope-and-pulley window sash took some coaxing, but finally Bree forced it up about six inches.

"What are you doing out there?" she asked.

"I know how it happened. They kill the girl and boy in dis very room. The others down de hall."

His accent was African. Nigerian was Bree's guess.

"How do you know so much?" she asked. "Why should I believe you?"

"I am the lookout, but soon they will make me go with them to kill others." He looked past Bree and Sampson to the scene inside. "I do not want to do dis. Please—I am Cat'lie."

"It's all right," Bree told him. "You don't have to hurt anyone. I'm Catholic too. Why don't you come down from there, and we can—"

"*No!*" He took a hand off again, threatening to jump and run. "Don't try nah tricks on me!"

"Okay, okay." Bree held up her hands, palms out. Then she knelt down a little closer. "Just talk to me. Tell me more. What's your name?"

"Benjamin."

"Benjamin, do you know anything about a man they call the Tiger? Was he here?" Alex had told her about the Tiger during their phone call. Supposedly the killer was in Africa now, but maybe Alex's information was wrong.

The boy nodded slowly. "I know, yes." Then he said, "More than one, though. Not just one Tiger."

That certainly stunned Bree—and she assumed it would surprise the hell out of Alex too.

"Many men are called the Tiger?" she asked. "You're sure about that?"

Another nod from the boy.

"Here in Washington?"

"Yes. Maybe two or three."

"And in Nigeria?"

"Yes."

"How many Tigers, Benjamin? Do you know?"

"They do not tell me, but dere are many. Bosses of gangs are all Tigers."

Bree looked over her shoulder at Sampson, then back again at the boy. "Benjamin, do you want to hear a secret?"

The question seemed to confuse him. His eyes went from side to side; he looked down again, checking his escape route.

And when he did that, Bree moved. Fast! Much faster than Benjamin thought she could.

Chapter 65

SHE REACHED IN through the bars and got her hand around the lookout's skinny wrist.

"Sampson, go!"

"Let go of me!" the boy yelled at her.

He tried to step away, and his weight wrenched her arm against the bar. There was no leverage from this angle. She could only try to ignore the pain, and hold on until Sampson got to the boy from below. *Hurry, John, I'm losing him!*

"Benjamin, we can keep you safe. You need to come with us."

He screamed at her. "No, fuckin' bitch! You lied to me!"

His transformation was startling. The scared eyes had gone fierce. He clawed at her hand and drew blood. Had he lied to her? Was he one of the killers?

Finally, Bree could hear Sampson's feet pounding somewhere outside. *Faster, John!*

Just when she thought her arm might break—the kid twisted free. He dropped to the porch roof and all but bounced another eight feet to the ground.

Two quick strides and then he was scrambling up a small ash tree, barely big enough to support his weight, much less an adult's.

Just as Sampson came running around the back, the boy flipped sideways over the top of a high cedar fence into a service alley beyond.

Seconds later, Bree came out the front door.

There was no gate to the alley. They had to sprint back through the house, out another door, and around the block, just to find out what they already knew: The boy named Benjamin was long gone.

The so-called lookout for the murders had gotten away from them.

Five minutes later, they had an APB out, but Bree wasn't holding her breath. Her thoughts had already turned to Alex, and how to reach out to him.

"He needs to know about this. Like, last week. Only I don't know how to reach him. I don't even know where he is now."

Chapter 66

THIS PART OF Africa wasn't recommended for backpacking or camera safaris. The yowl of hyenas was a constant reminder of where I was now. So were the road signs that said things like, WARNING — LIONS — CROCODILES!!

Getting out of Sierra Leone and back to Nigeria was proving to be even more complicated than I had expected. And dangerous too, treacherous at almost any curve.

Like right now. Two military-issue jeeps sat nose-to-nose across the road, blocking our way. This was no ordinary border crossing, though. We were less than an hour outside Koidu.

"Are these guys actually government?" I asked Moses. "Any way to tell?"

He shrugged and shifted uncomfortably on the seat of the Drifter. "Could be RUF."

There were six of them by my count, all wearing a mix of fatigues and street clothes and the familiar flip-flops. All of them were armed, including a mounted gunner in the back of one of the jeeps.

A lanky guy in a maroon beret came striding over to my window. His eyes were bloodshot, like he might have been stoned. He raised his rifle with one arm and held out the other hand.

"Papers."

I played it cool for now and showed him the police clearance and my passport.

He barely looked at them. "Fifty dollars. To pay for your visa."

Whether these men were government officers or not, I knew right then that this was grift, pure and simple. A holdup.

I raised my gaze and looked into his red eyes. "I just spoke with the US embassy in Freetown this morning. Deputy Ambassador Sassi assured me himself that my papers were in good order. So what's the problem here?"

He stared back hard at me, but I didn't flinch. Two of the other guards started over from the side of the road, but he held up a palm to save them the trouble.

"Still, it is ten for the passenger. Twenty, if it's in leones."

Somehow, we both knew I'd pay that one. I didn't want to push my luck. I gave him two American fives and we were on our way—to the next roadblock anyway.

We hit four of them before the actual border crossing. Each rite of passage went about the same. It got easier as we went, cheaper anyway, and by the time we finally crossed at Bo Waterside to Liberia, I'd paid out only another fifteen bucks or so.

The precious thing we did lose was time.

We didn't get into Monrovia until after dark, and with no guarantee of supplies east of there, we had to spend the night.

I worried through the night and didn't sleep very well. We were safe so far, but the speed we were traveling was no Tiger's pace.

He was getting away again.

Chapter 67

WE DROVE ALL the next day and into the second night, alternating at the wheel, trying to make up time. As we traveled, Moses told me that he was representative of most people here—not the RUF, and certainly not the Tiger and his murderous gang.

"There are many good people in Africa, sah, and no one to help them fight back against the devils," he said.

Less than half an hour east of Monrovia, we passed the last billboard and radio tower and entered dense rain forest that went on for hours.

Sometimes it opened up into clear-cut fields, with stumps like grave markers for miles in every direction.

Mostly, though, the road was a tunnel of bamboo, palm, mahogany, and vine-choked trees such as I'd never seen before—with leaves and low scrub slapping and slathering the sides of the truck as we pushed through.

Late in the afternoon, we were near the coast, driving through tidal flats and then wide swaths of open grassland that were the antithesis of the jungle we'd just left.

I saw a huge colony of flamingo around sunset, thousands and thousands of stunningly beautiful birds, an incongruous sea of pink in the orangish light.

Finally we had to stop for the evening. We were both too tired to drive. As I drifted off to sleep, I wondered how many fathers got to tell their kids they'd spent a night in a real African jungle.

Chapter 68

I WOKE UP some hours later. Moses was already laying out breakfast on the tailgate of the Drifter.

Canned sausages, a couple of bruised tomatoes, and a two-liter jug of water to sip from.

"Looks good," I said. "Thank you, Moses."

"There is a river. Over there if you wish to wash up." He pointed with his chin to the opposite side of the road. I noticed his shirt was soaking wet. "It is not far."

I bushwhacked with my arms, skirting a huge knot of thorny scrub the way Moses had obviously done before me.

About twenty-five yards in, the brush opened up and I came out onto a mud-and-gravel bank.

The river itself was a wide, murky green piece of glass. I could barely tell it was moving.

I took a step toward the water and sank up to my ankle in mud.

When I pulled back, the mud sucked the shoe right off my foot. Shit. I'd wanted to clean myself up, not get filthier.

I looked up and down the bank, wondering where Moses had gone to wash?

First, I needed my shoe back, though. I reached down into the guck and felt around. It was actually nice and cool down there.

Suddenly the water in front of me boiled up. Something rough, like a huge log, came to the surface very, very quickly.

And then I saw that it was a full-blown, honest-to-God crocodile. Its black eyes were set on me. Breakfast was on the table.

Shit. Shit. Shit. Good-bye shoe. Good-bye leg or arm?

I stepped back ever so slowly. So far, the croc showed just a layer of tiled skin at the water's surface. I could see the bulge of its snout. The great beast's eyes didn't leave me for a second.

Never taking a breath, I kept inching backward.

On the next step though, my foot turned in the mud. I fell! Like it had received a cue, the crocodile sprang forward.

Nine, ten, maybe as much as twelve feet long, it surged out of the water, slashing in and out of an S-shape as it leapt straight at me.

I tried to pull in my legs, if only to postpone the inevitable savage bite. How could this have happened? Everyone had been right—I shouldn't have come to Africa.

Suddenly a shot exploded behind me!

Then a second shot!

The huge croc let out a strange, high-pitched noise that was part scream, part gasp. It reared up off its front legs, then smacked back down into the mud. I could see a red ooze on the side of its head. It thrashed once more, then rapidly backed away into the river and disappeared.

I turned to see Moses standing behind me. He was holding the Beretta.

"I am so sorry, sah. I meant to say that you should take this with you. Just in case."

Chapter 69

AFRICA! WAS THERE anywhere in the world like it? I didn't think so.

We reached Porto Novo the next day and decided it would be best if I took the bus from there to Lagos. A man stood outside the public toilet at the bus station. He tried to get me to pay to enter, until I told him I would pee on his shoes first. He laughed and stepped away.

Then Moses and I parted, and he drove off proudly in his truck. I never found out whether he was a good Samaritan or an opportunist, though my nature favored the former. I will always think of Moses as my first friend in Africa.

Back at the hotel in Lagos, I showered off three days' worth of dust, sweat, and blood. I looked at my crooked nose in the bathroom mirror. *Alex, you are a piece of work.* Finally, I plopped down on the bed to call home.

I started with a call to Bree's cell this time. It was good

just to hear her voice again, but the warm hellos between us were quick.

She had news that couldn't wait—about a new murder, on Eighteenth Street, and about the young boy she'd found there and what he'd said: *There was more than one Tiger.* Flaherty had told me the same thing, but I was pretty sure I was looking for one killer—I could feel it in my gut.

Bree countered, "If this boy is for real, it's the closest thing we've got to inside information. He was in the gang, Alex. You could be doing just as much damage control in DC, maybe more. Come home."

"Bree, you're talking about a phantom witness back there. A young boy. I know that the man who killed Ellie and her family is here right now. He's in Lagos." *At least my instincts told me he was. Who knows now?*

"I'll see what else I can find out, specifically about *him*." Her voice was tight. We'd never really fought before, but this conversation was feeling pretty close.

"Listen, Bree," I said. "I swear, I'm not going to stay here any longer than necessary."

"I think we have very different definitions of what that means, Alex."

"You could be right about that."

I might have kept that to myself, but the only thing I could offer Bree right now was the truth.

"I miss you like crazy," I finally said, telling Bree another kind of truth, while trying to change the subject. "What are you wearing?" I joked.

She knew I was kidding and laughed. "Where do you think I am? I've got Ugly Fred looking at me across my desk"—I heard a shout of protest in the background—"and half the Major Case Squad's in the room with me. You want me to keep going?"

I took a rain check and we said our good-byes. Then, before I could dial home to Fifth Street, *I heard a rattle at my door.*

"Hello?" I called. "Who's there?"

The door swung open so fast I didn't have time to get off the bed to look. I recognized the front-desk manager.

But not the two dark suits with white shirts standing in the hall behind him.

"What are you doing in my room?" I asked the desk man. "What is this all about? Who are they?"

He didn't say a word to me. He just held the door open for the other two and then closed it from the outside as they moved across the room toward me.

I jumped up off the bed and set my feet on the floor. "What's going on here?" I said. "What's happening now?"

Chapter 70

"SSS!" ONE OF them shouted at the top of his voice. I had heard the initials before. *State Security Service,* if that's who these two men really were.

They went right at me, totally unafraid of any consequences. One of them bear-hugged my arms and shoulders; the other scooped my legs out from under me.

Now what was happening? Were they really State Security? Who had sent them for me? And why?

I struggled, but both of them were freaks sizewise, incredibly powerful men, quick and athletic too. They had my body twisted in a corkscrew and it was impossible to break free.

We crossed the room like that, with me tangled and helpless in their arms. Then I heard *a window slide open,* and I felt the rush of humidity on my skin.

My whole body tensed and I started to yell for help—as loudly as I possibly could to anyone who might hear me.

There was a blur of sky and earth and swimming pool and then *my back slammed hard into the hotel wall.*

I was suddenly *outside — and hanging upside down*!

"What do you want?" I screamed up at the one holding my legs. He had a very round face, flat nose, kind of a Mike Tyson squint. It was a struggle to keep still and not fight him, but I sure didn't want him to lose his grip.

The SSS man, or whoever he was, grinned down at me over the curve of my knees.

"You been here long enough, Cross. Time to cross you off." He laughed over his shoulder, sharing the joke with his partner.

Even if the swimming pool had been directly below me, which it wasn't, I figured I was too high to survive any fall. My blood coursed through me. I could feel it everywhere, especially in the growing pressure in my head.

But then my body was moving again. Inside!

My spine scraped hard against the aluminum window track, and I came down on the floor of my hotel room.

Chapter 71

I JUMPED UP and went at the nearest SSS man, until the other pressed his gun into my ribs.

"Easy," he said. "You don't want to get shot now, do you?"

I saw that my duffel was out on the bed.

And packed.

"Pick up the bag."

"Who sent you?" I asked them. "Who are you working for? This is insane!"

He didn't answer me. Instead, they grabbed me and moved me out into the hall. Freak One shut the door behind us and pocketed the key.

Then they both just turned and walked away.

"Go home, Detective Cross. You're not wanted here. *Last warning.*"

There was a bizarre half minute or so while they waited

for the elevator, talking low to each other. Then they calmly got on and left me standing in the hallway.

Clueless.

And keyless.

Obviously they'd taken this as far as it was going for now. Whoever they were, police or not, and whatever connection they might have to the Tiger, they didn't kill for him.

They hadn't even tried to put me on a plane.

But why not?

What was going on in this crazy country of theirs?

Chapter 72

IT WAS HARD to fathom or predict, but my situation in Lagos actually got worse over the next hour or so. The front-desk people at the Superior insisted that I had "checked out" and that no rooms were available, something I knew to be untrue.

I tried half a dozen hotels on the phone and got the same story everywhere—*credit card denied.* It was looking more and more like the two strong men who had evicted me from the Superior were indeed representatives of the state, whatever in hell that meant here in Lagos.

I tried Ian Flaherty several times and left a voice mail twice, but I didn't hear back from the CIA man.

So I did the next thing I could think of. I got a driver and asked him to take me to Oshodi Market. If I couldn't get hold of Flaherty, I'd go back to his valued informant. I was quickly running out of options.

I knew I was in the middle of something bad—but what was it? Why did everybody seem to want me out of the country? What did it have to do with the murder of Ellie Cox?

It took over an hour to get to the market and another fifty minutes of wandering and asking around to find the rug stall I was looking for.

A middle-aged man with one dead eye, not Tokunbo, was working today. His English was poor. He nodded at Tokunbo's name—I was in the right place—but then shooed me off for a customer!

I couldn't afford to just hang around hoping for a miracle, so I cut my losses and found my way back to the car. The only Plan C I could think of was to go to the US consulate.

But then, crawling through more traffic on the way to Victoria Island, I thought of something else. Plan D.

"Can you pull over, please?"

The driver stopped on the shoulder behind a burned-out old Ford Ranger. I asked him to pop the trunk, then went around and got my duffel.

I dug inside, looking for the pants I'd worn on that first day. I'd already trashed the shirt, but I was pretty sure—

Yes, here were the trousers, smelly and bloodstained from my time in jail.

I looked in the front pockets, but both were empty.

When I checked the back, I found what I was looking for, the one thing they'd missed when they took just about everything else at Kirikiri: *Father Bombata's card.*

I turned to the driver, who was waiting impatiently for me, half in, half out of the car.

"How much to use your cell phone?" I asked.

Chapter 73

TWO HOURS LATER, I was dining in style with Father Bombata in his office at the Redeemed Church of Christ, a sprawling complex right in the heart of Lagos.

"Thank you for seeing me," I said. "And for all of this. I was hungry."

We were sharing a meal of kudu, squash, salad and a South African Zinfandel, over the expansive desk in his office. The priest's tiny body was all the more dwarfed by a high-backed chair and the floor-to-ceiling windows looming behind him. Heavy red drapes kept out all but two slits of fading evening light.

"What happened to your face?" he asked me and actually seemed concerned. "Or should I ask, 'What happened to the other man?'"

I'd almost forgotten how I looked. The nose had stopped hurting somewhere around Ghana.

"Shaving accident," I told him and forced a crooked smile.

I didn't want to give one more person a reason to think I should go home on the next available plane. What I needed were allies, not more advice.

"Father, I've gotten some disturbing information about a killer called the Tiger. Do you think it's possible that there is more than one Tiger? Maybe operating in different locations? Like here *and* in the US?"

"All things are possible, of course," he said with a kind smile. "But that is not your real question, is it? Still, I suppose I would have to say yes, it is possible, especially if the government is involved. Or big business. There are a number of employers of killers-for-hire. It is a common practice."

"Why the government? Or a corporation?"

The priest rolled his eyes, but then he gave me a straight answer.

"They have the means for controlling information that others might not. And for controlling *misinformation* as well."

"Any idea why they would want to do that? Be involved, I mean."

He stood to pour me some more wine. "I can imagine any number of reasons. But it would be irresponsible of me to suggest that I actually think it's happening. Because, truthfully, I have no idea. The name is symbolism — *the Tiger*. You realize that there aren't any tigers in Africa. Maybe in a zoo someplace."

"I know that. In any case, I'm chasing at least one real man here," I said. "I need to find out where he's gone. He

killed my friend and her family. Other families were murdered too."

"If I may?" He looked at a mahogany clock facing him on
the desk. "From what you've told me, your more immediate
need is for somewhere to sleep."

"I wasn't going to ask."

"You don't have to, Detective Cross. I can't offer you anything here. It's a risk I would take for myself but not for my
congregation. However, I can take you to our men's shelter.
There's a five-night maximum, and it's no hotel—"

"I'll take it. Thank you," I told the priest.

"As for your mysterious Tiger, I'm in less of a position to
help."

"I understand." I was sorely disappointed but tried not to
show it.

Father Bombata held up a hand. "You think quickly, don't
you? Maybe sometimes your mind works too fast. What I was
going to say was that I can't help you there. But I do know
someone who might.

"My cousin, actually. She's the most beautiful woman in
Nigeria. But of course I'm biased. You be your own judge."

Chapter 74

HER NAME WAS Adanne Tansi, and, as promised by the priest, she was one of the most beautiful women I had ever seen in person. She was also a reporter with the *Guardian*, Lagos's biggest newspaper.

Her office was maybe 6 × 8, if that. As I entered, I only hoped that I didn't smell like I'd just spent the night in a crowded homeless shelter.

Over the next hour, Adanne told me that she had been covering the original Tiger and his gang for two years, but he was still something of a shadow figure.

"I am not certain there is more than one Tiger. But I have heard the rumor too. This could be gangster myth. Who knows, maybe he spreads it himself. Anyway, who can tell what a man like that could do to the newspaper if he wanted to."

"Or to a reporter?" I asked.

She shrugged. "Some things are worth more than a life. You're here, aren't you? You're taking chances with your life?"

I smiled. "I guess I am."

I found that I couldn't take my eyes away from Adanne Tansi, though I tried not to be rude. She was stunning in the manner of some actresses, and it was impossible not to notice her high cheekbones and her dark doelike eyes but also the way she carried herself. She seemed unafraid, and I wondered why that was so. She had much to lose but carried it lightly.

She picked up a pen. It had escaped me that she had a pad at hand among the mess of other papers at her work area.

"No notes," I said. "This isn't an interview. I'm just a tourist here. That's been made very clear to me."

Adanne immediately put the pen down, smiling as though she had had to at least give it a try.

I went on. "Do you have any sense of where the Tiger is now? Or any idea how I could find out?"

"No to the first," she said. "And I believe so to the second."

Chapter 75

I WAITED BUT she left it at that. After a few seconds, I realized that in Lagos even a newspaper office was a marketplace.

"In exchange for what?" I finally asked her.

Adanne smiled again. She was very coy—and clever. "A good story about an American detective looking for a criminal and murderer like the Tiger—that would be hard not to print."

I put my hands on the arms of my chair, ready to go. "No."

Suddenly her eyes were locked onto mine. "Detective Cross, do you realize how much good could come from a story like this? This human monster is responsible for hundreds of deaths, maybe more."

"I know," I said, working hard to keep my voice in check. "One of them was a friend of mine."

"And one was my brother," said Adanne. "So you can see why I want to write this story."

Her words resonated in the small room. She wasn't angry, just measured, and, within that, passionate.

"Ms. Tansi—"

"Please call me Adanne. Everyone does."

"Adanne. You obviously care a great deal about this, but I don't know you. I wish I could trust you, but I can't."

Her stare told me I hadn't lost her yet. "But I hope you'll help me anyway. I'm Alex, by the way. Everyone calls me that."

She thought about what I had said, and I could see she was conflicted. It was unusual to see this in a journalist, at least the ones I knew back in Washington—this kind of transparency.

Finally she stood. "All right," she said. "I'll see what I can do for you. I'm in." She picked up her pen again, a silver-topped onyx roller, the kind people give as gifts. "Where can I reach you? Alex?"

At the Redeemed Church of Christ men's shelter—that's where I live now.

I don't know if she noticed my pause. Whether or not it was wise, I found that I wanted to impress Adanne Tansi.

"I'll call you," I said. "First thing tomorrow. I promise."

She nodded, and then she smiled. "I believe you, Detective Cross. So far, anyway. Don't disappoint me, please."

How could I even think of it, Adanne?

Chapter 76

A BUSINESSMAN WITH rumored connections named Mohammed Shol stood like an expensively framed portrait of himself in the open double doors of his enormous home. The main building was twenty thousand square feet, and the guesthouse was another eight thousand. He was among South Darfur's wealthiest men and never missed an opportunity to show it off.

The gated compound with its high walls and attached citrus greenhouse made its own statement: *Who but the devil lives like a king in the middle of hell?*

Not that the Tiger minded dealing with devils; he did it all the time. This was his business, and if he had carried a card, a *black devil* might have been the logo.

Shol smiled broadly as he shook hands to elbows with the large and quite handsome fixer and murderer. "Welcome, my friend! Your team will wait out here, of course."

"Of course."

"They will be fed."

"They are always hungry."

The Tiger left Rocket in charge of the others and knew he would maintain discipline. The boys waited by the front gate, across the yard from Shol's two plainclothes guards, who watched the younger ones with unconcealed amusement. The guards at the estate had come up from the streets themselves.

Let them be cocky and sure of themselves, the Tiger thought as he eyed the older watchdogs. Underestimation had always worked in his favor.

He followed Mohammed Shol through the estimable front hallway and across an interior courtyard. Cooking smells, cardamom and beef, came from one side of the house. Boys' voices came from the other—reciting in Arabic, which further defined Shol's politics.

They came to a glass door at the far end of the courtyard.

An enclosed grove of exotic fruit trees showed on the other side. Shol stopped.

"We'll meet in here. Can I offer you tea? Or perhaps grapefruit juice?" The latter was a boast, since such juice was a delicacy here.

"Nothing," the Tiger said. "Only what I came for. Then I will be gone."

Shol dismissed his houseboy with a quick flick of the wrist, then used a key from his *jallabiya* pocket to let them inside.

It was pleasant in the greenhouse, temperature controlled with a waft of humidity lacing the air. The tiled floor was shaded under a low canopy of green. Above was the geometric pattern of a glass-and-steel ceiling.

Shol gestured for the Tiger to enter a small dining area in the back.

Four rattan chairs surrounded a luminescent bai wood table. Shol moved aside a potted sapling. Then he ran the combination on a floor safe hidden behind the tree.

Inside the safe was a paper envelope, stuffed thick. Shol took it out and placed it on the table between them.

"I think you'll find it's all there."

Once the Tiger had checked the contents, he set the package on the floor and sat back.

Shol smiled.

"You've done much here," the Tiger said, gesturing around the room. "It's impressive."

Shol smiled, puffed up by the compliment. "I've been blessed many times."

"Not just blessed. You've been busy. You are clever, I can tell."

"It's true. Between the legislature and my businesses, there's little time for other things."

"Travel," the Tiger said. "Meetings day and night? And your family, of course."

Shol nodded, clearly enjoying that the subject was him. "Yes, yes. On most days."

"Saying things you shouldn't. Putting your loved ones at risk."

The nodding stopped. Shol seemed to forget that he was afraid of looking the Tiger in the eye, and did it now. "No," he said. "Truly. I've not talked about my business dealings with you, or anyone else."

"Yes," said the Tiger, without moving. "*Truly.* You have.

You know *a reporter*—a woman? Adanne Tansi?" He reached up with one finger and tipped open his collar an inch. He spoke into a microphone.

"Rock da house! *Now*, Rocket. Spare no one. *Make an example of them.*"

Chapter 77

A FEW SECONDS later, the entire greenhouse reverberated with a half dozen or more gun blasts coming from outside. And then bursts of machine-gun clatter.

Mohammed Shol tried to get up, but the Tiger was fast and agile and already had his hands around the man's throat and was choking him. He slammed Shol into the far wall and a spider-web pattern blossomed in the glass.

"Do you hear that?" the Tiger shouted at the top of his voice. "You hear it? All your fault!"

There was more gunfire. Then screams—women first, followed quickly by boys, their voices high and pitiful.

"That," the Tiger told him, "is the sound of your mistakes, your greed, your stupidity."

Shol grappled with both hands at the Tiger's huge and unmovable wrists. His eyes reddened and veins appeared ready to burst at his temples. The Tiger watched, fascinated.

It was possible, he'd learned, to bring a man to the edge of death, and then keep him there for as long as he liked. He liked this because he despised Shol and his kind.

The greenhouse door shattered as two bodyguards arrived to rescue their employer. "Come in!" shouted the Tiger. In one motion, he spun Mohammed Shol around and pulled a pistol from the paddle holster at his ankle. He charged forward, Shol in front as a shield, firing as he came!

One bodyguard went down with a nine-millimeter hole in the throat. The other sent a bullet through his employer's outstretched hand, then into his shoulder.

Shol screamed, even as the Tiger launched him the last several feet across the floor, where he crashed into the guard. Both men went down. Then the Tiger shot the second bodyguard in the face.

"*Oga!*" Rocket said as he appeared in the empty doorway. *Oga* meant "chief" in Lagos street parlance. The Tiger liked the designation, and it came naturally to his young soldiers.

The screaming had all but stopped in the house, but there were still sounds of breakage and gunfire as his boys let off the last of their venom and steam.

"There was a tutor. Children being taught."

"Taken care of," said Rocket.

"Good." The Tiger watched as Shol struggled to stand. He fired once into his leg. "You'll need a tourniquet or you'll die," he said to the businessman.

Then he turned to Rocket. "Tie Mr. Shol up. Then put this in his mouth. Or up his ass, if you like."

"This" was an M67—a grenade.

"Pull the pin before you leave."

Chapter 78

EVERYTHING CONTINUED TO feel unreal and fantasylike to me.

All the doors at the church shelter for men were locked after nine o'clock. No one could get in or out. With traffic being what it is in Lagos, I barely made it back there in time.

My cot was at the far end of one of three lodges, long high-ceilinged dorms off the main corridor where breakfast would be served in the morning.

Alex Cross, I thought. *What have you come to? What have you done this time?*

The guy in the next bed was the same guy as the night before, a Jamaican man by the name of Oscar. He didn't talk much, but the strained look in his eyes and half-healed track marks told his story.

He lay on his side and watched me while I rooted around for a toothbrush.

"Hey, mon," he said in a whisper. "Dey is some shorty man o' God lookin' your way. He dere now."

Father Bombata was standing at the door. When I saw him, he beckoned with a finger, then walked back out of the dormitory.

I followed him outside and into a hall packed with last-minute arrivals. I pushed upstream toward the front doors, until I caught up with the priest.

"Father?"

I saw then that he was dialing a cell phone and wondered who he was calling. Was it good news or bad that I was supposed to hear?

"Ms. Tansi wishes to speak with you," he said and handed over the phone to me.

Adanne had news! An assassination in South Darfur had occurred that day. One of the representatives to the Sudanese Council of States was dead—and his family had been slaughtered.

"Any connection to Basel Abboud in DC?" I asked her.

"I don't know yet, but I can tell you that the Tiger does frequent business in Sudan."

"Weapons? Heroin?" I asked her. "What kind of business, Adanne?"

"Boys. His loyal soldiers. He recruits at the Darfur refugee camps."

I took a breath. "You might have told me about this earlier."

"I'll make it up to you. I can have us on an air freighter to Nyala first thing in the morning."

I blinked. "You said 'us'?"

"I did. Or you can fly commercial to Al Fasher and see about ground transport from there. I leave it to you."

Any other time I never would have considered it. But then, I'd never been five thousand miles from home without a lead and sleeping in a men's homeless shelter before.

I put my hand over the phone. "Father, can I trust this woman?" *With my life?*

"Yes, she is a good person," he said without hesitation. "And I told you, she is my cousin. Tall and beautiful, just like me. *You can trust her, Detective.*"

I was back on the line. "Nothing goes into print until we both say so? Do we have a deal on that?"

"Agreed. I'll meet you at the Ikeja Cantonment, at the main entrance by five. And Alex, you should prepare yourself emotionally. Darfur is truly a horrible place."

"I've seen a few horrors," I said. "More than a few."

"Perhaps you have, but not like this. Nothing like this, believe me, Alex."

Part Three

CAMP

Chapter 79

SO FAR, ADANNE'S connections were very good, and I was impressed by how quickly and efficiently she got things done.

It took her only one brief conversation on the tarmac, and then one radio call, before the African Union sergeant in charge allowed us to board the C-130 freighter the following morning.

We were in the air by six, the only civilian passengers on a plane carrying millet, sorghum, and cooking oil to Darfur.

The murder investigation continued, and now it was airborne and seemed to have more purpose than ever.

I borrowed a situation map from one of the flight crew and saw that Darfur was about the size of Texas. If I was going to get anywhere, I had to run with a few assumptions—one, that the Tiger had been in Nyala at the time of the massacre of the Shol family, and two, that Adanne's information was correct, and he might still be culling boys from camps for displaced persons in the area.

Given all of that, how far would he have gotten in the past eighteen hours? That was the next question that had to be answered.

During the flight, Adanne patiently told me much about Darfur and Sudan, and though she spoke in a low-key manner, there was no disguising the horrors—especially against women and children, thousands of whom were raped, then branded to increase their humiliation.

"Rape has become such a cruel weapon in this civil war. Americans have no idea, Alex. They couldn't possibly.

"Sometimes the Janjaweed will break a woman's legs first so she can't possibly escape and will be an invalid for the rest of her life. They like to flog victims; to break fingers one by one; to pull out fingernails," Adanne said in a voice that barely got above a whisper.

"Even some of the 'peacekeepers' are guilty of rape, and of using the refugees as prostitutes. What's worse, the government of Sudan is behind much of it. You won't believe what you will see here, Alex."

"I want to see it," I told her. "I made a promise to a man in Sierra Leone that I would tell Americans what was happening here."

Chapter 80

"THIS IS KALMA." She pointed at a yellow triangle on the map. "It's one of the largest camps in Darfur. I'd wager that the Tiger knows it well. Everyone around here does."

"What are the other colors?" I asked.

There were more than a hundred camps in all, Adanne explained. *Green* meant inaccessible during rainy season, and *blue* was closed to nonmilitary aid organizations, based on current fighting conditions. Kalma's *yellow* meant open.

That's where we would start our Tiger hunt.

"And these?" I ran a finger over a line of *red* flame icons. There were dozens of them.

Adanne sighed before answering my question.

"Red is for villages that are confirmed destroyed. The Janjaweed burn everything they can—food stores, livestock. They put human and animal carcasses down the wells, too.

Anything to ensure that no one comes back. In Arabic, Janja-weed means '*man with a gun on horseback*.'"

These were the Arab militias, widely believed to be supported by the current government in a vicious campaign to make life as unsafe as possible for black Africans in the region. An unthinkable two million people had already fled their homes and more than two hundred thousand had died. *Two hundred thousand that we knew of.*

It was Rwanda all over again. In fact, it was worse. This time the whole world was watching and doing almost nothing to help.

I looked out my porthole window at the Sahel landscape twelve thousand feet below.

It was actually quite beautiful from up here—no civil war, no genocide, no corruption. Just an endless, peaceful stretch of tan, sculpted earth.

Which was a lie, of course.

A beautiful, very diabolical lie.

Because we were about to land in hell.

Chapter 81

AT THE BASE in Nyala, we secured a ride out to the Kalma Camp with a five-truck convoy carrying sacks of grain and crates of F75 and F100 baby formula. Adanne seemed to know everyone here, and I found it interesting to watch her work. Her gracious smile, not her attractiveness, seemed to be her secret. I saw it succeed again and again with people who were overworked and stressed to their limits.

Camp seemed like the wrong word once I actually saw Kalma.

Yes, there were tents and lean-tos and stick-straw huts, but they stretched for miles and miles. One hundred and fifty thousand people lived here. *That's a city.* And one that was overflowing with unbearable suffering and heartbreak and death by everything from Janjaweed attacks, to dysentery, to childbirth without drugs, and usually without a doctor or midwife.

Around the camp's center were some signs of permanence, at least. A small open-air school was in session, and there were a few walled buildings with corrugated tin roofs, where limited food supplies were still available.

Adanne knew exactly where we should go first. She took me to the United Nations' Commission on Refugees tent, where a young soldier agreed to do some translating for us, although many of the refugees knew bits of English.

The soldier's name was Emmanuel, and he had the same kind of sinewy height, dark skin, and deep-set eyes I'd seen on many of the so-called Lost Boys who had emigrated to DC over the years. Emmanuel spoke English, Arabic, and Dinka.

"Most of the people here are Fur," he told us as we started down a long dirt avenue. "And eighty percent are abused women.

"Most of their men are dead, or looking for work, or for resettlement," added Adanne. "This is the most *vulnerable* city in the world, Alex. No exception. You will find out for yourself."

It was easy to see what Adanne and Emmanuel were talking about. Most of the people we found to speak with were women who were working outside their shelters. They reminded me of Moses and his friends, because of how eager they were to share their terrible stories with someone from the outside.

One woman, Madina, cried as she wove a straw mat and told us about coming to Kalma. The Janjaweed had destroyed her village and killed and mutilated her husband, her mother, and father. Most of her neighbors and friends were burned alive in their huts.

Madina had arrived with three children and literally nothing else. Tragically, all three of her children had died at the camp.

The sleeping mats she made were in demand because of dooda worms, which came out of the ground at night and burrowed into the refugees' skin. Whatever she earned went toward onions and grain, though she hoped to have enough to buy a patch of cloth one day. She'd been wearing the same *toab* since she'd gotten here.

"When was that?" Adanne asked.

"Three years ago" was Madina's sad answer. "One for each of my children."

Chapter 82

"I HAVEN'T LOST sight of your Tiger," Adanne said as we trudged along. "He recruits boys here. It's easy for him."

"You were right about the horror, Adanne," I told her.

I was eager to speak with people in as many sectors of the camp as possible, but when we came to one of the few medical tents, I had to stop again. I had never seen such a bewildering sight in my entire life.

The tent was overflowing with sick and dying patients, two and more to a cot. Bodies were jigsaw-puzzled into every available space. To make matters worse, long lines extended outside, at least three hundred very sick women and children waiting for treatment, or for a better place to die.

"Sadly, there's little to be done to stop their suffering," Adanne told me. "Medication is scarce, much of it stolen before it can get here. There is starvation, pneumonia, malaria. Even diarrhea can be fatal—and with the water and sanitation problems, there is no end to it."

I saw one doctor and two volunteer nurses. *That was it.* The entire hospital staff for thousands of very sick people.

"This is what they call the 'second phase' of the crisis," Adanne went on. "More people dying inside the camps than outside. Thousands. Every single day, Alex. I told you that it was horrifying."

"You understated," I said. "This is unimaginable. All these people. The children."

I knelt down by a little girl in one of the few beds. Her eyes were clouded and looked unreal. I brushed away a buzzing cluster of black flies gathered at her ear.

"How do you say 'God be with you'?" I asked Emmanuel.

"Allah ma'ak," he told me.

I said it to the tiny girl, though I don't know if she heard me. *"Allah ma'ak."*

Somewhere along the way today, I'd stepped away from a terrible, terrible murder investigation and into an unbelievable holocaust. How was this possible in our world? Thousands dying like this every day?

Adanne put a hand on my shoulder. "Alex? Are you ready to go? We should move on. You are here for the Tiger, not for this. There's nothing you can do about this."

I could hear in her voice that she'd seen all this before, many times probably.

"Not yet," I said. "What needs doing around here? Anything?"

Emmanuel's quick answer was not what I expected.

"That depends. Can either of you handle a rifle?"

Chapter 83

FOR THE NEXT few minutes, Adanne explained what should have been obvious to me—*that the simple act of gathering firewood was one of the most dangerous parts of life at Kalma.*

Janjaweed patrols were always present in the desert, and not far from the camp. Anyone venturing out took the risk of being raped, shot to death, or both. The wood gatherers, desperate women and their children, depended on AU escorts when they could get them; mostly, though, they were forced to take their chances alone. No firewood meant no way to feed your family.

Emmanuel secured me an older model M16, which had been retrofitted with a decent scope.

"Don't hesitate to fire," he told me. "Because, I promise you, the Janjaweed will not. They are skilled fighters, even while riding on horses or camels."

"I won't hesitate," I promised, and I felt Adanne grab hold of my elbow, then let go.

"You're sure about this, Alex?" she asked. "You want to get involved?"

"I'm sure."

An hour or so later, we set out with an intrepid group of two dozen women wood gatherers.

Several had swaddled babies on their backs. One had brought a donkey with an old fork-shaped cart for carrying wood.

I needed to do this, to help in some way if I could. I knew this about myself: It was my nature. Adanne came too because, she said, "I feel responsible for you now. I brought you here, didn't I?"

Chapter 84

YEARS OF WOOD foraging, moving farther and farther from the camp, had turned this into a long and scary walk.

I used the time to talk with as many of the women as possible. Only one, it turned out, had any information about the missing boys and possibly the Tiger.

"She says there is a hut in her sector," Emmanuel told me. "Three boys were sharing it. But now they are gone."

"I thought that wasn't unusual," I said.

"Yes, except they left their things behind. She says a large man in fatigues was sighted in the camp. She was told he was the Tiger."

"Did any of the missing boys have parents in the camp?" I asked.

"No parents."

"And did anyone see the boys leave?"

"They left with the enormous man."

After two hours of walking, we finally came to a long line of low, skeletal brush. The women spread gathering cloths on the ground and set to breaking down the brush. Adanne and I pitched in while Emmanuel kept watch for Janjaweed patrols on the horizon.

Without translation, we were mostly reduced to eye contact and gestures as we worked side by side with the gatherers. The women seemed oblivious to the scratches that appeared up and down their arms. They easily outpaced us newcomers and tried not to laugh at our clumsiness.

One young mother and I fell into a kind of unspoken communication, making faces at each other like little kids. She stuck out her blue-tattooed lip. I held up two sticks like antlers. That one got a real laugh out of her. She put her hand up to her mouth, not quite hiding a brilliant white smile.

But then the mother stopped short.

Her hand came down slowly as her eyes fixed on something in the distance.

I turned around—but all I could see was a far-off dust cloud.

And then Emmanuel started shouting for everyone to run!

"Go quickly! Now! Get out of here! Go back to camp!"

Chapter 85

JANJAWEED!

I could see them now. Maybe a dozen armed killers were riding toward us on horseback.

There was a vapor, a kind of mirage that made it hard to tell the exact number. Either way, their pace didn't leave much to the imagination. They were coming for us — fast.

Two of the women, one with a child fiercely holding on to her blouse, were still unhitching the communal donkey.

"Get them out of here!" I shouted at Adanne. "You go with them. Please, Adanne."

"Is there another weapon?" she yelled back.

"No," Emmanuel answered. "Distance is your weapon right now. Go! For God's sake, go! Take them back to camp."

Emmanuel and I had to make a stand.

We took up a position behind the abandoned donkey cart. I was using it as a brace for the rifle more than as cover.

Our best hope was that we were on the ground—while they would be firing from horseback.

I could see them through my scope now, eleven killers, bearded males in baggy fatigues, waving Kalashnikov rifles.

Just coming into range.

The first shots came from them.

Sand kicked up on either side of us. They rode a little wide of the mark, but still too close. They weren't amateurs. They were already yelling threats at us, confident about the final result. Why not? They outnumbered us eleven to two.

"Now?" I finally said to Emmanuel.

"Now!" he shouted.

We fired back four shots, and two were hits. The killers slumped on their horses—like someone had dropped their puppet strings—then fell to the ground. One of them was trampled under his own horse. It looked like his neck was snapped, maybe broken.

Even as I pulled the trigger again, it registered with me: *Everything changes now. First kill in Africa.*

I heard a scream behind me, and my gut seized. One of the fleeing women had been hit, either by a stray shot or on purpose.

Not Adanne, I saw with a quick check over my shoulder.

She was keeping low, trying to get to the wounded woman, who was writhing on the ground. She'd only been shot in the arm. *Only.*

When I turned toward the Janjaweed again, two of the riders had stopped. They were jumping down off their horses, not to help their brothers but to get off a better shot at us.

The others kept coming fast. They were maybe fifty to sixty yards away now.

Emmanuel and I had the same instinct. We fired on the lead riders, quick shot after shot. Then at the two who were on flat ground. Three more of the Janjaweed went down in the next half minute or so.

Then Emmanuel screamed, dropped, and began twisting in pain on the ground.

And the rest of the Janjaweed were on us.

Chapter 86

DUST WAS KICKED up everywhere. That was probably a good thing. They had to fire blindly—but so did I. The gunfire from all the rifles was deafening at this range.

One of the riders tore through the dust cloud and swept right past me. On instinct, I grabbed at his leg and held on. The momentum took me off my feet. I got dragged along for a second or two, and then the rider spun off his horse and crashed heavily to the ground.

I grabbed his rifle and kept it at my feet. I fired and wounded another of the riders. And then another, in the stomach. They had been cocky—because the wood gatherers usually couldn't fight back—but they weren't well trained, and not many men can fire accurately from horseback, despite what Emmanuel had said.

I saw three of the riders break ranks and retreat. It gave me some hope—not a lot, but some.

I rushed to the fallen rider I'd pulled from his horse. I pushed his head down into the ground, then got off a hard punch that struck the hollow of his throat.

"Don't move!" I yelled. He didn't need English to know what I was saying. He stayed very still where he was.

"Alex!"

A voice came from behind me.

It was Adanne.

She and another woman stood swinging pieces of firewood at the last rider's horse to keep him away. Several of the women were on the ground, hands over their heads. I'm sure they still thought they were going to die.

Adanne swung again, and the horse reared up onto its hind legs. The rider lost his grip and fell.

"Alex, go!" I looked and saw Emmanuel had propped himself up. He was covering the Janjaweed from his place on the ground.

I took off at a sprint.

The downed rider near the women was just getting up again. I yanked my rifle around as I came up on him. He looked at me in time to take the stock in the face. His nose exploded.

"Adanne, take his gun. Are you all right?" I asked her.

"I will be."

Emmanuel was calling to me, screaming. "Let them go, Alex! Let them go!"

I didn't hold back. "What are you talking about? We have to bring them in."

Even as I spoke, the truth of the situation settled over me. *Same game, different rules.*

"No use arresting the Janjaweed," Adanne said. "They know the government. The government knows them. It only brings more trouble to the camps. The UN can't help. No one can."

I kept the Janjaweed's rifle, but motioned for him to get on his horse.

And then the strangest thing happened. He laughed at me. He rode away laughing.

Chapter 87

THE UN CAN'T help. No one can. This was what the refugees in the camp at Kalma believed, what they knew to be true, and now I knew it too.

But the survivors at the camp also knew how to be thankful for small favors and good intentions.

That night, several of the women used their precious firewood to make a meal for the three of us, as thanks for helping them. I couldn't imagine taking food from these people, but Emmanuel told me it was the only proper response.

He shocked me by showing up for the supper, bandaged and smiling, with a bag of onions he'd nicked for the occasion.

Then we all shared *kisra* and vegetable stew around the cookfire, eating right-handed only from a common bowl. It felt like the right thing to do, almost like a religious experience, special in so many ways.

These were good people, caught in a terrible situation not of their making.

And yet, even they talked freely of frontier justice, the violent kind. A woman proudly told us how criminals were dealt with by the people in her village. They would all rush forward, stab the offending person, put a tire filled with gasoline around his neck, and then light it. No trials, no DNA testing, apparently no guilt from the vigilantes either.

Adanne and I were treated like guests of honor at dinner. There was a steady stream of visitors and a lot of laying on of hands.

When Emmanuel wasn't around to translate, I got the gist of the Dinka or Arabic from the warmth in the voices and the body language.

Several times, I heard something that sounded like *Ali* in the middle of sentences. Adanne picked up on it too.

She leaned near me at one point and said, "They think you look like Muhammad Ali."

"That's what they're saying?"

"It's true, Alex. You do look like him, when he was world champion. He's still very well loved here, you know." She nodded with her chin and smiled at a group of younger women hovering nearby. "I think you've made a few girlfriends in the bargain."

"Does that make you jealous?" I asked, grinning, happier and more relaxed than I'd been in many days.

A little girl crawled uninvited onto her lap and curled up. "The word's not in my vocabulary," she said. Then she smiled. "Maybe a little bit. For tonight anyway."

I was finding that I liked Adanne very much. She was

courageous and resourceful, and Father Bombata was right about her: *She was a good person.* I had seen her risk her life for the wood gatherers today, and maybe because she felt responsible for me.

We stayed late into the evening, as the crowd got steadily bigger. Actually, the adults came and went, but the kids pooled all around us. It was an audience I couldn't resist, and neither could Adanne. She was very free and easy around children.

With Emmanuel's help, I got up and told an improvised version of one of my own kids' favorite bedtime stories.

It was about a little boy who wanted nothing more than to learn to whistle. This time, I named him Deng.

"And Deng tried—" I puffed out my cheeks and blew, and the kids rolled all over one another as though it were the funniest thing they had ever heard. They probably liked that I could be silly and laugh at myself.

"And he tried—" I bugged my eyes and blew right in their faces, and when they continued to laugh, it was more than a little gratifying, like an oasis in the middle of everything that had gone on since I'd come to Africa.

"You like children, don't you?" Adanne asked after I'd finished the story and come back to sit beside her. She had tears in her eyes from the laughing.

"I do. Do you have children, Adanne?"

She shook her head and stared into my eyes. Finally she spoke. "I can't have children, Alex. I was...when I was very young...I was raped. They used the handle of a shovel. It's not important. Not to me, not anymore." Adanne smiled then. "I can still enjoy children, though. I love the way you were with them."

Chapter 88

THE NEXT MINUTE or so seemed like they couldn't be happening. Not that night. Not any night.

The Janjaweed had come back. They seemed to appear out of nowhere, like ghosts out of the darkness. The ambush was brazen and sudden; they had come right into the camp.

It was hard to tell their number, but there must have been a couple of dozen of them. I thought I recognized one, *the man I had released, the one who'd laughed at me.*

These Janjaweed were on foot—they had no horses or camels. They had guns and also knives and camel whips; a couple of them wielded spears.

One man waved the flag of Sudan as if they were here on the state's business, and possibly they were. Another carried a flag with a white fierce horseman on a dark blue background, the symbol of the Janjaweed.

The women and children of the camp, who had been

laughing and playing just a minute before, were screaming and trying to scatter out of harm's way now.

The attack was satanic in its viciousness; it was pure evil, like the murder scenes I'd visited in Washington. Grown men slashed away at defenseless refugees or shot them down. The thatched roofs of huts were set on fire not twenty feet away from me. An elderly man was lit on fire.

Then more Janjaweed arrived, with camels, horses, and two Land Cruisers mounted with machine guns. There was nothing but killing, cutting, slashing, screaming to heaven—no other purpose to this attack.

I fought off a few of the bastards, but there wasn't anything I could do to stop so many. I understood the way the people of this camp, of this country, understand: *No one can help us.*

But that night someone did. Finally, Sudanese regulars and a few UN troops arrived in jeeps and vans. The Janjaweed began to leave. They took a few women and animals with them.

Their last senseless and vengeful act: They burned down a grain shed used for storing millet.

I finally found Adanne, and she was cradling a child who had watched her mother die.

Then everything was strangely quiet except for the people's sobbing and the low winds of the harmattan.

Chapter 89

IT WAS GETTING close to morning when I finally laid myself down in a tent with a straw mat on the floor. It had been provided to me by the Red Cross workers, and I was too tired to argue that I didn't need a roof over my head.

The flap of the tent opened suddenly and I got up on one elbow to see who it was.

"It's me, Alex. Adanne. May I come in?"

"Of course you can." My heart pumped in my chest.

She stepped inside and sat down beside me on the mat.

"Terrible day," I said in a hoarse whisper.

"It's not always this bad," she said. "But it can be worse. The Sudanese soldiers knew a reporter was in the camp. And an American. That's why they came to chase away the Janjaweed. They don't want bad press if they can possibly avoid it."

I shook my head and started to smile. So did Adanne.

They weren't happy smiles. I knew that what she had said was true, but it was also ridiculous and absurd.

"We're supposed to share the tent, Alex," Adanne finally said. "Do you mind?"

"Share a tent with you? No, I think I can handle that. I'll do my best."

Adanne stretched herself out on the mat. She reached out and patted my hand. Then I took her hand in mine.

"You have someone — back in America?" she asked.

"I do. Her name is Bree. She's a detective too."

"She's your wife?"

"No, we're not married. I was — once. My first wife was killed. It was a long time ago, Adanne."

"I'm sorry to ask so many questions, Alex. We should sleep now."

Yes, we should sleep.

We held hands until we drifted off. Only that — hand-holding.

Chapter 90

THE FOLLOWING DAY, we left the camp at Kalma. Nine refugees had died during the nighttime attack; another four were still missing. If this had happened in Washington, the entire city would be in an uproar now.

Emmanuel was one of the dead, and they had cut off his head, probably because of his participation when we'd fought back earlier.

A mutual hunch took Adanne and me to the Abu Shouk camp, the next-largest settlement in the region. The reception there was more ambivalent than we'd gotten at Kalma.

A big fire the night before had made personnel scarce, and we were told to wait at the main administrative tent until we could be processed.

"Let's go," I said to Adanne after we'd waited nearly an hour and a half.

She had to run to catch up with me. I was already headed

up a row of what looked like shelters. Abu Shouk was much more uniform and dismal than Kalma. Nearly all of the buildings were of the same mud-brick construction.

"Go where?" Adanne said when she came up even with me.

"Where the people are."

"All right, Alex. I'll be a detective with you today."

Three hours later, Adanne and I had managed half a dozen almost completely unproductive conversations, with Adanne attempting to serve as translator. The residents were at first as friendly as those in Kalma, but as soon as I mentioned the Tiger, they shut down or just walked away from us. He had been here before, but that was all the people would tell us.

We finally came to an edge of the camp, where the sand plain continued on toward a range of low tan mountains in the distance, and probably bands of Janjaweed.

"Alex, we need to go back," Adanne said. She had the tone of a person putting her foot down. "Unfortunately, this has been unproductive, don't you think? We're nearly dehydrated, and we don't even know where we're sleeping tonight. We'll be lucky to get a ride into town"—she stopped and looked around—"if we can even find our way back to the admin tent before dark."

The place was like an impossible maze, with rows of identical huts wherever we looked. And so many displaced people, thousands and thousands, many of them sick and dying.

I took a deep breath, fighting off the day's frustration. "All right. Let's go. You're right."

We started picking our way back and had just come around a corner, when I stopped again. I put a hand out to keep Adanne from taking another step. "Hold up. Don't move," I said quietly.

I had spotted a large man ducking out of one of the shelters. He was wearing what I'd call street clothes anywhere else. Here, they marked him as an outsider.

He was huge, both tall and broad, with dark trousers, a long white dashiki, and sunglasses under a heavy brow and shaved head.

I took a step back, just out of sight.

It was him. I was sure it was the same bastard I'd seen at Chantilly. *The Tiger—the one I was chasing.*

"Alex—"

"Shh. That's him, Adanne."

"Oh, my God, you're right!"

The man gestured to someone out of sight, and then two young boys walked out of the shelter behind him. One was nobody to me. The other wore a red-and-white Houston Rockets jersey. I recognized him instantly from Sierra Leone.

Adanne gripped my arm tightly and she whispered, "What are you going to do?"

They were walking away but were still in plain sight.

"I want you to wait five minutes and then find your way back. I'll meet you."

"Alex!" She opened her mouth to say more but stopped. It was probably my eyes that told her how serious I was. Because I had realized that everything I'd been told was true. The rules I knew just didn't apply here.

There was no taking him in—no transporting him back to Washington.

I was going to have to kill the Tiger, possibly right here in the Abu Shouk camp.

I had few qualms about it either. The Tiger was a murderer. And I had finally caught up with him.

243

Chapter 91

I HUNG BACK, following the killer at a distance. It sure wasn't hard to keep him in sight. I had no specific plan. Not yet.

Then I saw a shovel sitting unattended outside somebody's hut. I took it and kept moving.

It was just past sunset, a time when everything looked tinted with blue, and sound carried. Maybe he heard me, because he turned around. I ducked out of sight, or at least I hoped so.

The huts along the footpath were packed in tightly. I wedged myself into a foot-wide gap between two of them. The walls on either side were crude mud-brick. They grated on my arms as I tried to push my way through and get the Tiger back in sight.

I had made it about halfway, when one of his young thugs stepped out into the alley.

He didn't move. He just shouted something in Yoruban.

When I looked over my shoulder, Houston Rockets was at the other end of the alley. I could see the white of his grin but not his eyes in the dim half-light.

"It's him," he called out in a high-pitched voice, almost a giggle. "The American cop!"

Something slammed hard into the wall inside the hut. The entire hut buckled, and large chunks of dried mud fell into the alley.

"Again!" Houston Rockets yelled.

I realized what was happening—they meant to crush me in the narrow passageway.

The whole wall exploded then. Bricks and debris and dirt poured down on my head and shoulders.

I waded forward, took a hard swing, and struck the nearest punk with my shovel.

And then—I found myself face-to-face with the Tiger.

Chapter 92

"NOW YOU WILL die," he said to me matter-of-factly, as if the deed were a foregone conclusion.

I didn't doubt that he was telling the truth.

He looked incredibly calm, his eyes barely registering emotion as he reached forward and grabbed me by the arm and throat. My only thought was to hold on to the shovel, and to swing it if I got the chance.

He threw me back down the alley as easily as if I were a child. No, a child's doll. I landed hard on splintering wood and plaster. Something sharp sliced into my back.

I registered Houston Rockets blocking the other escape route. There was nowhere for me to run.

The Tiger came charging at me. So I swung the shovel as hard as I could, going for the bastard's knees.

The shovel head connected — not a home run, but

maybe a double. The Tiger buckled, but he didn't go down. Unbelievable. I'd hit him in the kneecaps and there he stood, glowering at me.

"That's all you have?" he said.

It was as though he didn't feel anything at all. So I raised the shovel again and struck his left arm. He must have been hurt, but he didn't show it, his face revealing no more emotion than a wall of slate.

"Now—my turn," he said. "Can you take a punch?"

Suddenly a floodlight hit my eyes. There were voices behind it. Who was there?

"Ne bouge pas!"

I heard footsteps scuffing on the dirt and the metallic rustle of guns. Suddenly, green-helmeted AU soldiers were in the alley with us, three of them.

"Laisse la tomber!" one of the soldiers yelled.

It took a second to realize I was just as much a suspect here as the Tiger. Or, worse—maybe I was the only suspect.

I dropped the shovel and didn't wait for any more questions. "This man is wanted in the United States and Nigeria for murder. I'm a policeman."

"Tais-toi!" One of the soldiers said and put his rifle right in my face. Jesus! The last thing I wanted was to have my nose broken again.

"Listen to me! *Écoutez-moi!*" This was a Senegalese platoon, and my French wasn't the greatest. The scene was getting more insane and out-of-control by the second. "He's got two accomplices. *Deux garçons, vous comprenez?* They are all murderers!"

That last remark got me a punch in the gut. I doubled over, trying to catch my breath while the Tiger just stood there, mute, uttering not a word of protest.

Perfectly calm. Smarter than I was.

And in control? I wondered.

Chapter 93

THEY BROUGHT US both out of the alley at gunpoint and made us kneel in the dirt. A crowd had gathered, maybe a couple hundred people already.

There were only five AU troops on the scene, barely enough to cover us and keep everyone else back a few yards. Several people were pointing—at the Tiger. Because he was so large? Or because they knew who he was? Or maybe how dangerous?

"Alex? Alex?" I heard Adanne's voice, and nothing could have sounded more welcome to me.

Then I saw her push through the crowd to the front. Her eyes went wide when she spotted the Tiger kneeling a few feet away from me. He saw her too.

"Let me through! I'm with the *Guardian*." She took an ID out of her pocket, but a soldier shoved her back.

She called out to me again, and she kept yelling, risking

her own safety. "Alex! Tell them that the *Guardian* is doing your story! Tell them the *Guardian* is here. I will write their story."

But then my ears took in something else—the high-pitched whine of a vehicle traveling in reverse!

Was that right? Was I hearing it correctly? *Who was coming now?*

The crowd on one side started to stir, from the rear at first. Then people were scattering wildly, screaming or cursing.

Everything was turning to chaos, even worse than it had been.

I could see a black pickup truck now, *backing* toward us at high speed. It weaved recklessly along the very narrow street, taking out several shade canopies as it came. There were gunshots too, possibly coming from the truck.

The AU team scrambled back first. Then the truck stopped twenty yards away.

Houston Rockets was in the back, shielding himself with a young girl. She was maybe twelve or thirteen. He had one arm around her throat. His other hand—held high over his head—was holding a grenade for everyone to see.

The Tiger wasted no time. He jumped up and ran for the truck. The passenger door opened for him and he disappeared inside.

I saw his huge hand come out and slap the roof hard.

As the pickup raced away, the young girl was thrown from the back. Thank God for that anyway.

But as we watched in shock, she clawed the air with

both arms and hit the ground with her head. Then she exploded!

Houston Rockets must have shoved the grenade into the girl's clothing. They had no reason to kill her. The murder was just for show — or maybe for my eyes.

Or Adanne's?

Chapter 94

THE NEXT MORNING, we returned to Lagos, exhausted and with heavy hearts. Clearly, this kind of insanity happened often here. How could the people bear it?

Adanne insisted that her family put me up for a day or so. "Whatever you need, Alex. I want to get this killer as badly as you do. I've written about him enough."

She had her own apartment in the city, but we drove to her parents' house on a part of Victoria Island—to a side of this fascinating megacity that I hadn't seen before.

The streets here were wide and clean, with no buildings taller than two stories. Most of the homes sat behind yellow or pink stucco walls. Still, there was a familiar smell of fruit and flowers decaying in the air.

Adanne pulled up to a gate and punched in a code.

"Alex," she said before we got out of her car, "I prefer to

save my parents the stress and worry. I told them we've been in Abuja. They're worried about civil war."

"Okay," I agreed. "Abuja it is."

"Thank you. You're very kind," she whispered up close to my ear. "Oh, here they are. They'll think you're a new boyfriend. But I'll clear that up, don't worry."

Everyone was coming out through the carport to the parking pad as we pulled in. I was still pondering the idea *Adanne's new boyfriend.*

Two boys, adorable, smiling twins in school uniforms and undone neckties, appeared. They were elbowing each other to be the first to open Adanne's door.

There were hugs all around for Adanne and then introductions for me. I was *a policeman from America who was helping her with an important story.* I was *not* a new boyfriend. Adanne had everyone laughing about that absurdity within seconds. *Ha, ha, what a comedienne she was.*

Chapter 95

I MET HER mother, Somadina, her father, Uchenna, her sister-in-law, Nkiru, and the nephews, James and Calvin. They couldn't have been warmer or nicer people. It seemed utterly natural to them that a complete stranger should come stay in their home for an unspecified amount of time.

The house was a modest one-story but with lots of windows and interesting views. From the foyer, I saw a walled backyard with tamarind trees and flower gardens. I could smell the hibiscus, even from inside.

Adanne showed me to her father's office. The walls in here, like in Adanne's office at the *Guardian,* were covered with framed news stories.

I noticed that a couple of them dealt with a gang of killer boys, and the man who led them. The name Tiger wasn't used, however.

"Are these all yours?" I asked, looking around. "You've been a busy girl, haven't you?"

She was a little sheepish now, the first embarrassment I had seen from her.

"Let's say I've never had to wonder if my father is proud of me. My mother as well."

I also noticed a framed military portrait on the desk—a young soldier with Adanne's features and her eyes.

"Your brother?"

"Kalu, yes." She went over and picked it up. Instantly there was sadness in her eyes.

"He was with the Engineering Corps. My big brother. I adored him, Alex. You would have liked him."

I wanted to ask what had happened to him, but I didn't.

"I'll tell you, Alex. Two years ago, he went to Niku—for a meeting at the Ministry of Urban Development. There was a dinner that night. A private function at a popular restaurant. No one knows exactly what happened, but all fifteen people there were found dead. They were massacred with guns and machetes."

The Tiger? I wondered. *And his killer boys? Was that why she had written about him? And maybe why I was here now? Was everything finally coming together?*

Adanne set the picture down with a sigh. Then she absently ran her fingers through her braids. Once again, I couldn't help noticing how beautiful she was. Stunning, really. There was no getting around it.

"That was the first time I ever heard of the Tiger. Only because I did my own digging. The 'official' investigation by the police went nowhere. As usual."

"And you're still digging?" I asked.

She nodded. "Maybe someday I can tell my parents that Kalu's murder is solved. That would be the greatest thing, *'make my career,'* as they say. In the meantime, we don't talk about it here, you understand?"

"I understand. And I'm sorry."

"No need for that, Alex. I'm working on a story that's larger and more important than any particular killer. It's about the people who hire them, the ones who want to control our country. Honestly, the story scares even me."

For a few seconds, neither of us said anything, which was unusual for us. We looked at each other, and there was a sudden but undeniable charge in the silence.

Like most of the men she met, no doubt, I wanted to kiss Adanne, but I held myself back. I didn't want to insult her or dishonor her parents, or, more important, *Bree.*

She smiled at me. "You are a good man, Alex. I wasn't expecting that—in an American."

Chapter 96

I EXCUSED MYSELF for a few minutes and borrowed Adanne's mobile to make a call. I didn't think Ian Flaherty would pick up, but I wanted to at least try and reestablish contact with the CIA.

So I was surprised when Flaherty answered on the second ring, and then shocked when he knew it was me calling.

"Cross?"

"Flaherty? How did you do that?"

"Caller ID, ever heard of it?"

"But—"

"Tansi. Your girlfriend's name is on the AU flight record along with yours. I've been looking everywhere for you. Both of you—she's a celebrity too. Writes controversial articles, one after the other. She's a big deal down here. We need to talk. Seriously. You finally have my interest. And so does your killer, the Tiger."

"Hang on a second. Slow down." I'd forgotten how quickly Flaherty could piss me off. "You've been looking for me? Since when? I only tried you about sixteen times."

"Since I learned something you want to know."

"What do you mean?"

He didn't answer right away. "I mean, *I found out something you want to know.*"

It was suddenly obvious to me that he didn't trust the phone line. I stopped to regroup for a second and picked up a pen from the desk.

"Where can I meet you?"

"Let's say tomorrow, same time as before, at the place on that card I gave you. You know what I'm talking about, *Detective* Cross?"

He meant the bank on Broad Street but didn't want to name it, obviously. It was a Victoria Island location, so it was perfect for me.

"Got it. I'll see you then."

"And dress nice, Detective. Wear a tie or something."

"A tie?" I said. "What are you talking about?"

But he'd already hung up on me.

The prick.

Chapter 97

EVERYONE WAS WAITING for me on the patio after my call—with palm wine and kola nuts untouched until I got there.

First though, Adanne's father, Uchenna, blessed the nuts in the Yoruban custom, and the boys, James and Calvin, passed them around.

Adanne seemed to be finding my visit either very joyful or amusing, and she was smiling all the time. I could tell she was happy to be home.

Then the boys got me into a little backyard soccer. The twins were either polite or genuinely impressed that I could juggle the ball a little, even as they schooled me up and down the yard. But it felt good to be running around with the kids. Nice boys. Not killers.

Dinner was a chicken stew called *egusi*—and *fufu*, which is pounded yam for dipping in the broth. There were also fried plaintains, served with a spiced tomato sauce that could have taken the paint off a car. The family setting seemed familiar to me, yet different at the same time, and I ate easily the best meal I'd had in Africa.

Uchenna's favorite topic clearly seemed to be his daughter, Adanne. I learned more about her in those few hours than in all the time she and I had spent together before coming back to Lagos. Adanne jumped in to tell her own version of a few of her father's stories, but when Somadina dragged out the baby pictures, she surrendered and went off to the kitchen to clean up.

While she was gone, the conversation got more serious, and her father spoke of the tragic murders of Christians in northern Nigeria, and then of the reprisals by Christians in the east. He told me the story of a Christian schoolteacher who was recently beaten to death by her Muslim students.

Finally, Uchenna talked about the provocative newspaper articles his daughter wrote on a weekly basis and said how dangerous they were.

But mainly there was laughter in the house that night. Already I felt at home. This was a good family, like so many families here in Lagos.

After Nkiru took the boys to bed and Adanne rejoined the group, the conversation turned to politics and grown-up talk again. There had been four bombings in Bayelsa State that week, down in the Delta region near the oil fields. The pressure for Nigeria to split into independent states was growing along with the violence all around the country.

"It is all about bad men. All of it, always has been," Adanne said. "It's time that the world was run by women. We want to create, not destroy. Yes, I'm serious, Daddy. No, I haven't had too much wine."

"It was the *beer*," her father said.

Chapter 98

AROUND MIDNIGHT, ADANNE led me to a small bedroom where I'd be staying in the rear of the house. She touched my arm, came in behind me, and sat down on the bed.

I could see she was still in a playful mood, still smiling, a different person from the one who had taken me to Darfur a few days ago, and very different from the suspicious, serious-faced reporter I'd met in her office.

"They like you, Alex, especially my mother and sister-in-law. I can't see why. I don't get it."

I laughed. "I guess I fooled them. They'll catch on to me soon."

"Exactly right. Just what I was going to say. So now, we're thinking the same thoughts, I see. So—what are you thinking at this moment? Tell me the truth, Alex."

I didn't have a very good answer for Adanne. Well,

actually I did, but I didn't want to say it out loud. But then I did anyway.

"I think there's an attraction between us, but we have to let it go."

"That's probably right, Alex. Or maybe not."

She leaned in and kissed me on the cheek and held her lips there for a few seconds. She smelled nicely of soap, clean and fresh.

Adanne looked up into my eyes and she was still smiling. She had perfect white teeth. "I just want to lie here with you for a while. Can we do that? Just be here together without any more intimacy than that? What do you think? Can we do it two nights in a row?"

I finally kissed Adanne back, on the lips, but I didn't hold the kiss for very long.

"I'd like that," I told her.

"Me too," she said. "I have love in my heart for you. It's just a crush, I think. Don't say anything, Alex. Don't spoil this, whatever it is."

I didn't. We held on to each other until sleep took us both. I'm not sure if it took us farther away or closer together that night, but nothing happened for either of us to regret.

Or maybe I would come to regret that nothing happened.

Chapter 99

THE NEXT MORNING, Adanne was up early, making coffee and fresh-squeezed juice for everyone. Then she volunteered to drive me to my meeting with Flaherty. She was more serious and businesslike now, the way I'd seen her away from her family.

"Why are you wearing a dumb tie?" she asked. "You look like a downtown lawyer. Or a *banker*. Ugh."

"I have no idea," I told her and smiled. Now I was the one smiling all the time. "It's another Nigerian mystery, I guess."

"You're the mystery," she said. "I think so."

"You're not alone in that."

She stopped the car in front of the bank on Broad Street. "Be careful, Alex." She gave me a quick kiss on the cheek. "It is dangerous out there, more than ever."

Then I hopped out of the car and gave a wave, and she was off. I decided immediately not to think about her, but then

I was thinking about nothing else but Adanne—her smile, last night at her house, things that we didn't do.

Flaherty! I reminded myself. *What the hell does he want from me?*

The CIA man was nowhere to be seen, though. I waited about twenty minutes, just long enough to start getting paranoid, when his Peugeot skidded up to the curb.

He threw open the door on my side. "C'mon, let's go. I don't have time to waste." When I got in, I saw there was a blue folder on the seat and picked it up.

"What's this?"

Flaherty looked dirty and sweaty and totally stressed out, more weasely than usual. He pulled away and started driving. Typical of him, he didn't bother to answer my question.

So I opened the file. It was just a single photocopied form with a passport-size picture of a young boy stapled to it.

"Adoption papers?"

"Orphanage records. *That's your Tiger.* His name is Abidemi Sowande. Born Lagos, nineteen seventy-two, to wealthy parents. Both of them died when he was seven years old, no living relatives. Apparently little Abi wasn't exactly the picture of mental health. He ended up on a ward for a year after that. When he came out, the old family fortune was gone."

"What happened to it?"

Flaherty shrugged, and a little smoke from his cigarette got into his eye. He squinted and rubbed at it.

"Sowande was supposed to get transferred to state care, but somewhere between hospital and orphanage, he disappeared. He was a bright boy apparently. High IQ anyway. He spent two years at university in England. Then he disappeared until a few years ago here. That's it, all I have. No further record of any kind until now. We think he might have worked as a mercenary."

I stared at the picture in my hand. Could this *boy* be the *man* I'd seen in Darfur? The killer of so many people here and in Washington? Ellie's murderer?

"How do we even know it's him?" I asked.

"The dead guy in Sudan—Mohammed Shol? We got a source says he was bragging about doing business with 'the Tiger,' supposedly knew a thing or two about him. It seemed like a long shot, but then someone dug up this record and we got a print match to the crime scene at Shol's. Sweet, right?"

"I don't know," I said, holding up the folder. "I mean, really, what am I supposed to do with this? Seems a little convenient all of a sudden."

Flaherty glared over at me and swerved out of his lane. "Jesus, Cross, how much help do you want here?"

"Help?" I said. I wanted to hit him. "You hang me out to dry, then show up and give me the name of someone who doesn't seem to exist anymore? Possibly a mercenary, but who knows? Is that the kind of help you mean?"

"This is gravy, Detective. I told you not to count on me from day one."

"No, you told me that on day four—*after* I spent three nights in jail."

Chapter 100

FLAHERTY ANGRILY FLICKED his lit butt out the window and wiped the sweat off his face. "Do you even know why you're not dead yet? It's because everyone thinks you're CIA, and we let them think it. We've been babysitting you. I've been babysitting you. Don't bother to thank me."

I clenched my hands several times, trying to cap my anger. It wasn't just Flaherty's arrogance getting to me, or his condescension. It was this entire case. The Tiger was worse than any of the serial killers I had ever arrested—so why was he allowed to roam free here?

I looked over at Flaherty. "What is it you do, exactly—for the agency?"

"I service the copiers at the embassy," he said, deadpan.

Then he lit another cigarette and blew out smoke. "Actually, I'm on record here as CIA. Okay by you?"

"Fair enough. How about this, then? Why aren't you on

the Tiger's case yourself? Why pass me information instead of running with it? Abidemi Sowande is a murderer. You know that."

Something about the debate, just getting it out in the open, I guess, was diffusing the tension in the car. Plus, I was on a roll.

"For that matter, why in God's name am I wearing this stupid tie?"

For the first time, Flaherty smiled.

"Ah," he said. "That's one I can answer."

Chapter 101

AN HOUR LATER, I was in the waiting room at an executive suite on the thirtieth floor of Unilight International's administrative offices in Ikeja. I knew that Unilight was one of the most successful packaged goods companies in the world, but that was about it.

Glossy pictures of Lubra Soap and Oral Toothpaste hung on the walls, and I was trying to figure out exactly what I was doing here. Flaherty had dropped me out front with a business card and a floor number. "Willem de Bues wants to meet you, and you want to meet him."

"Dr. Cross?" A receptionist called over to where I was sitting. "The director will see you now."

I was shown down a hallway to a double door, which she opened for me, into a huge corner office with floor-to-ceiling windows.

Stranger and stranger. What did a successful multinational corporation have to do with a murder case?

A massive desk sat at an angle to the door with two comfortable chairs opposite it. A pair of tufted leather couches took up another corner, where two men in dark suits, white shirts, and clubby ties were just standing up.

"Dr. Cross," the taller of them said. A white man with close-cropped blond hair and heavy-framed rectangular glasses came over and shook my hand.

"I'm Willem de Bues." His accent was Dutch—I think. He motioned to the other man. "This is Thomas Lassiter, an attorney with our legal department."

"Nice to meet you," I said, not quite sure yet if that was true or not. How could I know? I half expected to be beaten up and to have my nose broken next.

"It's our understanding you've been following a local man known as the Tiger," de Bues said, throwing me for a loop. What could this businessman possibly have to do with a killer for hire?

"That's right," I said. "I came here from Washington, where he had committed a couple of savage murders. Savage by our standards anyway."

"Then, we might have something to talk about. Sit down," Mr. de Bues said. It was clear he was used to giving orders. "Your reputation as a policeman precedes you, of course. Your record for solving difficult cases."

"How about you tell me what this is about first? And why your attorney is here."

De Bues's demeanor didn't crack. In fact, he smiled.

"We'd like to help you find the Tiger. And, given that this is a rather…irregular situation, I want to make certain that I don't say, or offer, anything illegal in this meeting. Is that honest enough for you? Please, sit down, Detective. *Sit.*"

Chapter 102

"WHY WOULD YOU want to help a murder investigation?" I asked. I was genuinely curious.

"Unilight International has a considerable interest in Nigeria. Our cosmetics and skin-care business alone has grown enough to justify the expansion we have planned in the southeast. This is true of many multinationals, not just the oil companies."

"In the Delta?" I asked.

"Port Harcourt, yes. And, of course, Lagos. Whatever relationship we now have with local factions seems to be irrelevant to some of the Islamic extremist organizations that are now moving into the region."

"Are you saying the Tiger is Islamic? Because that's news to me."

"No, I have no idea about that. I doubt that he's a religious man.

"But it's no secret he deals in goods that bankroll these groups—conflict diamonds, lifted crude, that sort of thing.

Essentially, he creates inroads for them and makes life more difficult for all foreign corporations. And, as I'm sure you know, *Tiger* is the local term for 'killer for hire'."

"And you want somebody to help you get the killer, or killers, out of your way?"

De Bues looked over at his lawyer, who nodded, and then answered. "We want to help with your criminal investigation, that's all. We're the good guys here, Dr. Cross. Just like you. This is not a 'conspiracy,' like in one of the *Bourne* movies."

"Why not go through the local authorities?"

He smiled again, that nonsmile of his. "You condescend to me, Dr. Cross. The political situation, as we both know, is complex here. It is fair to say that civil war is almost inevitable for Nigeria, but war is like fire, yes? Even as it burns something away, it leaves fertile ground."

It seemed like every day in Africa, I was falling a little farther through the looking glass. This conversation was turning out to be no exception. The CIA had directed me to a multinational corporation — or maybe a clique of them — for help in a brutal murder case?

I stood up. "Thank you for the offer, Mr. de Bues. I need to think about it."

De Bues followed me to the door. "Please, Dr. Cross." He held out a business card. "At least take my number. We do want to help you."

"Thanks," I said and left it at that.

De Bues shook his head as I walked to his door. "You don't understand, do you? This part of the world is about to explode. And if it does, Africa could go the way of the Middle East. That is the key to your murder case, sir."

Chapter 103

FRUSTRATED AND CONFUSED more than ever, I took a car service to Adanne's office. Then we drove to her parents' house, brainstorming about the case, Unilight's involvement, and the Tiger's whereabouts.

My next stop would be to check local records—schools, hospitals, crime reports—any instance of an Abidemi Sowande from 1981 to the present.

Adanne had good suggestions for getting access to state-level information. She wasn't surprised that the multinationals were frightened and looking for help anywhere they could find it.

"Maybe your murder investigation is heating up," she said. "It feels like it to me."

"Yes, to me too."

Adanne took my hand and that was a distraction I needed.

"If you're good," she said, "I might even sleep with you again tonight."

I leaned in and kissed her cheek and wondered how much longer I could be good around Adanne?

"Remember Alex, I *know* what you're thinking. I'm probably thinking the same thing."

It wasn't until we came around the corner onto her parents' street that we realized something was wrong.

"*Oh, no,*" she groaned. "*Oh no, oh no.*"

Adanne stopped her car at the top of the block. At least half a dozen police and fire units were parked at urgent angles to one another in front of her parents' home. Hose lines snaked from the street through the open gate, and black smoke billowed up from behind the wall.

Adanne clawed at the seatbelt release until the strap flew away. "My God, my God! Oh, my God!"

"Adanne, wait a minute," I said and tried to grab and hold her back.

But she was already out of the car and running toward her parents' house. She was screaming in a full voice.

And then I was running too.

Chapter 104

I CAUGHT UP to Adanne just shy of the gate to the house. I grabbed her and picked her up. Her legs kicked off the ground and she struggled against me, reaching toward the gate even as I pulled her away from it.

"Adanne," I said. "You don't want to go in there and see. Trust me, please."

The house was still burning but it was mostly a ghastly, black skeleton of itself. From where we were, Adanne and I could see straight through to the back of the property. The roof was already completely gone.

The driveway and lawn were littered with smoking black debris. Clearly, there had been an explosion. It looked as though it might have been a firebombing.

When I saw two small lumps under sheets on the lawn, I grabbed Adanne tighter and pressed her head into my chest. The bodies had to be the twins, poor little James and Calvin. Adanne knew this too, and she was crying softly in my arms.

A police officer ran by and I caught his attention. "How many were inside?"

He looked me over before answering any questions. "Are you family? Who are you? Why do you want to know?"

"This is her parents' house. I'm a friend. She's Adanne Tansi."

"Three adults, two children," he said. He looked at Adanne, then back at me, and shook his head no. *No survivors.*

A deep shudder went through Adanne and then she began to sob. She was saying something; maybe it was a prayer. I couldn't make out the words or even the language she was speaking.

"I need to talk to your commander," I said to the patrolman standing with us.

"About what?"

"CIA," was what I said next.

The policeman opened his mouth again, but I cut him off. "Just get your commander. Get him over here right now."

As he walked away, I spoke softly against Adanne's forehead. "I'm here. You're not alone." She continued to sob in my arms, shivering like she was freezing cold in the ninety-degree heat.

I watched the commander approach, a tall, broad-backed man in a dark suit. I couldn't hear anything over the fire crew and the hiss of water jets, but I didn't need to.

I knew his face—the flat nose, those round cheeks, that idiotic Mike Tyson squint of his. The last time I'd seen it, he had been dangling me out a hotel window.

Chapter 105

"ADANNE, LISTEN TO me!" I was already pushing her back toward the car. "It's not safe for us here. We have to go right now. That man, the policeman, he almost killed me at my hotel."

She nodded and seemed to understand, and then we were walking quietly. I got her up the block to her car and into the passenger seat. "We have to go."

When I reached the driver's side, I could see the police commander through the windshield. He'd picked his way through the knot of emergency vehicles in front of the house. Then he broke into a run, heading straight for us. Two other men came running with him. I thought that I recognized one of them as the other man who'd come into my hotel room and tried to scare me out of the country.

"Adanne, fasten your seat belt! We have to get out of here. *Right now!*"

I put the car in reverse and checked over my shoulder. The intersection behind me was too busy; I couldn't wait for the traffic to clear, though.

So I changed my mind.

I shifted into drive and drove right at the approaching cops. I began to blare the horn, hitting the wheel again and again.

Adanne's car was only a little Ford Escort, but I caught the cops off guard. I floored it and stayed the course directly at the men. The "commander" didn't budge from his path.

At the last second, I braked hard, but I still struck him. His eyes looked huge with fear—probably the same way mine did when I was hanging out that hotel window.

Now I threw the small car sharply in reverse. He took one of the windshield wipers with him as he flew off and rolled into the street.

I backed all the way up to the corner and spun the wheel hard to face the other direction. A horn blared as an Audi wagon clipped the car, nearly shearing off the rear bumper.

I picked a direction arbitrarily and punched those four cylinders for all they were worth.

"Where are we going?" Adanne sat up a little straighter, almost like she was coming out of a trance.

"Into the city," I told her.

If there was one thing Lagos might be good for, it was crowds we could get lost in.

Chapter 106

"ADANNE?" I REACHED over and held on to her shoulder. "We have to get away from here. The policeman back there—when I was staying in Lagos—he nearly killed me. I'm sure it's the same man. It's all connected somehow, it has to be."

Adanne didn't argue with me. She just nodded and pointed to the right.

"Turn here for the Mainland Bridge. It's the best way, Alex. We'll go through Benin."

"Hold on tight, brace yourself!"

"It's too late for that, way too late."

I took the turn—without slowing down. We came out onto a wide boulevard lined with low-slung stucco shops, open lots, and old dusty cars and trucks. A freestanding billboard advertised Grace of Light Church, with an illustration of a woman in a choir robe, eyes on the sky and arms open to God.

But it certainly wasn't God that I heard next.

It was the deafening chop of a helicopter, loud and very close to the roof of the Escort.

They'd found us already.

They were on top of us, right over our heads.

"It's the police!" said Adanne. "They'll kill us, Alex. *I know things they don't want in any newspaper.*"

Chapter 107

I CRANED MY neck to see what was up, literally. The small bird with white struts was almost directly overhead. There were no police markings, and the low altitude was another bad sign.

The pilot was being increasingly reckless and didn't seem to care about the safety of people down on the street, or about his own well-being, for that matter.

The Mainland Bridge was still a mile or so off. I scanned the area for any kind of cover—parking garage, construction site. There was nothing obvious, nowhere for us to hide from the helicopter.

What was worse, within a few blocks I saw lights in my mirror—red-and-blue spinners, at least three cruisers moving very fast, gaining on us.

"Shit! That's definitely police."

"I'm serious, Alex. They'll kill us if they catch us. I'm not being paranoid."

"I believe you. But why, Adanne?"

"Alex, I know terrible things. I'm writing a story about it. I have to tell somebody what I found out."

"Tell me," I said.

In the next frantic few minutes, that's what Adanne did; she told me secrets that she hadn't shared before. One of the secrets was that Ellie Cox had visited her in Lagos. They had shared sources and information. They had talked about Abidemi Sowande — the Tiger. And the group that he worked for.

"Alex, he is one of the most dangerous mercenaries in the world."

I sped up and weaved through the traffic as best I could. But when I checked the mirror again, the police cars were still close. I was a little numb from hearing what Adanne knew about the Tiger and so much more. I still couldn't believe that she and Ellie had met.

Suddenly Adanne grabbed my arm. *"Alex!"* she shouted. *"There!"*

A police car had hopped the curb from a vacant lot on the left and was pulling across our path right now.

I jammed down on the brakes — *too late.*

The Escort skidded and caught the cruiser broadside.

Our front end folded right in on itself, as if it were made of molding clay. No wonder Ford was losing market share. My chest hit the steering column hard, and I saw Adanne's head smack the windshield.

Already the other police cruiser was right behind us, siren screeching, spinners going like crazy.

"Adanne?" I sat her up and saw that her forehead was swabbed in red. She raised her eyebrows and blinked several times.

"You all right?" I asked.

"I think so. Don't tell them anything, Alex. More people will die. Don't tell them a thing I told you. Do you promise? Alex?"

Chapter 108

BLUE-UNIFORMED COPS WERE running up on either side of our car. When they threw open the doors and grabbed at us, Adanne came out easily. I was a lot more work for them.

When I was finally pulled from the front seat, I came up swinging, crunching a straight right fist into somebody's chin. It felt good.

Then two of them flung me down hard onto the pavement. That didn't feel so good. Something popped in my shoulder. Jesus!

My arm flew up reflexively, and a wave of pain crashed over me, even as I felt the joint slip back into place. I wasn't sure if I could move the arm again, though. How could I fight them now?

The police were yelling on all sides, at least four of them screaming in a mishmash of languages I couldn't understand.

Then one of them fired his service revolver into the air to make his point crystal clear.

Adanne was shouting too. "I'm with the *Guardian*! I'm a reporter. Press!"

I could see under the car to where she was lying facedown on the other side. There were pairs of black shoes moving all around her. Then a pistol was pointed at her head.

But that didn't stop her from yelling at them. "Adanne Tansi! I'm with the *Guardian*!"

She shouted it over and over, not just for them, but for anyone who could hear in the neighborhood. We had already stopped traffic on both sides of the street.

With any luck, Adanne had just gone from anonymous suspect to known entity. It was a good move — especially given her state of mind after what had happened at her parents' house.

I saw two of the cops who were standing over me exchange a look. One reached down to pull my hands back and cuff me. When he did, my shoulder felt like it was being torn in half.

Then I was punched and kicked in the small of the back. Everything was getting hazy and surreal again in a hurry. I couldn't let myself black out.

"Alex!" Adanne's voice came again. "Alex! I'm over here! Alex!"

I turned my head to look for her. The heel of a shoe came down on my cheek and temple. But I saw her anyway. The police were dragging her away. Past a standard cruiser — to an unmarked black sedan.

Going where?

"She's with the *Guardian*!" I yelled at the top of my voice. "She's with the *Guardian*! She's press!"

Adanne kicked and twisted, and I tried to roll the two cops off my back.

But it was too little too late. Adanne was still shouting when they stuffed her into the black sedan, slammed the door, and drove off in a hurry.

Chapter 109

A FEVERED VOICE inside my head was screaming for me to help Adanne, but I knew I should think things through before I tried anything.

I had no idea, and no way to find out, if the car they had put me in was following Adanne's. I was in a police unit, though. Small and cramped by DC standards. Smelling strongly of tobacco and sweat and somebody's urine. *Were these men policemen?*

I sat sideways on a ripped vinyl seat in back. My hands were cuffed, and a rusted metal security grate was a few inches from my face. My shoulder throbbed and I was afraid it was broken. But that was the least of my worries right now. What I cared about most was Adanne and what was happening to her.

"Where did they take her?" I asked. The two uniforms

in front wouldn't even turn to look at me. I couldn't provoke them.

"Talk to me. Tell me where we're going," I demanded to know.

Then I saw for myself, and it couldn't have been any worse.

The first thing I recognized was the signpost at the turn-off for Kirikiri. Then the familiar concrete walls and razor wire crisscrossing the top.

Oh hell, no.

I felt like I'd fallen into some kind of hell on earth. Going in here the first time had been bad enough, but heading back when I knew what to expect?

It took the two cops and two more prison guards to get me out of the car and inside the jail.

I thought they would drag me up to the wards—but we went *down* instead. *Down* couldn't be good. Where was Adanne? Was she here too?

My feet bumped over stone steps, then onto the compacted dirt floor of a barely lit corridor. It looked and smelled like the cell block upstairs, but when we passed through one of the reinforced steel doors, I saw they all opened onto the same enormous space.

There was a low ceiling that dripped some kind of sludge, and a row of retrofitted support columns ran right down the middle of the room. They extended into deep shadows on either side.

A blank space. For torture? Interrogation? Execution?

Everything was left to the imagination—on purpose, I was sure.

The police and guards left me there, with my hands cuffed tightly behind my back, secured around one of the posts. The column was rusted steel, about four inches thick, and going nowhere. Just like me.

I stopped struggling as soon as they walked away. Better to save my strength, I figured.

I didn't know who wanted me here—the Tiger? The police? The government?

Someone else?

A multinational corporation, for God's sake? Maybe that was it. Anything was possible here.

If I was extraordinarily lucky, Flaherty would come looking for me again; and if I was even luckier, he'd be able to find me down here. But that could take days, and then more time to find Adanne.

If she was still alive.

If they hadn't gotten the secrets out of her.

If... if... if...

Chapter 110

A LIGHT CAME on... *two* lights actually

Quickly, one after the other.

I didn't know how many hours had passed. Or what time of day it was. I knew that I hadn't slept.

The man I now thought of as the police commander, the one I'd hit with Adanne's car, stood by one of the doors.

His hand was still on the wall switch. Two single-bulb fixtures shone brightly overhead. They weren't meant to be easy on the eyes, or the brain, or the soul.

"Tell me what you know about the Tiger," he said as he strode forward. I noticed he'd changed suits—and that there was a rectangle of gauze taped to his forehead.

"Where's Adanne Tansi?" I said.

"Don't make me *cross*, Cross." The commander chuckled softly; he'd been a jackass joker the last time too, I remembered. The accent was Yoruban and the voice was calm. Too calm. He had more self-control than I would have thought he should, given that I'd tried to run him over and put tire marks on his ugly face.

"Just tell me if she's alive," I said. "That's all I need to hear from you."

"She's alive. Somewhat." He spread his hands. "Now — the killer you chased here? What do you know? Are you CIA? Or are you working with her? The *reporter*?"

At least he wanted something from me. Quid pro quo was better than nothing, I guess.

"There are lots of Tigers, killers for hire," I said. "You know that. The one I'm after is physically large. He operates internationally, with teams in Lagos and Washington at the very least. I believe his name is Sowande.

"As of two days ago, he was in South Darfur. I don't know where the hell he is now." I paused and stared into his eyes. "I'm *not* CIA, definitely not CIA. Tell me where she is."

His shoulders barely shrugged. "She's here. At Kirikiri. No need to worry about her. She's close by. Look! Look at that. There she is now. The news reporter is here."

Chapter 111

A POLICE OFFICER I didn't recognize was pushing Adanne into the room. She shuffled ahead of him, with a wad of tape stuffed over her mouth. Blood streaked both her cheeks.

Her braids had been cut short; they stuck out at angles from her head. One of her eyes was swollen shut and colored blue-black. She saw me and nodded that she was okay. I didn't believe it for a second.

"Now maybe there's more that you can tell me," the commander said. "Something I don't *already* know about the Tiger. Why did you come here? Not to solve a murder case. Why would I believe that? How do you know Adanne Tansi?"

I began to shout at him. "What the hell is the matter with you? I'm a cop, just like you. I'm investigating a murder case. It's that simple."

The cuffs tore at my wrists. Then the pain in my shoulder turned to nausea. I thought I was going to throw up.

The commander nodded once at the cop who'd brought in Adanne. The underling threw a hard uppercut into her stomach. I felt the cruel blow in my own body.

Adanne groaned behind the tape and fell to her knees. The dirt on her face was streaked with tears, but she wasn't crying now. She was watching me. Blood from her mouth was turning the tape red. Her eyes were pleading. But for what?

"Why are you doing this?" I spit between clenched teeth. I could imagine my hands around his throat. "My friend was killed in Washington. *That's why I'm here.* That's all there is. I'm not part of some conspiracy."

"Take the tape off her mouth," the commander ordered.

The guard ripped it away and Adanne said, "Alex, don't worry about me."

The commander turned to the cop. "Again. Hit her." He turned back to me. *"Alex! Worry about her."*

"Okay!" I cut him off. "The Tiger's name is Abidemi Sowande. He disappeared in nineteen eighty-one, when he was nine years old, turned up in England at a university for two years, and hasn't used that identity since.

"He's murdered a lot of people, here and in America. He uses wild boys. He may control other Tigers. That's all I know. That's everything I have. You know about the diamonds, the gasoline, the illegal trading."

The commander kept his hand in the air to hold off the next punch. "You're sure that's it?"

"*I'm sure, goddammit!* I'm just a cop from Washington, DC. Adanne has nothing to do with this."

He squinted, thinking about it, and then seemed satisfied. His hand came down slowly. "I should kill you anyway," he said. "But that's not my choice."

Then I heard another voice in the room. "No, that would be *my* choice, Detective Cross."

Chapter 112

A MAN STEPPED out of the shadows, a large man—*the mercenary soldier known as the Tiger. The one I'd been chasing.*

"No one seems to know much about me. That's good, don't you think? I want to keep it that way. She writes stories in newspapers, the London *Times,* maybe the *New York Times.* You get in the way a lot."

He walked over to me. "Unbelievable," he said. "Some people fear you, eh? Not me. I find you to be a funny man. Big joke. The joke is on you, Detective Cross."

My body eased just a fraction. He didn't seem angry, and he wasn't concerned about me, but he was huge, and musclebound, as fierce as any man I'd ever seen.

Then, with his eyes still on me, he said, "Shoot her. Wait. No, no. Give me a gun."

"*NO!*" I yelled.

That's all I got out. Adanne's good eye flew open and she found me in this unbelievable nightmare we were sharing.

The Tiger took a quick step forward. "Pretty girl," he said. "Stupid bitch. Dead woman! You did this to her, Cross. You did this, not me."

Blam.

Blam.

Chapter 113

HE HAD FIRED a police service revolver close to her head. Twice. He missed on purpose, and he laughed merrily at the prank.

"People find it difficult to believe that a black man can be clever and intelligent. Have you found that to be true, *Doctor* Cross? How about you, Adanne?"

She didn't answer, but she spit at him. "Murderer," she said.

"One of the best—and proud of my accomplishments."

Then he fired a third shot, right between Adanne's eyes. Her body lurched forward, and she landed facedown on the ground. Her arms spread out like wings. Adanne didn't move.

As fast as that, as insane, she was gone. Adanne was dead in this horrid jail cell, murdered by the Tiger as the police looked on and did nothing to stop him.

Rage poured out of me. There were no words for what I was feeling. A cord tightened around my throat, another around my forehead.

Don't worry about me, Adanne had said. She *knew* they were going to kill her; she knew it all the time.

Her killer stood over her and he watched me. Then he grinned. He dropped his trousers, went down on his knees, and committed his final outrage against Adanne.

"Pretty girl," he growled. "You did this to her. Never forget that, Detective. *Never.*"

Chapter 114

ALEX, DON'T WORRY about me.

Don't worry about me.

Don't worry.

Night had become morning somehow, and I was still alive. I could see that it was light through the black fabric of a hood they made me wear. What's more, I was being moved.

The neck cord kept me oxygen hungry and weak as they dragged me outside. They threw me like cargo into the backseat of a truck or van, a vehicle with a high step and a diesel engine.

Then we drove for a long time. I kept my eyes open inside the hood. Still, all I could see in my mind was the last moment when Adanne was alive, and then . . .

The Tiger had killed her, and worse. He thought I was a joke. He said I was no threat to him. Just another policeman. We'd see.

If I lived through the next few hours or so.

As the ride continued, I prayed for Adanne and for her family. I told them, in my own way, that this wasn't over yet. Not that it mattered to them. But it did to me. I wondered why I was still alive. It made no sense to me. Another mystery.

When we finally stopped, car doors opened on either side of me. Now what?

Somebody shoved my head down into the seat. The cuffs were roughly removed. Powerful hands pressed into the small of my back and pushed hard. "You go home now. *Go!*"

I went flying through the air — but only for a few seconds of uncertainty and terror.

Then I landed on stone or cement. By the time I'd gotten up and untied the hood, they were gone, out of sight, whoever had brought me here.

They had dropped me on a side street next to an official-looking building, the sort of white stone box you might find in downtown DC.

I could see through an iron fence and across a manicured front lawn to a gatehouse out front.

An American flag flew above it, flapping in a light breeze.

This was the American consulate. Had to be. The embassy was in Abuja. That must be where I was now.

But why?

Chapter 115

SOMETHING WAS GOING on here at the consulate. Something big. And dangerous-looking. Hundreds of people were gathered in the streets outside the front gates. Actually, it looked like there were two separate crowds. Half of them were lined up like they were waiting to get in. The other half, on the opposite side of a concrete barrier, were demonstrating against the United States.

I saw hand-lettered placards that read US PAYS THE PRICE, and DELTA PEOPLE, DELTA RULE, and NO MORE AMERICANS.

Even from a distance, I could tell it was the kind of scene that could turn ugly, or violent, at any time. I didn't wait around for that to happen.

I walked around the corner, and leading with my good shoulder, I started pushing through the crowd. People on both sides grabbed at me, either because I was cutting in line or, maybe, because I looked like an American. The shouting on the street side blocked out any other noise around me.

One guy got hold of my shirt. He ripped it all the way down the back before I knocked his arm away.

The shirt didn't matter to me. Nothing did anymore. Once again I wondered why I was still alive. Because they thought I was CIA? Because I had friends in Washington? Or maybe because they finally believed I was a cop?

I made my way to the main gate. Standing there, filthy and barefoot, with no passport to show, I told the double-chinned marine who got in my face that my name was Alex Cross, I was an American police officer, and I had to speak with the ambassador right away.

The marine didn't want to hear it, not a word.

"I was kidnapped. I'm an American cop," I told him. "I just witnessed a murder."

Out of the side of his mouth the marine muttered, "Take a number."

Chapter 116

I WAS GOING more than a little crazy now, but I had to hold my emotions in. I had stories to tell someone, information to give, Adanne's secrets to share with someone who could make a difference.

I got several minutes of healthy skepticism at the gate before I finally convinced a marine guard to call in my name. The response came back right away: *Bring Detective Cross inside*. It was almost as if they were expecting me. I wasn't sure if that was a good sign or not. Given my recent history, probably not.

The consulate lobby, with its metal detectors and bulletproof glass on all the windows, felt like an urban police station. People were lined up at every desk and window, most of them clearly agitated, waiting to be seen.

All the American accents—and a portrait of Condoleezza

Rice presiding over the room—played tricks with my mind about where I was, and exactly how I had gotten here.

Once inside, I was met by a nonmilitary escort in an off-white suit. He was "Mr. Collins," a Nigerian of some unspecified position here.

Unlike the marine who'd brought me this far, Collins was friendly and animatedly answered a few questions as we walked.

"There's been at least one rebel attack in Rivers State today," he explained, gesticulating the whole time. "Much bigger than we've seen before. The government won't admit to it, but the independent media is calling it the beginning of a civil war."

The populist buzz on the first floor gave way to crisp officiousness and hushed conversations on the second.

I was taken straight to the ambassador's consular suite, where I waited outside his office for several minutes—until a dozen men, black, white, and four who looked Chinese, walked out all at once. Each of them appeared somber and nervous. No one met my gaze, or perhaps no one was in the least interested that I was sitting there barefoot and in rags.

Mr. Collins politely held the door for me, and then he closed it from the outside.

Chapter 117

AMBASSADOR ROBERT OWELEEN was tall and willowy, almost too thin, a silver-haired man of maybe sixty. He stood behind his large antique desk flanked by American and Nigerian flags. Two aides stayed where they were, on a small couch in an alcove off to one side.

"Mr. Cross." He shook my hand, unsmiling. "My God, what happened to you?"

"A lot. I won't waste your time. I'm here about a man, a killer, known as the Tiger. It's a matter of Nigerian and American security."

He swept my words away in the air. "I know why you're here, Mr. Cross. I've been getting all kinds of pressure from Abu Rock about you."

"Excuse me—Abu Rock?"

"The capital. It seems that the only one who wants you

in Nigeria is you. The CIA has actually saved your life here, haven't they?"

Now I was a little dumbstruck, to add to my general numbness and dizziness about what had happened recently. The American ambassador knew about my presence here? Was someone taking out billboards about me or something?

"We're sending you home today," Oweleen continued, with finality in his voice.

I looked at the floor and back at him again, trying to keep it together. "Sir, the man I'm chasing is a mass murderer. He may have government ties here. He's definitely involved with the police in some mysterious way. If I could just have a chance to reach my CIA contact in Lagos—"

He cut me off. "What exactly do you think your authority is, Mr. Cross? You're a visitor in this country, nothing more than that. You can take this up with the State Department if you wish. *In Washington*."

"He needs to be stopped, sir. Yesterday he murdered a reporter for the *Guardian* named Adanne Tansi. I saw him kill her. He murdered her entire family. He's responsible for at least eight deaths in Washington."

Finally, Oweleen exploded. "Who the hell are you? I never even heard of you until three days ago, and now I'm taking time out for *this*? Do you have any idea what's going on here?"

He waved his hand at the plasma TV on the wall. "Turn that up."

One of the aides pushed a button on a remote—and then I watched the TV in shocked silence and with dread.

Chapter 118

THE TV WAS tuned to CNN. A British reporter was speaking over an image of an upscale housing complex—white two-story buildings in neat rows, shot from high above.

The overlay read "Breaking News—Summit Oil Residential Compound, Bonny Island, Nigeria."

"Never before have families been taken," the reporter was saying, "and certainly never this number of live hostages. In an e-mail to the international press, People for the Liberation of the Niger Delta now have claimed responsibility for the incident—with these shocking images attached to their message."

The screen switched to grainy infrared video.

Dozens of people sat along the floor of a dark hallway. Their heads were covered and hands tied, but it was easy to tell there were men, women, and children on the film. Some of them were crying, others moaning piteously.

"Those are British and American citizens," Ambassador Oweleen informed me. "Every one of them. Consider yourself lucky to get a flight out of here at all."

"What flight? When?"

He held up a hand, looking back at the TV. "Look at this, will you? Do you see what's happening?" Armed troops were streaming out of a truck single file.

The British reporter went on: "Government forces have established a perimeter around the entire complex, while economic pressure mounts internationally.

"With more attacks promised, oil-production facilities are shutting down regionwide, approaching an unprecedented seventy percent slowdown, which is considered to be catastrophic."

"Chinese, French, Dutch, and of course US interests in particular are at stake. Under normal trade conditions, Nigeria provides about twenty percent of American oil."

A phone buzzed on the desk. Ambassador Oweleen picked it up. "Yes?" he said, and then, "Send them in."

"Sir," I tried again. "I'm not asking for much. I just need to make one phone call—"

"We'll get you a shower and some fresh clothes right away. And we'll take care of any immigration issues. We can get you a new passport right away. But then you're gone. Forget about your manhunt. As of right now, it's over."

I finally snapped at him. "I don't need a shower! Or fresh clothes. I need you to listen to me. I just witnessed a reporter named Adanne Tansi being murdered at the Kirikiri Prison. She was writing an important story that has relevance to the violence near the oil fields."

The doors to the office opened, and Oweleen's eyes shifted right past me. It was as though the moment I raised my voice, I'd lost him. He didn't even respond to what I'd said.

He spoke directly to the double marine escort waiting there. "We're all done here. Take Detective Cross downstairs and get him cleaned up for travel back to the US."

Chapter 119

THE TWO MARINES were polite and respectful enough but very mission oriented as they escorted me to a subbasement locker room.

It had tall wooden lockers and a faded carpet, a tiled steam room and whirlpool, and a small area for showering. As promised, I was given a fresh towel.

One of the marines asked me my trouser, shirt, and shoe size and then left. The other marine told me I had about ten minutes to shower and dress, so I ought to get started. Both of the marines were black—probably no coincidence there.

There were four stalls, each with a curtained changing cubicle in front. I stood inside the last one, my mind racing while the clock ran down on my time in the country.

What was I going to do? There were no windows in the

room, and there was only one exit. I turned on the water, just to sound busy.

Then I leaned in and let it pour over my head.

Suddenly my whole body was shaking. I was remembering Adanne, and that had to stop, for now, anyway.

A minute later, I heard someone moving around outside. A curtain slid open and closed. One of the other showers was turned on.

Someone was humming that James Blunt ballad that was always on the radio, the one where he keeps repeating the word *beautiful*.

I took off the remnants of my shirt. Then I stuck my head under the water again, and leaned back out, dripping on the floor.

"Hey, can you get me another towel?" I asked the guard.

I had noticed there were stacks of them by the entrance when we'd come in.

"Why do you need two?" he leaned inside the shower and said.

"Are you kidding? You saw the way I look. And smell."

He shook his head but went to get the extra towel.

"Thanks," I called.

I immediately stepped over to the other cubicle, holding the curtain rings to keep them from singing on the bar.

Whoever was showering next to me had hung his clothes on a hook in the changing stall.

I rifled through the pants pockets and found just what I was hoping for—*a cell phone*.

Seconds later, I was back in my own stall—just before the marine looped a white terry towel over the top of the bar. "You'd better pick up the pace," he said from outside the curtain.

I turned the shower up as hard—and as loud—as it would go.

Then I dialed Ian Flaherty's number.

He answered himself.

Chapter 120

"FLAHERTY," I SAID. "It's Alex Cross."

"Cross? Where are you?"

"I'm at the consulate. I'm in Africa. They're sending me out of the country. It's going down right now. I need you to talk to someone and get it stopped. I'm close to the bastard, the Tiger."

He didn't even pause before he answered. "No can do. I can't cover for you anymore."

"I don't need you to cover for me. Adanne Tansi is dead—he killed her. I need you to make a call or two. I can break this case now."

"You don't get it," Flaherty said. "You're done over here. Game over. Go home and stay there. Forget about Abi Sowande. Or whatever his name is now."

The water in the other shower stopped. The man in there started whistling. I hit the heel of my hand against my forehead, putting it all together. *Flaherty hadn't been covering for me at all. I had this all wrong, right from the beginning.*

"I was covering for *you*, wasn't I?" I said.

The whistling in the next stall stopped for a second and then continued.

"That's why you wanted people thinking I was CIA. I was out in the open. While you played covert, I was a useful distraction."

"Listen." I could hear in Flaherty's voice that he was done. "I've got to run. We saved your bacon a couple of times. Be thankful. There's a war going on here. Get the hell out of Dodge — call me from the States."

"Flaherty!"

He hung up at the same time that the shower curtain flew open.

The marine who'd fetched the towel was there and looking totally pissed off. He pushed me into the wall and pinned my wrist. I didn't struggle with him. For one thing, my shoulder was howling with pain. When he reached for the cell phone, I just opened my hand and let him take it.

Game over, all right.

I was going home.

Whether I wanted to or not.

Honestly, I had mixed feelings.

Chapter 121

I LEFT THE consulate pretty much the way I'd left Kirikiri—*as a captive.* This time, of the American government. I wondered if I could possibly get away again. And did I really want to?

One of the marine escorts drove, while the other sat in back with me. Worse, they had handcuffed me to him. I guess they'd decided I wanted to do this the hard way.

The main gates to the consulate were closed as we drove toward them. *No one was waiting to get in anymore.*

The demonstrators had swollen in number, though. They were lined along the fence, holding on to it like they would jail bars, cursing against all things American, as well as the life that fate had dealt them.

Once we were through the main gates, the crowd closed in around us.

Bodies pressed against the car windows, palms slapped

on the glass, and fists beat the roof. I could see anger and fear in their eyes, the frustration of lifetimes of injustice and misery.

"What do these people want?" the young marine in back with me asked. His name tag said Owens. "Those hostages in the Delta are Americans and Brits. They're probably going to die."

"What do they want?" the marine at the wheel said. "They want us not to be here."

And nobody wants me here, I was thinking, *not even the Americans. Nobody wants to hear the truth either.*

Chapter 122

THE ROADWAYS TO Murtala were even more crowded and bustling than the last time I'd been here—if that was possible. We parked at the very same airbase Adanne and I had used to go to Sudan. We had to take a shuttle from there.

The bus was jammed with American families presumably headed home or at least out of Nigeria. Everyone was talking nonstop about the terrifying hostage drama in the Delta. No one had been freed yet, and everybody was afraid the hostages would be killed soon.

The surprise to me was how little attention anyone gave to two men handcuffed together. I guess these people had other things on their minds besides me and my marine guard.

The terminal at the airport was overflowing, noisy, and as chaotic as the scene of a bombing. We burrowed our way in to a security office to arrange a walk-through to the plane.

Apparently the handcuffs weren't coming off until I was buckled in tight and pointed toward home.

The waiting area was packed, like everywhere else, with all eyes turned toward a single TV. It was tuned to an African channel.

The female reporter had a Yoruban accent, just like Adanne's, and it was the strangest thing, but that's what finally put me over the edge. Tears started to roll down my cheeks, and I began to shake as if I had a fever.

"You okay, man?" the marine cuffed to me asked. He seemed like a good man, actually. He was just doing a job, and doing it well.

"Yeah, yeah," I said. "I'm fine."

Still, I wasn't the only one crying in the room. With good reason. Nigerian troops had moved in on the Bonny Island complex in what was supposed to be a "rescue mission." Instead, all thirty-four hostages were now dead. Open fighting had broken out all through the Delta region. Riots were reported in at least two other states in the south.

The images of the slaughtered hostages were shocking by American news standards. The hostages were lying on the floor of the corridor, adults and children, both. The bodies were slumped and fallen, draped over one another, with bloodstained clothes, and hoods still over their heads.

One woman near me let out a piercing scream. Her family was still down in the Delta. Everyone else was quietly fixated on the screen.

"Governors' offices in Rivers, Delta, and Bayelsa states have issued warnings," the reporter went on. "Local citizens are urged to avoid all but the most necessary travel for at least the next twenty-four hours. Full curfew is in effect. Violators will be arrested, or possibly shot."

The marine cuffed to me, Owens, spoke. "Your plane is boarding. Let's go, Detective Cross. Hell, I wish I could go with you. I'm from DC myself. I'd like to go home. I miss it. You have no idea."

I took a number from Owens and promised to call his mother when I got back.

A few minutes later we were all being led out to the airplane. I heard someone call my name and I looked to one side, toward the terminal building.

What I saw there froze my blood and seemed to change everything.

Father Bombata was looking right at me, and he raised his small hand and waved.

Standing beside him, towering over the priest — if he was indeed a priest — was the Tiger. Abi Sowande. The monster ran his thumb across his throat.

What was that supposed to mean — *that this wasn't finished?*

Hell, I knew that.

It wasn't over by a long shot. I had never given up on a case yet.

But maybe the Tiger already knew that.

Part Four

HOME AGAIN, HOME AGAIN

Chapter 123

I KNEW I had failed.

And I knew, and had known for a long time, that I'd already witnessed and investigated enough murders and bloodshed to last me for a couple of lifetimes. Nothing had prepared me for the insane mayhem and horrors of the past few weeks: torture and episodes of genocide; suffering by innocent women and children; finally, the senseless murders of Adanne Tansi and her family.

I wanted nothing more than to escape into sleep for a few hours on the plane to London, where I would eventually connect with a flight to Washington.

But I couldn't stop the terrible nightmare images from my time in Africa: *Again and again I saw Adanne's murder and rape by the monstrous Tiger.*

And what had come of the murders of Adanne and her family? What had been accomplished beyond a failed chase after the killer called Tiger? What of all the other deaths here that would never be avenged, or even properly memorialized? What of the secrets Adanne had shared with me?

I woke with a shiver as the flight descended into London's Gatwick. I had slept some and now I felt groggy and had an upset stomach and a splitting headache.

Maybe it was just my paranoia, but the Virgin Nigeria flight attendants seemed to have avoided me for most of the trip.

I needed water now and an aspirin. I signaled the attendants, who were collecting cups and soda cans before we landed. "Excuse me?" I called out.

I was certain the women had seen me signal, but I was ignored by them again.

Finally, I did something I don't remember ever having done on a flight. I hit the "Attendant" button. Several times. That got me a stern look from the closer of the flight attendants. She still didn't come to see what I needed.

I got up and went to her. "I don't know what I've done to offend you—," I began.

She cut me off.

"I will tell you. You are a most *ugly* American. Most Americans are that way, but you are even more so. You have caused suffering to those you came into contact with. And now you want my help? No. Not even a cold drink. The seat belt light is on. Return to your seat."

I took her arm and held it lightly but firmly. Then I turned and looked around toward the cabin.

I was hoping to see someone watching us, someone who had spoken to the flight attendants about me.

No one seemed to be looking our way. Nor did I recognize anyone.

"Who told you about me?" I asked. "Someone on the plane? Who was it? Show me."

She shook herself loose. "You figure it out. You are the detective." Then she walked away and didn't look back. That angry face of hers and the mystery of her anger toward me followed me all the way home.

Chapter 124

THE NEXT TWELVE hours of the trip passed very slowly, but finally I arrived in Washington. I wasn't able to reach Nana to tell her I was home. So I just grabbed a taxi waiting at Reagan International and headed to Fifth Street.

It was a little past nine and the nighttime traffic was heavy, but I was glad to be in DC again. Sometimes it feels that way when I come home after a long, hard trip, and this time certainly qualified. I couldn't wait to be in my own house, my own bed.

Once I was in the cab, I got lost in a kind of jet-lagged reverie.

No one had any idea about the carnage and suffering until they actually visited parts of Nigeria, Sudan, Sierra Leone—and there were no easy answers or solutions either. I didn't believe that the violence I had seen came from regular people being evil. But those at the top were, at least some of them.

And then there were psychopaths on the loose, like the Tiger and the other killers for hire, the wild boys. The fact that terrible conditions might have made them killers hardly seemed to matter.

The irony that kept jabbing at me was that I'd spent the last dozen years chasing murderers in the States, and it seemed like child's play now, nothing compared with what I'd seen in the past weeks.

I was shaken out of my reverie when the cab slid over to the side of the road. *What was wrong now?* I was home, and still misfortune followed me? What — *a flat tire?*

The driver peered back and nervously announced, "Engine trouble. I am sorry. Very sorry." Then he pulled a gun and yelled, *"Traitor! Die!"*

Chapter 125

SOMEBODY WAS STUBBORNLY ringing the front-door bell at the Cross house. Ringing it again and again and again.

Nana was in Ali's bedroom, putting him down the way he liked her to, lying in bed next to him until the sweet boy drifted off to sleep as she whispered the words of a favorite story.

Tonight the book was *Ralph S. Mouse,* and Ali wouldn't stop giggling at every page, often a couple of times on the same page, saying, "Read it again, Nana. Read it again."

Nana waited patiently for Jannie to get the front door. But it rang again, and then again. Persistent and rude and maddening. Jannie had been making a cake in the kitchen. *Where was that girl? Why didn't she answer the door?*

"Now, who can it be?" Nana mumbled as she pushed herself up and out of Ali's bed. "I'll be right back, Ali . . . *Janelle, you are trying my patience, and that's not a good idea.*"

But when she got to the living room, Nana Mama saw that Janelle was already at the door—which was flung wide open.

A strange boy in a red Houston Rockets basketball shirt was *still* ringing the bell.

"Are you some kind of a crazy person?" Nana called out as she hobbled quickly across the foyer. "Stop that bell ringing this instant! Just stop it now. What do you want here so late? Do I know you, son?"

The boy in the Rockets jersey finally took his hand off the bell. Then he held up a sawed-off shotgun for Nana to see, but she kept coming forward until she protectively held Jannie.

"I will kill dis stupid girl in a second," he said. "And I will kill you, ol' woman. I will not hesitate jus' 'cause you de detective's family."

Chapter 126

IT ALL HAPPENED so fast in the taxi and caught me completely off guard and unprepared, but I saw a chance, and I had to take it.

I didn't think the cab driver was an experienced killer. He'd hesitated instead of just pulling the trigger and shooting me.

So I lurched forward and grabbed the gun and his hand at the same time.

Then I smashed his wrist against the taxi's metal partition. I smashed it again as hard as I could.

The man yelped loudly and he let go of the gun. I pulled it away and swung it toward him.

Suddenly he ducked low and then flung himself out the front door.

I jumped out the back door, but he was already scampering down a grassy hill. Then he disappeared into a thicket of woods off to the side of the highway.

I had a shot with his gun, but I didn't take it. He'd called me "traitor." Just like the flight attendant.

Did he believe that, or was he doing what he'd been told?

I pictured the man's face, gaunt, a goatee, maybe in his midtwenties. A soldier? A thug? His accented English showed hints of a Nigerian dialect. So who had sent him after me—the Tiger? Somebody else? Who?

I tried not to speculate on conspiracy theories right now. Not here, not yet.

The keys were still in the ignition, and without much deliberation I decided to drive the taxi home. I'd call Metro once I was there.

But what would I tell them—how much of this strange and disturbing story?

And how much would I tell Nana? She wouldn't be happy to see me like this: driving a cab—taken from the driver, who had wanted to kill me.

Chapter 127

IT TOOK ONLY a few minutes for me to get to the house on Fifth Street.

I parked the cab out on the street. Suddenly I was sprinting toward the house. On the way home, I had started to worry about Nana and the kids.

Was everyone all right? Maybe this was just more paranoia on my part. But maybe it wasn't. The Tiger went after families, didn't he? And someone had just tried to kill me. I wasn't making that up.

I was startled by Rosie the cat, who snuck up behind me on the front lawn.

Who had let Rosie out? She was a committed indoor cat. I could see she was highly agitated. Why was that? What had happened? What had Rosie seen?

"Nana," I called as I ran up the front steps. "Nana!"

I turned the knob — *and the door wasn't locked.*

That wasn't right either. Nobody left their doors unlocked in Southeast, especially Nana.

"Nana! . . . Kids!" I called as I let myself in and began hurrying though the downstairs part of the house. I didn't want to scare them just because I was frightened out of my skull.

Still?

I stopped in the kitchen because it was a complete disaster area. I'd never seen it like this. It looked like someone had been making a cake and had stopped in the middle of things.

But that wasn't all that had happened here. Chairs had been turned over. Plates and glasses were broken on the floor.

So was a mixing bowl that looked like it had held vanilla frosting. Nana had been making a cake— lucky for me.

I pulled out the gun I'd taken from the taxi driver.

Then I started upstairs, unable to get my breath. I tried not to trample on Rosie as we hurried up there together.

Quietly.

And quickly.

Chapter 128

I CHECKED ALL the bedrooms on the second floor. Then my office in the attic. Finally I went down to the cellar.

There was nothing, no one, anywhere in the house.

Finally, I called Metro and reported the possible kidnapping of my family.

Within minutes, three cruisers pulled up in front. Their roof lights were flashing ominously. I came outside just as Sampson arrived.

I explained to John what I knew so far. He stood with me on the porch, where I was holding Rosie, holding on to her for support, really. Everything felt unreal and I was numb from my head to my feet.

"It's the Tiger, has to be him. Something about what happened in Africa," I said to John. "I almost got shot on the way from the airport." I pointed toward the taxi sitting on the street. "Cab driver pulled a gun on me."

"They're alive, Alex," Sampson said and put an arm around me. "They have to be."

"I hope you're right. Otherwise, they would have killed them here, like Ellie and her family."

"They must think you know something. Do you, Alex?"

"Not very much," I told Sampson. But it was a white lie.

I heard a woman's scream then. *"Alex! . . . Alex!"*

Bree! She was running down the block from where she'd had to leave her car. The police had completely blocked off Fifth Street now. It was starting to look like one of those gruesome crime scenes that I hated to be called in on. Only this time, it was my house, my family.

"What is it, Alex? I just got the call. Saw the address. What happened?"

"Somebody took Nana, Ali, and Jannie," Sampson told Bree. "That's what it looks like."

Bree came into my arms and held me tight. "Oh, Alex, Alex, no." She made no empty promises, just gave me the only comfort she could. Her embrace, a few whispered words.

"No note, no message?" she finally asked.

"I didn't find anything. We should look again. I don't think I was too clearheaded the first time I looked. I know I wasn't."

"You think you ought to go back in there right now?" she said and took my arm.

"I have to. Come with me. Both of you, *come*."

We all went back into the house.

Chapter 129

WHILE BREE AND Sampson started looking around, I called Damon's school and talked to the headmaster, then got Damon on the line. I told him to pack some things. We would be moving him soon. Sampson had already made the arrangements for him to be picked up. "Why do I have to come home?" Damon wanted to know.

"You're not coming home right now. Not yet. It isn't safe here. Not for any of us."

I joined Bree and Sampson and we searched the house for several hours, but there was nothing for us to find. No message left anywhere. The only evidence of a struggle was the mess in the kitchen and a tangled runner in the foyer.

I thought to check my computer, but there was nothing there either. No messages had been left anywhere. No threats. No explanation of any kind. *Was that the message?*

I decided to place a call to Lagos next. It was eight a.m. there.

I reached Ian Flaherty's office, but he didn't pick up himself this time.

"Mr. Flaherty is not here at the moment," said his assistant. She sounded nervous.

"Do you know where he is or when he's expected back?" I asked her. "It's important that I talk to him."

"I'm sorry, I don't. There is a lot going on here, sir. It's a very bad situation."

"Yes, I know. May I leave a message for him?"

"Of course."

"Tell him that Alex Cross is back in Washington. They've taken my family. I think it's the Tiger or his people who did this. I need to talk to him. Please make sure that he gets this message. It could be a matter of life or death."

"Yes, sir," said the assistant, "it always is."

Chapter 130

SAMPSON, BREE, AND I stayed in the house another hour or so. We searched every room again, looking for anything to work with.

But I understood that the two of them were here to make sure I was all right, especially since I was showing a few cracks.

Finally I told John to go home to his family and get some sleep.

No one had called or tried to get a message to me.

"There are two squad cars outside," Sampson said. "They'll stay here the rest of the night. Don't argue with me about it."

"I know. I can see them."

"That's the idea, Sugar. They're supposed to be seen."

"Make sure they're on their toes," Bree said. "I'll be here too. Tell them I'll be checking."

Sampson hugged Bree, then did the same with me. There

was no cop humor tonight, no making light of this. "*Any-thing*—you call," he told me.

Then he started out the kitchen door. He stopped and turned back. "I'll talk to the men outside. Maybe put on one more car."

I didn't bother to agree or disagree. I was in no shape to make decisions right now. "Thank you."

"We'll be fine," Bree said.

"I have no doubt," Sampson said and nodded. "Call me if *anything* happens!" Finally he shut the door behind him.

I went over and locked the door, which would give us an extra few seconds if somebody tried to come in. Maybe we'd need it.

"You all right with this?" Bree asked.

I nodded. "You staying with me? Of course I am."

She drifted over and hugged me again. "Let's go upstairs, then." She took my hand. "Alex, come."

I let Bree take me upstairs. I was numb and in a faraway dreamscape anyway.

"There's a phone in here," she said as we entered the bedroom. Then she hugged me again and reached down and started to unhook my belt. I didn't think that was what I needed, but I was wrong about that.

Until the phone in the bedroom rang.

Chapter 131

THE CALLS TO the house started at a few minutes past four in the morning. *Hang-ups,* one after the other, virtually nonstop.

The calls were emotional torture for me, but I answered every time; and I didn't dare take the phone off the hook. *How could I?* The phone was my lifeline to Nana and the kids. Whoever was calling had them. I had to believe that.

Bree and I held each other through the night, probably the worst night of my life.

I told her some of what I'd done and seen in Africa—about the horrors and Adanne and her family—their senseless murders. But I also talked about the goodness and natural-ness of the people; their helplessness, caught in a nightmare they hadn't created and didn't want.

"And this Tiger, what more did you learn about that bas-tard, Alex?"

"Terrorist, assassin—seems to work both sides of the street.

Anyone who pays him. He's the most violent killer I've ever seen, Bree. He likes to hurt people. And there are others like him. It's a name they have for killers for hire: *Tiger*."

"So he took Nana and the kids? He did this? You're sure about that?"

"Yes," I said as the phone rang again. "And that's him."

The phone kept ringing—and I began to pace around the house, going from room to room, thinking about my family all the while. Rosie followed me everywhere.

In the kitchen, Nana's favorite cookbook was still out—*The Gift of Southern Cooking*. I checked and saw it was open to a starred recipe for chocolate-pecan cake.

Nana's famous gabardine raincoat was draped over the back of a kitchen chair. How many times had she told me, "I don't want another raincoat. It took me half a century to get this one worn in right"?

I walked around Ali's room.

I saw his Pokemon cards laid out carefully on the floor. His beloved plush toy *Moo*. A hand-painted T-shirt from his fifth birthday party. A copy of *Ralph S. Mouse* spread open on the night table.

When I got to Jannie's room, I sat down heavily on the bed. My eyes ran over her precious collection of books. And the wire baskets brimming with hair accessories, lip glosses, fruit-scented lotions. Then I spotted her reading glasses, prescribed only a month or so ago. That got to me. There was something so vulnerable and telling about her new glasses sitting on the desk.

I sat there holding Rosie and heard the phone ring again. Bree picked it up.

She said, very quietly, "Fuck you."

And she hung up on whoever it was this time.

Chapter 132

I WAS GOING to get my family back. I had to believe that. But was it true? What were the real odds that I would? They were definitely getting worse.

From six-thirty until close to seven that morning, I sat out on the front porch and tried not to go completely crazy. I thought about taking a drive, to see if it would relax me.

But I was afraid to be away from the house for any length of time.

At a little past seven, the phone hang-ups stopped and I got about an hour of sleep.

Then I showered and dressed and called in one of the patrolmen from the street. I told him to take any calls for me and gave him a cell number where I could be reached.

At nine, Bree and I attended an emergency meeting at the Daly Building.

I was surprised to find about a dozen officers inside the

conference room. These were top people too, the best in Washington. I understood that it was a show of support and concern for me. Most of the detectives were people I'd worked with on other cases. Chief of Detectives Davies, Bree, and Sampson had reached out to officers with street connections who might help locate my family.

If anyone could.

Chapter 133

FROM THERE, THE day got stranger and stranger for me.

At eleven o'clock, I faced a smaller group inside a windowless conference room at CIA headquarters out at Langley. The atmosphere in the room couldn't have been more different from the one at Daly. Everyone except me wore a suit and tie. The body language was stiff and uncomfortable. No one wanted to be there except me—I needed their help.

A case officer from the National Clandestine Service named Merrill Snyder greeted me with a firm handshake and the unpromising line "Thanks for coming to see us, Dr. Cross."

"Can we start?" I asked him.

"We're just waiting for one more," Snyder said. "There's coffee, soft drinks."

"Where's Eric Dana?" I asked, remembering the leader's name from the last time I'd been out to Langley.

"He's on vacation. The man we're waiting on is his superior. Sure you don't want some coffee?"

"No, I'm fine. I don't need any more caffeine this morning, trust me."

"I understand. You still haven't heard from whoever abducted your family?" Snyder asked. "No communication?"

Before I could answer him, the door to the conference room swung wide open. A tall, dark-haired man in his early forties, wearing a gray suit and silver-and-red-striped tie, entered. He carried himself like someone important, which he probably was.

And right behind him came . . . Ian Flaherty.

Chapter 134

THE MAN EVERYONE had been waiting for introduced himself as Steven Millard. He said he was with National Clandestine Service but gave no rank. I remembered now that Al Tunney had mentioned his name before I went to Africa. Millard was the group chief, who'd been involved from the start.

All Flaherty said was, "Dr. Cross."

"Has there been any word about your family?" Millard wanted to know right off.

Snyder cut in. "No word so far. They haven't contacted him."

"There are cops from Metro at my house now," I told them. "They'll answer my phone and call me."

"That's good. About all you can do," said Millard. I couldn't figure out what to make of him. I was sure he knew about my meeting with Eric Dana before I'd left for Africa, but how much more did Millard know?

"I need whatever help you can give me," I finally said. "I really need some help."

"You can count on it," said Millard. "But I have a couple of questions you might be able to help us out with first. Detective Cross, why did you go to Africa in the first place?"

"A friend of mine and her entire family were killed. I had a lead that the killer fled to Lagos. It was my homicide case."

Millard nodded and seemed to understand. "Tell me this, then, what did you learn in Africa? Something useful, I assume? Otherwise, why would this professional killer want to come after you and your family in Washington?"

"I was hoping maybe you could help me out with that. What's going on in Nigeria and here in Washington too? Can you tell me?"

Millard clasped, then unclasped, his hands. "Did you see anything unusual or unsettling in Nigeria? We need to figure out why this killer would want to come after you here? You're a well-known police officer. This Tiger, or whoever it is, wouldn't want to take the risk unless he had to. I can't imagine that he would. Unless you really pissed him off."

"You know it's him, then?"

"No, no, I don't know for sure. It just makes sense. Ian agrees. So what do you know, Dr. Cross?"

I looked at Flaherty, then back at Millard. "You're not going to help me find my family, are you? You just want to pump me for information again?"

Millard sighed, took a beat and then said, "Dr. Cross, regretfully, we think your family is dead."

I stood up much too quickly from my chair, almost tipping it over.

"How can you say that? What do you know? What aren't you telling me? Why would they call me all night if my family's dead?"

Millard stared into my eyes, then rose from his seat too. "You were advised not to get involved in this. I'm sorry for your loss. We'll help if we possibly can."

Then he felt compelled to add, "We're not the bad guys here, Detective. There is no big conspiracy at work."

If that was true, why did everybody have to keep saying it?

Chapter 135

THOSE CIA BASTARDS! Even though they had been a little more human this time, I knew they were hiding something.

Maybe that's why I didn't tell them what Adanne had revealed after the slaughter of her family. The meeting had been typical of my experience with them over the years.

And Flaherty? After the meeting, he had gone to Langley for a "previously scheduled series of meetings." No way that was the whole truth, or anything close to it. At least I didn't think so.

That night, I went home to an empty house. I'd told Bree that it might be better if I was in the house alone. I was so desperate, I was ready to try anything now.

Millard's words kept coming back. *Dr. Cross, regretfully, we think your family is dead.*

I fixed a sandwich but only nibbled the corners away. Then I watched the news stations—CNN, CNBC, FOX—but there was almost nothing about the civil war in the Delta.

Unbelievable. A Hollywood actress had killed herself in LA, and that was the big story; it was being covered on every station—almost as if they all had the same news source and used the same journalists.

Finally, I switched the story about the dead actress off, and the silence wasn't a good thing either. I was nearly overwhelmed by sadness and fear that I had lost Nana, Ali, and Jannie.

For a long time I stayed in the kitchen, holding my head in my arms and hands. I remembered certain images, and feelings, and sensations from the past: Ali, just a little boy, and such a sweetheart; Jannie, still my "Velcro" girl, my living memory of her mother; Nana, who had saved me so many times since I'd come to DC at ten after both my parents had died.

I didn't see how I could continue to live without them. Could I?

The phone began to ring again and I snatched up the receiver. I hoped it was the Tiger, wanting something, wanting me.

But it wasn't.

"It's Ian Flaherty. I just wanted to check on you. See if you're all right. See if you remembered anything that could help."

"Help you?" I said in a tight voice. "My family's been taken. *My family*. Do you have any idea what that's like?"

"I think I do. We want to help you, Dr. Cross. Just tell us what you know."

"Or what, Flaherty? What else can they do to me?"

"The proper question is…what can they do to your family?"

Flaherty left me a number where I could reach him at any time of the day or night.

At least the bastard was staying up late too.

Chapter 136

THE SOUND OF a ringing telephone woke me from a shallow snooze on the living-room couch. I picked up the phone, still half asleep, my extremities tingling.

"Cross."

"Go to ya moto car now. We watchin' ya house, Cross. Lights on upstairs and in di kitchen. You was sleepin' in living room."

A male speaking. English with a pidgin accent. I'd heard a lot of it in the past few weeks, but I was particularly tuned into it now — every syllable.

"Is my family all right?" I asked. "Where are they? Just tell me that."

"Bring your cell phone wit you. We have numba and we wan ya follow directions. And don't call no one or your family dead. Go now, Cross. Listen up."

I was sitting up now, staring out the window in the living room, sliding my feet into my shoes.

I didn't see anyone outside. No cars or lights were visible from where I was.

"Why should I listen to you?" I asked the caller.

A second voice cut in. *"Because I say you should!"*

The phone at the other end clicked off. The second voice had been gruff, older than the first. And I recognized it instantly.

The Tiger. He was here in Washington. *He had my family.*

Chapter 137

SUDDENLY I HAD even more questions.

They had the number of the cell phone I had borrowed. How did that happen? I wondered.

Not that it was impossible to get — but how had a gang of hoodlums from Nigeria managed to do it?

I wasn't inclined to conspiracy theories, but it was getting harder and harder to deny the obvious. Someone wanted to know what I had found out in Africa. And to shut me up for good.

Maybe a minute after the call ended, I walked out on the front porch, which I'd decided to keep dark for now. I still couldn't see anyone watching on the street.

Were they here? Had they left already? Did they have Nana and the kids in a nearby truck or van?

I didn't want to play the target any longer than I had to.

I hurried down the steps and got into the Mercedes—the family car that I had bought for safety.

I started it up, then began to back out of the driveway, feeling the car's power. I felt like I needed that—the help of some external force.

The cell phone shrilled—and I stopped.

"You continue to be a fool." It was the older male again. I wanted to curse him out, but I said nothing. He might have my family. That was a hard thing to hope for, but I did anyway. I had to hope for something.

He laughed into the phone.

"What's funny?" I asked him.

"You are. Don't you want to know which way to turn out of your driveway?" he asked.

"Which way?"

"Make a *left*. Then you follow my directions straight to hell."

Chapter 138

HE STAYED ON the line as I drove along Fifth Street but didn't say much of anything—and nothing to help me figure out what I should do next. I was trying to think things through, to make some kind of plan—anything that might work, maybe even a wild hunch.

"Let me speak to my family," I spoke again.

"Why should I?"

I thought about stepping on the brakes, making a stand here, but he had every advantage right now.

"Which way?" I said.

"Make a right, next corner."

I did as I was told.

"The fight in Africa is not your fight, white man!" I listened to the Tiger spitting rage as I drove along Malcolm X Avenue in Southeast. "You should drive faster," he said, as if he were right there in the front seat, watching me.

He directed me onto I-295 heading south toward Maryland. I'd been on that road countless times before, but it seemed unreal and unfamiliar tonight.

Next, I merged onto 95 and then Route 210 and followed it for nearly fifteen miles, which seemed much farther than that.

Eventually I found myself on 425.

His voice went low. "Let me tell you something that's true. You are only coming to collect the bodies. You want the bodies, don't you?"

"I want my family back," I said. He only laughed at that.

I said little more to the Tiger unless he asked me a direct question, and he didn't seem to care. Maybe he wanted to hear himself talk.

I needed to put the rational part of my mind in another place. So I listened to his threats, his cruel insults, but I just let them flow over me. It wasn't hard, because I was numb anyway. *I was here, but I wasn't.*

Chapter 139

"PULL OFF THE road!" he commanded.

I did as I was told.

There didn't seem to be any other vehicles around. I didn't think I had passed anyone since I'd gotten onto Layloes Nick Road, somewhere in Maryland—around Nanjemoy.

But I wasn't completely sure. How could I be?

I was that out of it. That nervous and afraid, that petrified.

"Take the next right. At the corner. Don't miss the turn. You better hurry now! Hurry!"

I made the turn, then drove straight ahead, as I was told to do. The trees and bushes surrounding the road appeared black and very thick, possibly because my peripheral vision was narrowing in the dark.

Above me was a big sky filled with stars. I was reminded

of Jannie, her love of the stars, but then I forced the sentimental thought out of my mind.

Nothing sentimental. Not now.

Maybe never again.

"Stop your motor, get out! Do exactly as I say!"

"That's what I'm doing."

Chapter 140

"YOU SEE THE farm ahead? Come and get your family. You can collect the bodies now! I know you can't believe it, but it's true. They're all dead, Dr. Cross. Come to the farm and see."

My heart was floating as I started sweeping forward through tall grass and bushes toward the small farmhouse that was still a couple of hundred yards away. My legs and arms felt numb, like they were part of somebody else.

I tried to calm myself by taking slow, deep breaths. Then by not thinking at all. Finally, by gathering my hatred for the Tiger into a small, tight ball that could explode at the proper time.

"You remember how you found the Cox family in George-town? This is better," he taunted me. "You made it happen, *Detective*."

I wanted to tell the rabid monster that my family had done

nothing to hurt anybody ever, but I kept it inside. I didn't want to give him anything else. I couldn't stop my brain from working that way, but I was trying to concentrate on the danger and the horrors ahead.

This had to be a trap, I told myself. Somebody wanted me here. They needed to find out what I knew about the war in Nigeria. It didn't matter. I had to be here, no matter what.

"Are you ready, Detective?"

The last sound—*his voice*—wasn't coming from the cell phone in my hand.

Then the Tiger stepped out from the bushes. "You ready for me?" he asked. "You want the mystery solved?"

Chapter 141

"FINALLY, YOU LISTEN. Only it's too late, fool," the killer spoke in a loud, cocky voice as he moved toward me. Two young thugs were at his sides—Houston Rockets, and a blunt-faced boy who aimed a flashlight at my eyes.

"Where's my family?" I said, staying on message as best I could under the circumstances.

"What difference does it make—*one family?* You make me laugh. All you pitiful Americans. Everyone laughs at you, all over the world."

He pulled out a hunting knife and showed the long, thick blade to me. He didn't say anything about the knife; he didn't have to. I had seen what it could do at Ellie's house.

"Where are they?" I asked again.

"You think you get to ask the questions? I can make you scream. Beg for death. Your life is nothing to us. We say 'ye ye'—'useless, worthless.' Your family—*nothing. Ye ye.* It means useless."

The Tiger came up close and I could smell his sweat and tobacco on his breath. He held the knife close to my throat.

"Say it—'I am nothing.' Say it! You want to know about your family?" he screamed in my face. "Say—'I am nothing!'"

"I am nothing."

He cut me, across the biceps. I didn't look at my arm but I knew I was bleeding. I wouldn't show him weakness. No matter what happened to me now.

"Flesh wound!" he said and laughed. His killer boys found it funny too, sick little bastards. I wanted to take all of them down.

He motioned with the knife. "You want to see your family so bad, come on. You can see what's left. *Ye ye!*"

Chapter 142

I STUMBLED FORWARD toward the deserted-looking farmhouse standing in shadowy darkness, and I wondered if Nana, Ali, and Jannie really were in there.

The closer I got, the less likely it seemed to me. I was afraid I had been living in denial all this time—for days now.

Suddenly I found it hard to walk, to stand, even, but I made myself go on, step by step, toward the dark farm that held secrets I maybe didn't want to know.

There was a narrow dirt path winding up to the house and I trudged along a few paces in front of the Tiger and his killers. Were these the same bloodthirsty devils who had murdered Ellie's family?

Was the one in the Houston Rockets shirt the bad lieutenant? Had he traveled back and forth from Africa with the Tiger? What was their connection with what was happening in Lagos and down in the Delta? Could a civil war become a world war? Was it starting in Africa this time?

Suddenly I was struck hard in the small of my back. I lurched forward, and almost went down, but somehow I kept my balance.

Then I whirled around and saw Houston Rockets holding the butt end of his rifle. He was going to hit me with it again.

"Stop right there!" I yelled. "You punk, you little coward." I wanted to go after him so badly, to wring his neck and break it.

The Tiger laughed, either at me or at his vicious killer. "No, no, Akeem! I want him conscious. Open the front door, Cross. You are the detective. You made it all the way here. Now you will see. Open the door! Solve the great mystery."

Chapter 143

I TURNED THE rusty knob, then pushed hard on the sticking wood-frame door. It opened with a loud whine.

At first I couldn't see much, even with the faint glow from the flashlight held behind me.

"Where are they?" I asked.

"Go in an' see," said the Tiger. "You wanted this—proof of death."

I walked into the house and still couldn't see anyone in there. My heart was racing. Everything in the first room smelled of mildew, of dirt and age, maybe of death.

"I can't see anything. It's too dark."

Suddenly a light went on. A living area was illuminated—two small sofas, easy chairs, standing lamps—but I still didn't see anyone else in the room.

I whirled to look at the Tiger, who loomed behind me. *Where are they?* I yelled. "There's no one in here!"

"Tell me what you know," he said, seeming serious and businesslike. "What did the she-bitch Adanne tell you? What do you know about the Delta? Tell me!"

I stared back at him. "Do you work for the CIA too? They wanted to know what Adanne told me."

He laughed out loud. "I work for *anybody* who pays me. Tell me what you know!"

"I don't know *anything*. I found out nothing in Africa. If I had, don't you think I'd tell you? I saw you kill Adanne Tansi. That's what I know, only what I saw with my own eyes."

Someone stepped out of an adjoining hallway. I turned to see Ian Flaherty there in the farmhouse.

"I don't think he knows anything. You can kill him," he said to the Tiger. "Then he can be with his family. Go ahead. Get it over with."

A terrible look crossed my face. "So the CIA was in on this from the beginning?"

Flaherty shrugged. "Not the agency, no. Just me. *Kill him now*. Get it over with."

Then another voice was in the living room. "*You* get to die first, asshole."

Sampson stepped into view. The car I drove had a tracker on it. John had followed the signal all the way down into Maryland. And he wasn't alone.

"It will be a dead tie," said Bree. She came up alongside Sampson. "You and the Tiger both die. Unless you start talking to us. Where are Nana and the kids?"

The punk in the Houston Rockets shirt pumped his gun. Bree shot him in the left cheek under his eye. He screamed, then dropped.

The Tiger dove back out the front door.

"I'm not armed," said Ian Flaherty and raised both hands in the air. "Don't shoot me. I don't know what happened to your family. That wasn't my doing, none of it. Don't shoot me!"

I drove my shoulder hard into Flaherty's chest and then ran past him after the Tiger. Sampson threw me a gun on the way out.

"Use it!" he yelled.

Chapter 144

IT WAS DARK outside, scarily black, and cold as the middle of winter. Just a sliver of moon was visible, with low clouds sliding fast across the night sky. I didn't see the Tiger anywhere.

But then I caught a wisp of movement to the right of the dirt trail we'd taken to the house.

"Alex!" I heard Bree call behind me. I didn't call back to her. I ran ahead and hoped she wouldn't follow, that she couldn't see me in the darkness. I wanted to get to the Tiger first, just me and him.

"Alex!" Bree shouted again. "Don't do it this way. Alex! Alex!"

I continued to track movement, the faint outline of a man running up ahead. Or just noise sometimes, the rustle of branches. I was concentrating on that—when a shadow flew at me out of the brush.

I spun sideways and fired a shot into the chest of a killer in a white tee and white baseball cap. One of the boys! He grunted and fell over in a heap. I kept on running after the Tiger.

He was moving fast, but so was I. Two downhill skiers on a dark slope. I was gaining on him a little but not enough. I didn't call out. I just ran with everything I had in me. There was nothing in my mind except catching him. No caution, not anymore. No fear for myself.

I could hear his heavy footfall, and his breathing, which sounded ragged. Still, I didn't call to him. I held my gun out — and I fired twice. I fired low so I wouldn't kill him by mistake. I needed to keep him alive so I could find out where my family was.

I didn't think I hit him, but he turned his body, and that caused him to stumble. I put on an extra burst of speed. I was gaining on him now. I could make out more details, see him clearly.

Then I dove for his legs!

I nearly missed, but I caught him around the ankles and he crashed down on his chest and face and hit his head hard on a rock.

I crawled over him on my hands and knees. Then I went up on my haunches and punched down with all my strength.

My fist connected with his jaw. Sweat and blood flew out to the sides.

"Fucker! Traitor!" he yelled at me, growling like a jungle cat under attack.

"My family — *where are they?* What happened to them?" I shouted.

Then I punched him again, with everything I had, all the anger and rage living inside. This time he lost a tooth, but he was strong, even hurt like this, and he finally threw me off.

Then he was on me! I shielded my head with my arms and he struck my wrist, perhaps breaking it, I thought. But I didn't make a sound. I arched my body several inches. I managed to grab him around the neck and hold on. I didn't know where the strength was coming from, or how long it would last.

I tried to head-butt him, and because of the odd angle I was at, I connected with his Adam's apple. He gagged, then spit phlegm and blood.

"My family!" I yelled again.

"Fuck your family!" he cursed. "Fuck your kids! Fuck you!"

Then he got to the hunting knife. I was still thinking that I had to keep him alive—not that *I* had to survive this, but that *he* did. I held his knife hand at the wrist, but I was losing my grip. The fight was turning his way. This was it; this was how I died. I would never know about Nana, Ali, Jannie. That was the worst part, not knowing.

A shot rang in the night.

The Tiger straightened up, but then he came back down at me with the knife. "Die!" he yelled. "Like your family died!"

A second shot struck where his right eye had been glaring at me a second before.

"Where are they?" I yelled again. "Where is my family?"

He didn't say another word. His good eye was all hatred. The rest of his face was a bloody mess. The Tiger couldn't answer. He collapsed on me, dead.

"Where are they?" I whispered.

Chapter 145

BREE CAME RUNNING up as I pushed the massive corpse away from me. Even now that he was dead, I still hated the bastard with all my heart and soul. Bree knelt on the ground and hugged me. "I'm sorry, Alex. I'm so sorry. All I saw was the knife. I had to shoot him."

I kept holding on to her and rocking. "Not your fault. Not your fault." But then I began to shudder and shake. I knew what I had lost here, knew that the Tiger had been my last chance to find my family.

We left the body and trudged back to the farmhouse. Police cars from the neighboring towns were arriving, and the trees were lit with a crimson-and-blue glare from their domes.

Sampson came out of the farmhouse as we approached. "I've gone through every room. There's no one here. I don't see any sign of them either, Alex. No blood anywhere, nothing obvious anyway. I don't think they were ever here."

I nodded, trying to register crime scene facts and to comprehend their meaning. "I want to look again anyway. I need to look for myself. What about Flaherty?" I suddenly thought to ask.

"The state police have him for now. He showed them he was CIA. I don't know what happens next. I don't think they can hold him."

Chapter 146

WE SEARCHED THE house and a nearby work shed, and a barn — until first light of day.

Then we began to comb the surrounding grounds. At this point there were more than thirty police officers and FBI agents searching at the scene, but it still didn't seem like enough manpower to me.

Everything was feeling even more unreal now. *I was here, but I wasn't.* I had no idea about the passage of time either; it seemed as if I could have been at the farm for a couple of days or for just a few minutes.

Proof of life, I thought. *That's what I want, isn't it? And if not that, then proof of death.*

We found a Nissan minivan that had to be the vehicle the Tiger and his killer thugs had come to the farm in. The van held small arms, clothing, and video games in cardboard boxes.

But there was no sign of blood inside, no rope to tie anyone up with. Nothing to make us believe Nana or the kids had been inside the vehicle.

There were more tire tracks up near the house, but nothing seemed unusual. Judging from the look of the place, I figured it hadn't been a working farm for at least a couple of years. Town records showed that it belonged to a Leopoldo Gout, but we hadn't been able to contact the owner yet. Who was Leopoldo Gout? What did he know about what had happened here?

Finally, at around four that afternoon, Bree walked me to my car. Then she drove me home to Fifth Street. I was in no shape to continue looking, she said, and she was right.

I hoped against hope for a good ending, but there was no one there at the house. The mess in the kitchen remained as I had found it, and I left it just that way.

For memories' sake.

Nana's kitchen. Her favorite place to be.

Chapter 147

IT WAS ALL so baffling, so incomprehensible, wrong in so many ways.

Bree and I brainstormed for a while, but I couldn't concentrate. My thinking was too chaotic; I was too crazy in the head, too disturbed and lost. I didn't want to talk, didn't want to eat, and I couldn't sleep. I couldn't even keep my eyes shut the one time I lay down on the living-room couch. I thought about taking a drive, then decided no, not right now.

"I'm going to go for a run," I finally told Bree. "Clear my head. There has to be something I'm missing."

"Okay, Alex. I'll be here. Have a good run."

She didn't offer to come, understanding that I wanted to be alone now. I did need to be by myself, to plan, to do something that would make some sense of what had happened.

I ran, at first along familiar streets close to my house, but then on the streets winding off Fifth, where I didn't remember ever coming on foot before.

Finally I was able to concentrate a little better, and I began to think about what Adanne had told me in Lagos. Had her secrets caused any of this — the death of her family, her own murder, whatever had happened to Nana, Ali, and Jannie?

"Alex, I know terrible things," she'd told me. *"I'm writing a story about it. I have to tell somebody what I found out."* She was afraid that something would happen to her.

Well, something had happened to Adanne.

I continued to run and I found that I was getting stronger physically, or moving faster, anyway. What a cruel world this could be sometimes. Jesus. That wasn't how I looked at things usually. That wasn't me. Only now it was.

I didn't notice anything, until a gray van stopped suddenly at the curb and the sliding door flew open. Three men jumped out. Suddenly they were all over me, knocking me down, pushing my face into the grass and dirt on somebody's lawn.

Then I felt a sting in my thigh.

A needle?

Three men, not boys. Not the Tiger's team.

Who then?

Who was holding me now?

What did they want?

Chapter 148

THE WAS A damp cloth over my face, some kind of a hood that reeked of rubbing alcohol. Then I was being pulled to my feet. I'd been unconscious, but I didn't know for how long.

I had no idea where I was now, but it wasn't a five-star hotel. I could smell, almost taste, body odor, feces, and urine. The ground under my feet was rough stone, maybe concrete. Did that tell me anything?

"Put your hands flat against the wall and spread your legs. Stay just like that. Don't move, or you'll be shot."

"Where's my family? Where the hell are they? Who are *you?*"

Instead of an answer to the question, I heard an amplified whirring sound in the room.

"Stay just like that—or you die right here and now. Then you'll never know about your family. Never is a long time, Dr. Cross. Think about it."

I thought about other things first. Who had grabbed me off the street in Southeast and was holding me now?

Could it be another Tiger? Somebody else from Nigeria?

The voice didn't sound like it. No accent. American. Could it be the CIA?

"Where's my family?" I asked again.

No one answered, and I stayed there with my hands tied and held flat against the wall over my head. I knew this particular kind of torture had a name, *wall-standing*. I was also made to wear a hood and was subjected to loud noise and sleep deprivation. I'd heard about these torture techniques before. Now I was the victim.

No one answered any of my questions, and I wondered if I was alone. Was I delirious? Was I dreaming all this?

My hands went numb first.

Then I could feel pins and needles stinging my ankles and feet. Then shooting pains moving up and down my legs.

My head began to swim and I thought I was going to pass out.

"I have to pee," I said. "I have to go."

No answer.

I held it as long as I could, then let go down my legs, over my bare feet. No one reacted. Was anyone there? Was I alone now?

Wall-standing. Some American government officials had said that it was okay to use techniques like this on suspected terrorists.

Was I a terror suspect? What had I done to deserve this? Who was torturing me?

My hands were completely numb and I badly wanted to

sleep. I could think of little else and would have given anything just to lie down on the floor. I couldn't give in, though.

Wall-standing. I can do this.

I thought about stepping away from the wall and what the consequences might be. I held internal debates with myself. They wouldn't kill me, would they? What would be the point of it?

Finally, I turned my body so that only *one hand* was on the wall. Did that count? Was it a violation of the rules?

Immediately I was kicked hard behind the knees! I went down hard on the floor. Cold to the touch. A bed—finally!

But I was yanked right back up and thrown hard against the wall. Still, no one spoke. But I assumed the position. Not just my legs were trembling now. Everything was—my entire body was shaking terribly.

Who else was with me in the room?

What did they want from me?

Chapter 149

THEN I WAS talking to Jannie. I was hugging her, and I was so happy that she was all right. "Where's Ali? Where's Nana?" I asked in an excited whisper. "Are you okay, sweetheart?"

Suddenly I came to and realized that I had been sleeping on my feet. Jannie wasn't here.

It was only me.

I had the sense that I was in the second day of captivity. Or may be the third day. Suddenly I was startled as someone pulled the cloth hood up around my nose, still keeping my eyes in darkness.

"What?" I muttered. "Who are you?" As I spoke, I realized how dry my lips and mouth were.

I was given water, which splashed from somewhere, maybe a bottle, pouring down my throat and all over my face.

"Don't be greedy, now," someone said and snickered. A

captor with a cruel sense of humor. "Eat this! Slowly. Don't make yourself choke."

I was fed three crackers, one right after the other. I didn't choke, but I was afraid I was going to throw them up as fast as I'd eaten them.

"Water?" I asked. "More water, please?" My throat was tightening up again.

There was a long pause, but then the bottle was returned to my lips. Once more, I drank greedily.

"Too fast," someone said. "You'll cramp up. Don't want you to be uncomfortable."

Then I was pushed into position again.

Wall-standing.

Chapter 150

SOMETIME AFTER THAT, I began to seriously hallucinate and I wondered if there was something in the water, or maybe even the crackers I'd eaten.

I was convinced that I was back in Africa and that I was lost somewhere in a vast desert. I knew I was going to die soon, and that didn't seem like such a bad thing. I actually welcomed death and wondered if I would meet Nana, Jannie, and Ali on the other side. Would Maria be there too? And others I had lost?

I was struck hard in the back—and I fell to my knees again.

"You were dreaming—asleep on your feet. That's not allowed, hotshot."

"Sorry."

"Of course you are. Now, would you like this to stop? Would you like to sleep? I'll bet that you would."

More than anything I've ever wanted in my life.

"Where—?" I began to say.

"Right—Where is your fucking family? You're nothing if not consistent, or is it stubborn? Or stupid? Now, listen to me closely. I *will* let you sleep. I *will* give you closure about your family....Are you with me so far?...Are you following what I'm saying?"

"Yes."

"Yes *what?* Tell me what you are agreeing to."

"You'll tell me about my family. Let me sleep."

"Provided that what?"

I don't attack and kill you, you sonofabitch. Where there's a will...

"Provided I answer your questions."

"Very good. Would you like more water, hotshot?"

"Yes."

The cloth hood was lifted halfway and the water bottle was returned to my lips. I drank as much as I wanted to, but then there was silence. It frightened the hell out of me. Had he gone away? The one who knew what had happened to my family? The one who had actually talked to me for a minute or so.

"I saw terrible things in Africa, especially in Sudan," I said. "I don't think any of that interests you. A family—the Tansis—were murdered. In Lagos. Maybe because they were talking to me. Or because of what Adanne wrote in the newspaper....You can get her articles.

"Are you there? You wanted me to talk, right? Are you listening now?

"Anyway, Adanne Tansi and I were taken to a prison," I

continued. "She was murdered there. I saw it happen. The Tiger killed her. I don't know who the other men holding us were. *I don't know who the hell you are!*

"Before we got to the prison, Adanne told me about a long piece she was writing—it was to appear in the London *Times . . . The Times.* Maybe some other papers. I'm not sure.

"She had learned that the United States might be manipulating factions in the Delta . . . to ensure the oil fields would stay in the right hands. Adanne had tapes of interviews. They were taken from her.

"Whoever captured us . . . must have them now. You have the tapes, don't you?"

I stopped talking and waited for an answer, any kind of response.

But no one said anything. That was the technique—and guess what? It worked. I kept talking.

"Adanne told me the man known as the Tiger was also being paid by our government. I don't know if that's true. You probably know, don't you?"

I stopped again, then went on. "By the CIA, maybe. The oil companies? By someone from here. Adanne wrote that, and she told another writer, named Ellie Cox. She was killed because of what she knew.

"That's what I know. That's what Adanne found out. *That's all of it.*"

I stopped again. There was still no response, not a word from the interrogator.

I waited.

I waited.

I waited.

Chapter 151

YOU THINK YOU know what's going to happen in life. But you never do. And usually the surprises aren't good ones either.

No one spoke to me for a long time, and I kept waiting for somebody to put a gun to my head, to finally pull the trigger.

Hours after I was interrogated, I heard footsteps in the room where I was being kept. More than one person. At least two.

I pulled myself away from the wall and moved forward. I stumbled and fell to my knees. I pushed myself back up and somebody grabbed my arm.

"Fucker can't even walk by himself."

I heard a door being slid open and then I felt cool air hit my face. I was pulled forward and then shoved inside some kind of van or truck.

"Let's go!" said someone in the front. "We don't have much time for this."

For what?

What was happening now?

I had no idea where I was going now, but I knew the chances were good that I was going to die. At certain times in the past, I'd been pleasantly surprised that I'd lasted as long as I had. Still, it felt unreal that I would probably die in the next few minutes. I prayed for my family; and then I said a prayer for myself.

Good, moderately lapsed Christian that I am, I even said a prayer of contrition.

Then the van pulled to a stop. This was it. "End of the line!" I heard one of the bastards say.

I was pushed out and landed hard on the street, and then I heard the vehicle drive away, gravel crunching under spinning tires.

I crawled up and over a curb and then just lay there, partly on grass, partly on a sidewalk or walkway.

They hadn't killed me.

I was still alive.

Finally—I slept.

Chapter 152

THEN I WAS awake; at least I thought I was.

"I'm Officer Maise, with the DC Metro police. Are you all right, sir?" The patrolman spoke to me even as he lifted the hood that covered my head.

"Why are your hands tied? What happened to you?" he asked next.

"I'm Alex Cross. I'm a detective with Major Crimes.... I was kidnapped."

He had the hood all the way off now, but I couldn't see much of anything yet, not even his face. My eyes were slow to adjust to the light—to the streetlights mostly. It was dark outside. Night.

"Yes, sir, Detective Cross. We've all been looking for you," patrolman Maise said. "Let me call it in."

"How long...you been looking?"

"Three days."

Finally, I could see his face, which showed concern but also surprise. *He had found me. I was alive. I'd been missing for three days.*

"Can you get these binds off?" I asked.

"I'll call it in first. Then I'll get the ropes off you."

"No press," I told him.

"Of course not. Why would I call the press?" the patrolman asked.

"I don't know," I said. "I guess I'm not thinking straight yet."

Chapter 153

I WAS TAKEN home by Officer Maise. The house on Fifth Street was dark and obviously empty. Bree had been staying with us off and on, but she had kept her place, so I figured she was at her apartment tonight. Why would she stay here by herself?

I would call Bree soon, but I needed to go inside the house right now. I entered through the sunporch, passing the silent piano on my way, imagining playing it for the kids or, sometimes, just for myself.

No, I guess I was *remembering*.

The kitchen had been cleaned up since the last time I'd been there. Probably Bree had done it.

Now it was neat, *as if nobody lived here.*

I continued walking from room to room, everything quiet, and I felt unbearably sad. I turned on lights as I went, feeling like a visitor in my own house. Nothing about my life felt right, or even real. The world *had* become such a cruel, unsafe place. How had it happened?

How much blame should America take, and did accepting blame really help anybody? Wasn't it time to stop offering criticism and start providing solutions? It was easy to be a critic; it took no imagination. Problem solving was the bitch.

I finally made it up to my office in the attic, and I sat at my desk, looking down on the street, wondering if there was anyone out there watching me.

Had the interrogators believed me? Did it matter? It struck me that I didn't really know that much about the world, the larger picture, anyway. But who did these days?

None of us, maybe. That's what made it so daunting and scary—and took away hope too. That's what gave us a feeling that everything was out of our control. So who was in control? Somebody had to be—but who? Somebody had to have some answers. *Somebody* had just imprisoned and tortured me.

I continued to wander around the house. I needed to call people—Damon, who I hoped was still safely stashed away, and Bree and Sampson. But I couldn't make the calls yet. I didn't know what to tell any of them, or how to face them.

No, that wasn't it exactly. The truth was, *I didn't want to put them in danger.* Somebody out there might still think that I knew something, something dangerous and important, or maybe just embarrassing to them.

And the really scary part?

They were right.

Chapter 154

I HAD TOLD my interrogators about the possible CIA and Tiger connection, but that wasn't important to them. They'd let me go, hadn't they? They could deny all that—and besides, the Tiger was dead. I had cleaned up that particular mess for them.

But the thing I hadn't told them was the real subject of Adanne's story: The Americans, the French, the Dutch, the British, and several very important corporations were working with the Chinese in the Delta. China needed oil even more than we did. China was cutting corners. They were ready to pay top dollar for oil and willing to make deals, whatever it took. And because of these business ventures, thousands of Africans had died—men, women, and children. That was the one thing that I knew for certain. It was what Adanne had been researching and writing about.

It was what she had contacted Ellie Cox about; she had

talked to Ellie about her research. That was what got her family murdered in Georgetown.

Adanne had told me horror stories during our time together, especially about life and death in Sudan. Rape was the weapon of war there, and girls of age five and up were abused, sometimes by "peacekeepers." Hundreds and hundreds of mass graves had been discovered but were rarely reported on. Police corruption and brutality, some of which I'd witnessed myself, were rampant—an epidemic, really, and kidnappers were working in the Delta area, especially around Port Harcourt.

On the couch that had been in Nana's living room since I was a boy, I slept, finally. But not like a baby. That kind of sleep would never come to me again. The truth was, I had accepted that my family was gone, just like so many other families that had been murdered before them. Nothing would ever be the same for me again.

Chapter 155

I WAS WOKEN up early in the morning. *Somebody was coming into the house!*

I could tell that it was more than one person.

I jumped up from the couch, trying to collect my thoughts in a hurry, to focus on how to get to my gun in the den, when two men burst into the living room!

I was surprised—no, I was shocked—to see Steven Millard and Merrill Snyder from the CIA. Millard spoke first, "Detective Cross, we didn't know you were here. We—"

Someone else walked into the living room behind Millard and Snyder. My God, it was Ali.

And he looked all right to me—unharmed.

He looked just incredible—safe, alive, home.

"Ali!" I called and went forward to him. *"Ali!"*

"Daddy! Daddy!" he shrieked as he ran and threw himself

into my outstretched arms. My little boy was crying and shaking uncontrollably.

No, no — I was the one crying and shaking. Ali was just holding on to me incredibly tightly. He kept repeating, "Daddy, Daddy, Daddy!" I couldn't hear the words enough times.

What was happening here? I wondered, looking to the CIA men for answers. Now I saw that Eric Dana and my friend Al Tunney had come to the house as well.

Then I heard, "Alex? Is that you in there? Alex, is that you?"

The voice was Nana's, but the next person entering the living room was Jannie.

She had her arms stretched out, and she was sobbing as she ran and crashed into my chest. "Oh, my sweet girl, my darling girl," I whispered as she pressed into me. "Oh, Jannie, sweetheart. Oh, my baby, my baby."

"I'm okay, we're okay," Jannie said. "They kept us in a room. They asked us so many questions. We didn't know why, Daddy, we didn't know anything."

"No, of course you didn't."

Then Nana slouched into the living room, and she looked terrible and wonderful all at the same time. She came to us, and then we were all group hugging. The CIA agents just looked on, warmly, it seemed to me, but they said nothing.

"They didn't harm us," said Nana. "Thank God, we're all here together. We're all safe."

That was enough for this unbelievable moment, the most emotional one of my life — we were all together, and we were safe.

Chapter 156

THE GOOD MOOD was broken by Steven Millard from the CIA. "Detective Cross, can we have a moment? Whenever you're ready," he said.

I went out with Millard, who I took to be the highest-ranking of the CIA representatives at the house. He was the group chief, right? There were four of their vehicles parked outside. Three agents two of them women, stood around on the sidewalk. I wondered if they had been picked to make it easier for my family when they were brought home.

"Where were they? Where did you find them?" I asked Millard. "Who took them?"

He walked ramrod straight and I decided he had probably been military before he came to the CIA. He seemed very sure of himself, confident about who he was and his role here. *So what was it? Who the hell was Steven Millard? What was his role?*

"I told you before, Detective, we're the good guys—we're *still* the good guys. Most of us are busting our asses to do a good job and help keep this country safe....Ian Flaherty wasn't. He sold us out, maybe a couple of times. The last time, it was to the Chinese. Maybe to a bad apple from their basket."

"My family," I said, reminding Millard of my question.

"We had Flaherty under surveillance from the moment he reached Washington. Trust me on that one. He led us to your family. I don't know if they would've been released. A couple of mercenaries were with them—they were working with Flaherty. Flaherty was working for the Chinese. Your family was questioned, but mostly they were just insurance, in case it was needed. Flaherty was afraid you might have found out about him in Lagos."

I shook my head. "Bribery has become a way of life there. Adanne Tansi knew the Chinese were involved with oil trading in the Delta. Thousands of Nigerians have been murdered down there, as you know."

"Yes, we know," said Millard.

"And you knew the civil war was coming, but you did nothing to stop it."

"There was nothing we could do. We don't need another Iraq, do we?"

I stared into his eyes. "Where's Flaherty now?"

Millard didn't flinch as he answered. "We have him. We're talking to him now. Eventually he'll talk to us. We know that Mr. Sowande, your Tiger, worked for him."

"That's all you can tell me?"

Millard shook his head. "No. I can tell you this. Go home

to your family, Detective Cross. They're special. You've been away from them too much."

I nodded at Millard. He wasn't going to level with me, so there was nothing else to say. I turned around and began to walk back to my house.

He was right about one thing: *My family was special.*

They were waiting for me on the porch, and as I got close, another dark sedan pulled up in front. Damon stepped out, and he looked my way. He half waved, half saluted.

But then Damon came running, and so did I.

The Cross family was back together again. Maybe that was all that mattered.

Epilogue

THE LAST OF
THE GOOD GUYS

Chapter 157

I COULDN'T LET it end like that—it just wasn't in me. One night a couple of weeks later, I arrived at the house in Great Falls, Virginia, at a little past three in the morning. Interesting to me, and more than a little creepy, I had received a call from the psychopath Kyle Craig earlier in the week. Cool as ever, Kyle said he was glad I had gotten my family back, and then he hung up before I could say a word to him.

I focused and walked to the front door of a red-brick colonial that was obsessively well kept. I rang the bell a couple of times and waited. I looked at my watch. *3:11.* After a few minutes, the overhead porch light flicked on. Then the door slowly opened.

The CIA's Steven Millard stood there wearing a dark blue terrycloth robe, his legs and feet bare. He didn't look so impressive without a suit and tie. I heard a woman's voice call from upstairs, "Steve, is everything all right down there?"

"Go back to sleep, Emma. It's just work," he called back.

Then Millard's eyes came back to mine. "What do you want at my house at three in the morning, Detective Cross? This better be worth it."

"Why don't you invite me in and I'll tell you all about it. I could use some coffee. So could you."

Chapter 158

WE WENT INSIDE and sat in the kitchen, which looked as though it had been refurbished recently. Millard didn't offer coffee or anything else to drink, so I started to tell him why I'd come out to Virginia in the middle of the night.

"I spent some time at Ellie Cox's before I went to Africa. Your people did a good job in there. I found her partial manuscript, of course. Even some notes she made while she was in Nigeria. Everything looked just fine, though. Nothing incriminating."

Millard listened patiently, nodded, waiting for the punch line.

I stared at him for a while, and I was thinking about the idea of "good guys." Were there any left? I thought so. I sure hoped so.

"So that's why you're here? To let me know that everything is fine?" Millard spoke again.

"*Looked* fine. Just like it was supposed to. But last week I went back to the Cox house. At that point I had enough time to be a real detective again. I talked to Ellie's editor at *Georgetown Press*. He hadn't gotten the last section of Ellie's manuscript, which surprised him. That was the part that detailed her trip to Nigeria."

"Maybe she never got to write it," Millard suggested. "That would make sense, wouldn't it, Detective? It could be why she was targeted and murdered."

"I guess so. But if that was true, why would I be here at three in the morning, when I could be home sleeping?"

Millard's brow furrowed. He was starting to show some irritation and I couldn't blame him. "Maybe because you never properly thanked me for finding and bringing home your family? You're welcome. Now you can go. *Go.*"

I hit Steven Millard then. It was a strong right hand that lifted him right out of the kitchen chair, and knocked him onto the pinewood floor. His nose was bleeding, but he didn't go out. I could tell he wasn't sure where he was; his hands were feeling around the floor for some purchase.

"That's for taking my family in the first place," I said to him.

"Ellie had a typist for her manuscripts," I went on. "A woman in DC named Barbara Groszewski. I found that out through some checks Ellie paid every month.

"The good news, the reason I'm here, is that Barbara Groszewski had the last part of Ellie's manuscript, the section where she traveled to Lagos and met Adanne Tansi among others. Ian Flaherty is mentioned several times in the pages.

So are you, Millard. Adanne was aware of what you and Flaherty were up to.

"In fact, you were the one who set up the oil meetings with the Chinese. *You* took their bribes. And *you* were the one who hired Sowande, the Tiger.

"You're under arrest, Millard, and the Central Intelligence Agency isn't going to protect you. They've already given you over to us. So maybe there still are some good guys left."

Millard actually smiled. "A manuscript? Part of one? A writer's notes? You have nothing to hold me on."

"I think we do," I told him. "I'm sure of it."

I opened the kitchen door and let in several agents from the FBI, including my buddy Ned Mahoney. These were definitely the good guys.

I turned back to Millard. "Oh, I left out the best part, the most important. We found Ian Flaherty. You lied about holding him. In fact, we have Flaherty now. He's talking. That's why I'm arresting you. You're going down, Millard. You made a big mistake in judgment."

"What was that?" Millard finally asked.

Now it was my turn to smile. "You should've killed me when you had the chance. I'm very persistent. I don't ever give up."

Thus spake the Dragon Slayer.

On my way home, at around five that morning, my cell phone started to ring. I grabbed it off the seat and answered with my name.

I heard a voice that I didn't want to hear, not ever again, but especially not now.

"You are so damn impressive, Alex. I'm awfully proud of you," said Kyle Craig. "Believe it or not, I was right there in Millard's house with you. Guess I'm kind of special myself. *And I don't give up either.*"

Then Kyle clicked off.

And as always, he was scarier than anyone else.

Join us as Alex Cross sits on the couch and answers some burning questions

How do you think your childhood impacted on your career choices?
I had to toughen up at an early age. My parents died when I was young – my father was an alcoholic and my mom died from lung cancer when I was only nine years old. I was sent to Washington DC to live with my grandmother, Nana. I had a fortunate upbringing but I lived in a less fortunate neighbourhood so I guess I developed a pretty tough outlook from a young age. I learnt how to do stuff for myself and gained independence early on and developed a sense of spirit and fight I guess too.

What and where did you study?
I studied psychology. I received a doctorate from John Hopkins University in Baltimore, Maryland and worked as a psychologist for a while in my own private practice. I still hold appointments with a few patients and that work is very rewarding for me.

What made you join the police force?
I became disillusioned with the politics of the medical community and realised that there was plenty I could do to really make a difference in my neighbourhood. I realised I could help clamp down on crime on the streets. I like hands-on action. I left the FBI to open up my own private psychology practice. After a while though, I had to keep on being involved, I rejoined

407

WCPD as a consultant. I still have that hunger. I want to take matters into my own hands. I won't rest until a case is solved. I am the dragonslayer.

When you joined the police force, do you think your psychology education helped you?

Absolutely, my primary role is as a profiler. I can get right inside the minds of even the sickest of killers. It can be pretty terrifying but sometimes it seems there is no rhyme or reason to what some of these guys are willing to do. If you search deep enough inside though, you can usually work out what makes them tick, how their minds work and why they are intent on causing such harm. You just have to hope you reach those conclusions before they do too much damage.

Tell us about your first case.

The case name of the first one that really got to me was Along Came a Spider. This guy, Gary Soneji, was a control freak, he was totally sadistic and he really played us for some time there. He was a schizophrenic and unlocking his dual personality was a really tricky task. Even when I cracked it and got him put away, he haunted me for several years.

Was he the worst criminal you have come across?

Well he was certainly up there but there have been a few others. The Tiger was probably the most fearsome. His terror knew no boundaries and he had such influence over a whole gang of kids. He knew how to find people who didn't have much hope in life and got them on board to help fight for him. People would throw their own lives away for his respect.

That is such a frightening use of power. The Mastermind has been a nemesis of mine too, of course he turned out to be someone a lot closer to home than I thought.

How did it feel when you first solved a case? How did it change you?
When you're in the middle of working on a big homicide case, it is all-consuming. It takes every ounce of you to piece it all together, to try and get the job done and do the right thing. I quickly learnt that you can't always play by the rules and that you have to do whatever it takes. When one case is solved you just have to move straight onto the next and often you have several to solve at once. It's a demanding job but you just have to get back up again and live to fight another day. I try and make time to spend with the family – I need their love and support.

Tell us about your family.
I have three children: Damon, Jannie and Alex Junior. They are great kids, they are growing up fast and are so smart but they keep me grounded and keep me sane. Damon and Jannie's mother, my wife, Maria was killed when they were babies and little Alex's mother lives in Seattle, she found it hard to cope with my work load. So I'm bringing the kids up on my own but Nana is a lifesaver. We live with her and she looks after them when my work takes me away.

What do you like to do in your spare time?
I don't get an awful lot of spare time. When I'm not working, I spend time with my family – I don't get to do that often

enough. I play the piano to relax too. I also help out at St Anthony soup kitchen. To the guys there, I'm neither a psychologist nor a detective, I'm 'the peanut butter man'.

What is your neighbourhood like?
I live in the slums of Washington DC, it's not the nicest area but I'm a part of the community now; this place is home and I want to protect it and I want to protect my neighbours. I guess I could have moved away by now but somehow that didn't feel right.

Your partner at work is John Sampson – tell us more about your relationship with him and what it is like to work together.
John and I have been best friends since we were ten years old. He's not just my partner, he's my best friend. And he's Jannie's godfather. We go way back. I can always count on that guy and we've worked on some real tough cases together. Some people find us pretty intimidating, he's a man mountain, so I call him! Sometimes I have to go it alone but he is always supportive of that and let's me do what I have to do. He's always got my back though and I'll always be looking out for him. I'd lay my life on the line for him. He's the only person in the world who gets to call me 'Sugar'!

Do you find it hard to get close to people given the dangers of your job?
Sometimes you don't know who you can trust. I've gotten close to some people in the past who haven't turned out to be who I thought they were and that is hard to take. I've learnt to only really trust myself. It takes me a while to really get close

to people now. The job makes it tough to get too emotionally involved. That said, Bree Stone is an incredible woman and we met on the job.

How does it feel to get inside the mind of your suspects?
How does it feel knowing that this is something your colleagues can't do and therefore that you are going to be drawn right into the heart of a case?
It can be incredibly tough, inside the mind of some of those guys is a really tough place to be. Some of them are so hard to crack and you desperately just want to know what they are going to do next so you can stop them in their tracks before they get a chance to act. I guess it means that people see me as a way in and that means I've been put into some intense situations that others around me can't handle. Everyone on the team has their role to play and everyone works really hard on every case. Sometimes I'm just drawn right into the heart of a case though, that's when it becomes personal too.

If your children wanted to follow your line of work would you encourage or discourage it?
If that is what my kids want to do then I'd support them. They're so smart I reckon they could handle it. You never stop worrying about your kids though right?

The safety of your family and yourself have been called into question many times and their lives threatened due to the nature of your work – how does that make you feel and have you ever considered giving it up to protect them?
Yeah it is tough. I don't want people to get hurt. God help any sick guy out there who tries to bring my family into this.

It shouldn't be about them but I guess some people see my family as my weakness, as a way of getting at me. But I've worked on some of the hardest cases and no one has been strong enough to crack me yet, sure, they've hurt me, caused me physical and emotional pain but I'm strong and I keep on getting stronger. They also haven't reckoned with Nana, even at 88 she's one hell of a woman! It only serves to motivate me and I'll always defend my family.

You have been involved in some very intense and often personal cases, which has been the toughest for you?
I came back into the police force because John had a lead on a case involving the guy I thought had killed Maria. I couldn't pass up that chance to come face to face with the son of a bitch who took my wife from me. I invested so much in that case, it totally consumed me.

In terms of scale, the case I've just completed was huge. I started out investigating the murder of an old college friend and I had no idea what I had got myself in to. I've been across Africa, seen the most horrific things, fought for my life, been crossed and double-crossed but I came out the other side. Sometimes some things, like the plight of some of the people I met, the poverty and the violence, that is beyond what we can do in the police on one case. But I'll certainly do my best to help out where I can.

Have we seen the last of Detective Alex Cross?
No. There's always more to give. I ain't giving up this fight just yet. I love my work – the stuff with DCPD and with my patients. I'm not giving any of that up.

Read on for a sneak preview of

I, ALEX CROSS

Prologue

FIRE AND WATER

One

HANNAH WILLIS WAS a second-year law student at Virginia, and everything that lay ahead of her seemed bright and promising—except, of course, that she was about to die in these dark, gloomy, dismal woods.

Go, Hannah, she told herself. *Just go. Stop thinking. Whining and crying won't help you now. Running just might.*

Hannah stumbled and staggered forward until her hands found another tree trunk to hold on to. She leaned her aching body into it, waiting for the strength to take another breath. And then to move another burst of steps forward.

Keep going, or you'll die right here in these woods. It's that simple.

The bullet lodged somewhere in her lower back made every movement, every breath an agony, more pain than Hannah had ever known was possible. It was only the threat of a *second* bullet, or maybe worse, that kept her on her feet and going at all.

God, the woods were almost pitch-black back in here. A quarter moon drooping over the thick forest canopy did little to light the ground below. Trees were shadows. Thorns and brambles were invisible in the underbrush; they pierced and raked her legs bloody as she pushed through. What little she'd been wearing to begin with—just an expensive black lace teddy—now hung in shreds off her shoulders.

None of that mattered, though, or even registered with Hannah anymore. The only clear thought that cut through the pain, and the panic, was *Go, girl.* The rest was a wordless, directionless nightmare.

Finally, and very suddenly—had it been an hour? more?—the low canopy of trees opened up around her. "What the . . ." Dirt turned to gravel underfoot, and Hannah stumbled to her knees with nothing to hang on to.

In the hazy moonlight, she could make out the ghost of a double line, showing the curve of a country road. It was like a miracle to her. Half of one, anyway; she knew she wasn't out of this mess yet.

When a motor sounded in the distance, Hannah leaned on her hands and pushed up off the gravel. Summoning strength she didn't know she still had, she stood again, then staggered into the middle of the road. Her world blurred through sweat and fresh tears.

Please, dear God, don't let this be them. This can't be those two bastards.

You can't be so cruel, can you?

A red truck careened around the bend then, coming at

her fast. Too fast! Suddenly, she was just as blind as she'd been before, in the woods, but from the truck's headlights.

"Stop! Please stop! Pleee-ase!" she screamed. *"Stop, you sonofabitch!"*

At the last possible second, the tires squealed on the pavement. The red pickup skidded into full view and stopped just short of flattening her right there into roadkill. She could feel heat coming off the engine through the grille.

"Hey, sweetheart, nice outfit! All you had to do was stick out your thumb."

The voice was unfamiliar—which was good, really good. Loud country music was blasting from the cab too—*Charlie Daniels Band*, her mind vaguely registered, just before Hannah collapsed onto the pavement.

The driver was down there on the road a second later as she regained consciousness. "Oh, my God, I didn't...What happened to you? Are you—*what happened to you?*"

"Please." She barely mustered the word. "If they find me here, they'll kill us both."

The man's strong hands wrapped around her, grazing the dime-sized hole in her back as he picked her up. She only exhaled, too weak to scream now. A cluster of gray and indistinct moments later, they were inside the truck and moving really fast down the two-lane highway.

"Hang in there, darlin'." The driver's voice was shaky now. "Tell me who did this to you."

Hannah could feel her consciousness slipping away again. "The men..."

"The men? *What men,* sweetheart? Who are you talking about?"

An answer floated vaguely through Hannah's mind, and she wasn't sure if she said it out loud or maybe just thought it before everything went away.

The men from the White House.

TWO

HIS NAME WAS Johnny Tucci, but the boys back in his South Philadelphia neighborhood all called him Johnny Twitchy, on account of the way his eyes jumped around when he was nervous, which was most of the time.

Of course, after tonight, the boys in Philly could go screw themselves. This was the night Johnny got into the game for real. This was man time. He had "the package," didn't he?

It was a simple job but a real goody, because he was alone and had to take full responsibility. He'd already picked up the package. Scared him, but he'd done just fine.

No one ever said so, but once you started making deliveries like this, it meant you had something on the family, and they had something on you. In other words, there was a relationship. After tonight, there'd be no more running numbers for Johnny, no more scrapping for crumbs in southside neighborhoods. It was like the bumper sticker that said, *Today is the first day of the rest of your life.*

So naturally, he was pumped—and just a little bit nervous.

His uncle Eddie's warning kept playing like a tape in his mind. *Don't blow this opportunity, Twitchy,* Eddie had said. *I'm way out on a limb here for you.* Like he was doing him some kind of big favor with this job, which Johnny supposed maybe he was, but still. His own uncle didn't have to rub his face in it, did he?

He reached over and turned up the radio. Even the country music they played down here was better than listening to Eddie's nagging in his head all night long. Turned out, it was an old Charlie Daniels Band tune, "The Devil Went Down to Georgia.". He even knew some of the words. But the familiar lyrics couldn't keep Eddie's voice out of Johnny's head.

Don't blow this opportunity, Twitchy.

I'm way out on a limb for you.

Oh, fuck!

Blue flashers danced off his rearview mirror—coming out of nowhere. Two, three seconds ago, he could have sworn he had I-95 all to himself.

Apparently not.

Johnny felt the corner of his right eye start to twitch.

He goosed the gas; maybe he could make a run for it. Then he remembered the piece-of-shit Dodge he was driving, lifted out of a Motel 6 parking lot back in Essington. *Goddamnit! Should have gone to the Marriott. Got a Jap car.*

Still, it was possible the stolen Dodge hadn't been flagged yet. Whoever owned it was probably sleeping back at that motel. With any luck, Johnny could just eat the ticket and no one would ever have to know.

But that was the kind of luck other people had, not him.

It took the cops forever and a day to get out of their cruiser, which was a bad sign—the worst. They were checking the make and the plates. By the time they came up on either side of the Dodge, Johnny's eyes were going like a couple of Mexican jumping beans.

He tried to be cool. "Evening, officers. What seems to be—"

The one on his side, a tall dude with a redneck accent, opened the driver's door. "Just keep your mouth shut tight. Step out of the vehicle."

It didn't take them any time at all to find the package. After they checked the front and back seats, they popped the trunk, pulled the spare-tire cover, and that was that.

"Holy mother of God!" One of the troopers shone his light down on it. The other one gagged at the sight. *What the hell did you do?*

Johnny didn't stick around to answer the question. He was already running for his life.

Three

NOBODY HAD EVER been any deader, or dumber, than he was right now. Johnny Tucci knew that, even as he broke across the tree line and started slip-sliding down a ravine at the side of the highway.

He could hide from these cops, maybe, but not from the Family. Not in jail, not anywhere. It was a fact of life. You didn't lose a "package" like this without becoming one yourself.

Voices came from up the slope, and then dancing flashlight beams. Johnny dropped down low and threw himself under a clump of bushes. He was trembling all over, his heart was going so fast it hurt, and his lungs were heaving from too many cigarettes. It was almost impossible to keep still and keep quiet.

Oh shit, I am so dead. I am so, so dead.

"You see anything? See that little bastard? That freak?"

"Nothing yet. We'll get him. He's down here somewhere. Can't be far."

The troopers fanned out on either side of him, working their way down. Very deliberate and efficient.

Even as he caught his breath now, the trembling only got worse, and not just because of the cops. It was because he'd started to figure out what he had to do next. Strictly speaking, there were only two real options. One involved the .38 he had holstered to his ankle. The other, the package—and who owned it. It was only a question of which way he wanted to die.

And in that cold moonlight, it didn't really seem like much of a question at all.

Moving as slowly as he could, he reached down and pulled the .38. With a badly shaking hand, he fitted the barrel in his mouth. The damn metal clacked hard against his teeth and tasted sour on his tongue. He was ashamed of the tears coming down his face, but that couldn't be helped, and who would ever know but him anyway?

Jesus, was it really going down this way? Crying like a punk, all alone in the woods? What a crummy world this was.

He could just hear the boys now. *Sure wouldn't want to go out the way Johnny did.* Johnny Twitchy. They'd put it on his gravestone—just for spite. Those heathen bastards!

The whole time, Johnny's brain was saying *pull,* but his trigger finger wouldn't do it. He tried again, both hands on the grip this time, but it was no go. He couldn't even do this right.

He finally spit the gun barrel out, still crying like a little kid. Somehow, knowing he was going to live another day didn't do a thing to stop the tears. He just lay there, biting his lips, feeling sorry for himself, until the cops got as far as the stream at the bottom of the ravine.

Then Johnny Twitchy crawled real fast back up the way he'd come, ran across the interstate, and dropped into the woods on the other side — wondering how in Christ he was going to make himself disappear off the face of the earth, knowing that it just wasn't going to happen.

He'd *looked*. He'd seen what was in "the package."

THE NEW ALEX CROSS NOVEL, AVAILABLE FROM
NOVEMBER 2009

I, Alex Cross

James Patterson

**Alex Cross must battle against the very people he works for
to catch a sadistic killer with powerful contacts . . .**

Detective Alex Cross is celebrating his birthday when he receives an
urgent call from work. An all-too-regular occurrence for Cross.
There's been a homicide, nothing new there either. But then comes
news Alex wasn't expecting – this time the victim is his niece.

Devastated and grief-striken, Cross vows to track down the killer.
Although, as he investigates he discovers far more than he would
wish to know about his niece – she was a high-class prostitute at
a very expensive and very exclusive club located just outside of
Washington DC. It is clear that this case will test Cross as he never
has been before.

As more women working at the same club disappear, it becomes
obvious that there is more going on at the sordid mansion than
illegal prostitution, and Cross will stop at nothing to solve the
mystery of these brutal murders. But he is being foiled at every turn
by bureaucracy and a cover-up that stretches as far as the White
House. But what are they hiding? And why? Alex can trust no one
and will have to do this alone.

Century · London

I'm proud to support the National Literacy Trust, an independent charity that changes lives through literacy.

Did you know that millions of people in the UK struggle to read and write? This means children are less likely to succeed at school and less likely to develop into confident and happy teenagers. Literacy difficulties will limit their opportunities throughout adult life.

The National Literacy Trust passionately believes that everyone has a right to the reading, writing, speaking and listening skills they need to fulfil their own and, ultimately, the nation's potential.

My own son didn't used to enjoy reading which was why I started writing children's books – reading for pleasure is an essential way to encourage children to pick up a book. The National Literacy Trust is dedicated to delivering exciting initiatives to encourage people to read and to help raise literacy levels. To find out more about the great work that they do visit their website at www.literacytrust.org.uk.

James Patterson